LORD CUCUMBER

and

THE BOY HAIRDRESSER

LORD CUCUMBER

and

THE BOY HAIRDRESSER

two novels by

Joe Orton
and
Kenneth Halliwell

Introduction by Francesca Coppa

Methuen

Published by Methuen 2001

1 3 5 7 9 10 8 6 4 2

First published in Great Britain in 1999
(as *The Boy Hairdresser and Lord Cucumber*) by Nick Hern Books
This paperback edition published in 2001 by
Methuen Publishing Limited
215 Vauxhall Bridge Road, London SW1V 1EJ

Published in agreement with the University of Leicester
as owners of the original typescript of this work

Published by arrangement with Nick Hern Books

Introduction © 1999 by Francesca Coppa

Methuen Publishing Limited Reg. No. 3543167

A CIP catalogue record for this book
is available from the British Library

ISBN 0 413 74910 X

Printed and bound in Great Britain by
Cox & Wyman Ltd, Reading, Berkshire

INTRODUCTION

In May of 1951, an asthmatic, eighteen-year-old, wannabe actor named John Kingsley Orton came to London to study at RADA, the Royal Academy of Dramatic Art. Orton's acceptance at RADA was a triumph of major proportions, the culmination of years of planning and hard work. The juvenile diaries Orton kept from 1949 to 1951 illustrate his attempt to study drama with the few resources he had available to him in Leicester: library books, BBC radio plays, amateur drama readings, small parts in local productions. Orton saved what money he could for elocution lessons, for copies of Shakespeare's plays, for greasepaint and tubes of cold cream. But even within Leicester's amateur theatre community Orton remained a loner, an outsider, without friendly support or helpful connections:

> 3 April 1949. Spent afternoon and most of evening at Little Theatre rehearsing (or rather spent evening as I appear as a messenger and soldier at the end of the play.) Must check growing tendency to think:
>
> A) Nigel P. (he plays Rivers, Norfolk, and Largest Messenger) got his parts through influence (his dad is Ass. S.M.) [Assistant Stage Manager]

B) that because quite often I sit and read on my own
(I hardly know anyone) people think how lonely I must
be (which is ridiculous.)

But Orton's quiet diligence was to pay off: he was
accepted into RADA and won a rare grant from the
Leicester Education Committee to help pay for his
schooling. RADA offered Orton the chance to be part
of a new city and a new community, and his juvenile
diary reflects his enthusiasm, bursting into ebullient
banner headlines:

> 15 May 1951 Started at RADA. O bliss!
> 16 May 1951 Met Florentic G. A sister. You are she.
> 17 May 1951 An actor's life for me.
> 18 May 1951 Digs in Gower Street. Such fun.
> 19 May 1951 Oh the larks. *Memo:* Someone in the other
> class keeps looking at me.
> 20 May 1951 Did nothing.
> 21 May 1951 Mr. Constable's special movement. Was
> eyed.

Clearly Orton is enjoying his new classes (he wrote to
a friend in Leicester about his movement class, in
which he was asked to flop about 'in the most obscure
positions'), and meeting new people. He is also clearly
enjoying what he perceives to be sexual attention
('Someone in the other class keeps looking at me,'
'Was eyed.') – and what are we to make of the description of Florentic G.?: 'A sister. You are she.' From later
entries ('Florrie ate all the biscuits,' 'Florrie ate all the
cheese,' 'Florrie ate all the eggs,' 'Fuck Florrie,'),
Florrie sounds like a man, a mate, a target for friendly

teasing. Is Orton telling us that Florrie is homosexual, and identifying with him? Is this theatrical camp? 'You are she?'

Florrie is the first person to rate a mention in Orton's diary after he starts at RADA; very shortly after, however, another name appears: Ken.

> 15 May 1951 Met Ken and John at Charing Cross Road. *Memo:* I don't quite understand Ken.
> 1 June 1951 Met Ken and John again. This time with Rex Butler.
> 2 June 1951 Flo rang Ken. *Memo:* Am beginning to understand Ken.
> 8 June 1951 Met Ken. He invites us to live with him.

As is often the way with diaries, as events get more exciting, the descriptions of those events become more elliptical. Having little to do in Leicester, Orton wrote long entries detailing his irritation and boredom; now, in London, in the midst of apparently snowballing developments, Orton gives us only the minimum information. Or, to see things another way, the future playwright is already demonstrating an instinctive flair for dramatic concision:

> 12 June 1951 Ken offers to share flat again.
> 13 June 1951 I say no.
> 14 June 1951 Ken offers again.
> 15 June 1951 We accept because we must.
> 16 June 1951 Move into Ken's flat
> 17 June 1951 Well!
> 18 June 1951 Well!!
> 19 June 1951 Well!!!
> 20 June 1951 The rest is silence.

The rest *was* indeed silence: Orton's juvenile diaries end with that playful Shakespearean quotation. After those three teasing exclamations, Orton maintains a tactful silence about whatever follows; it would be fifteen years before Orton would break that silence in his candid adult diaries, having deciding that, 'the whole trouble with Western Society today is the lack of anything worth concealing.' The mature Orton – confident in both his prose and his sexuality – would tell all about practically everything.

However, it is appropriate that Orton's first diaries end with the appearance of the mysterious 'Ken': Kenneth Halliwell would radically change John Orton's life. Halliwell's impact on Orton's development simply cannot be overestimated, although it is often difficult to evaluate that constructive impact in the light of the horrifying fact that Halliwell murdered Orton in August of 1967. Halliwell's murder of Orton makes him the de facto villain of the Orton story, the gruesome nature of that act understandably overwhelming his more positive contributions to Orton's life and work. And yet it is true that, without Kenneth Halliwell, there might never have been a Joe Orton at all.

In order to understand Halliwell's impact on Orton, we must banish the image of the broken, desperate man of 1967 and try to summon up the Kenneth Halliwell of 1951, the man John Kingsley Orton met at RADA. Halliwell was seven years older than Orton, a sophisticated twenty-five to Orton's eighteen. Halliwell was middle class, the only child of a senior chartered accountant at a large company, and grew up in

Bebington, a suburb of Liverpool. In contrast, Orton was firmly working class, brought up on a council estate in Leicester with his brother and two sisters; his father was a gardener and his mother was a machinist in Leicester's garment industry. Halliwell had been a promising student and was sent to grammar school, where he excelled in classics and was expected to go on to Oxford or Cambridge. Orton failed his eleven-plus exam, and had been sent to Clark's Commercial College where he learned shorthand and typing. Orton had fought hard to win minor acting roles in Leicester; in Bebington, Halliwell had been cast again and again in substantial parts, and his acting had been positively reviewed by the local press. By the time that Halliwell was twenty-three both of his parents were dead (his mother by an accident, his father by suicide): this left Halliwell independent and with inherited money to spend. And, perhaps most import-antly, Halliwell considered himself both an actor and a writer, whereas John Kingsley Orton's 'literary' work before meeting Halliwell was confined exclu-sively to the juvenile diaries within which he charted his personal and theatrical aspirations.

Moreover, for Kenneth Halliwell, the literary was both political and personal; in this too, he would im-press and become a role model for the young Orton. Actively homosexual himself, Halliwell's only play, *The Protagonist* (1949), is thinly veiled homosexual propaganda played out with heterosexual characters. *The Protagonist* dramatizes the story of the actor Edmund Kean, whose career was ruined through sexual scandal and blackmail. In Halliwell's hands, the story of Kean's affair, blackmail, trials, and eventual decline into poverty is constructed so as to evoke the life of another theatrical artist – Oscar Wilde – as well as the contemporary plight of homosexuals in the late 1940s, who were then living in the great age of sexual blackmail. While theatrically ponderous, *The Protagonist* is thematically in advance of its time. Terrence Rattigan (who later met Halliwell, and disliked him) would do little better with his own coded homosexual drama *Separate Tables*; Halliwell's Kean is shunned from society owing to an adulterous affair with a scheming blackmailer, whereas Rattigan's protagonist suffers his decline for the far more implausible crime of groping a girl at the pictures.

But in 1951 *Separate Tables* had not yet been written, and even mild closet dramas were ahead of the popular taste. Halliwell, in his own way, was politically avant-garde: his Kean is a sexual nonconformist, a defiant, unrepentant, heroic figure – and at that point in the history of gay representation there would have been few protagonists like him. But Kenneth Halliwell, who had been well and widely educated, was deeply interested in gay representation – in what is now coming to be called the queer literary canon. Halliwell had identified a strain within the broader literary tradition to which he wished to contribute as a writer. *The Protagonist* was his first attempt to add to this canon – a failed attempt, since the play was never produced or published. However, Halliwell would one day fulfil his goal: he would train Joe Orton, helping to bring into being the most influential gay playwright of the twentieth century. And in his adult diaries, Joe Orton would step into the role of Halliwell's ideal protagonist; like Halliwell's Kean, Orton would reject shame and refuse to keep his life a dirty secret.

In 1951, all of this was well in the future; at that time, Orton and Halliwell had their hopes pinned on acting. It was only after their acting careers fizzled out that the two men began their productive literary partnership. Halliwell encouraged Orton to write; it is doubtful as to whether Orton, conscious of his meagre education and his lack of literary skill, would have dared to attempt something so ambitious on his own. But Halliwell took Orton on as a literary partner, and unselfishly and effectively nurtured his talent.

Still, in the early days, there was no question as to who was the *senior* partner. Charles Monteith, an editor at the publishers Faber and Faber to whom they had submitted their work, gives us a rare snapshot of the pair in the early fifties:

> I had a very clear impression at the first meeting that Kenneth was the one that did the writing. Kenneth was the talker. He liked to turn words around and savour them. Kenneth's talk, his appearance, his age vis-à-vis Orton certainly gave the impression that Kenneth was the literary figure. I thought that John was quite simply his young, pretty, and rather vivacious boyfriend.

But Orton was applying the same quiet diligence to writing that he had previously applied to acting. He was studying Halliwell's queer canon, from the ancient Greeks to Marlowe, Wilde, Firbank and Genet; he was developing his vocabulary, compiling pages of unusual adjectives (affably, athletically, allergically, apocalyptically); he was testing the way words fit together, composing page after page of impressionistic Firbankian sentences:

> The sea was grey, marbled with glittering crests.
> Brown and silver gardens came down to the pink water.
> Pendant globes of orange and blue striped fruit.
> A picture of a gold woman with crimson eyes, wrapped in fur.
> Windows like three orange eyes peering out of the fog.
> A sea like luminous milk.

It took ten years and over ten full-length works for John Orton, Kenneth Halliwell's 'young, vivacious boyfriend', to become Joe Orton, the author of *Entertaining Mr. Sloane*. When Orton finally broke through and became successful, he took great pains to present himself as a novice talent, a new writer. However, by 1964, Orton was already in the third stage of his literary career. In hindsight, the demarcations between these three stages are clear. In the earliest part of his literary career, 1953 to 1956, Orton wrote as a junior partner in collaboration with Halliwell. Together they produced *Lord Cucumber* (1954), first published in this volume, as well as at least four other novels, now lost, including *The Silver Bucket* (1953), *The Mechanical Womb* (1955), *The Last Days of Sodom* (1955), and the first of three works to be entitled *The Boy Hairdresser* (1956). While these novels attracted the attention of various publishers, they were all ultimately rejected – largely, if you read between the lines, on the grounds of their being too queer. In the latter part of 1956, Orton and Halliwell decided to sever their literary partnership. From 1956 to 1962, John Orton wrote as an independent author, producing two novels, *Between Us Girls* (1957) and *The Vision of Gombold Proval* (1961; published in 1971 as *Head to Toe*) and two plays: *Fred and Madge* (1959) and *The Visitors* (1961) (first published, in one volume, in 1998). During this second phase of Orton's career, he and Halliwell reunited to produce the second novel in this volume, which was also the second work called *The Boy Hairdresser* (1960). While *The Boy Hairdresser* also failed to find a publisher at the time it was written, Orton was not finished with it; he rewrote it, radically, as a radio play, and submitted it to the BBC, where it was championed by John Tydeman. Retitled *The Ruffian on the Stair*, the play became Orton's first accepted work, and thus marks the beginning of Joe Orton's mature career.

The two novels you are holding in your hand, *Lord Cucumber* and *The Boy Hairdresser*, are very special novels; in many ways they are literary rarities. They are, in the first place, collaborative works, and novels with two authors are extremely unusual. But, it is important to note that they are not, in fact, written by exactly the same team: *Lord Cucumber* is by Kenneth Halliwell and John Orton, whereas *The Boy Hairdresser* is written by John Orton and Kenneth Halliwell. The switch in billing is significant: John Orton's name rises above Halliwell's on the latter novel, out of alphabetical order or order of seniority. The two novels themselves are seamlessly written, providing us with no specific evidence as to how these two authors collaborated; did they alternate chapters? or sit at the typewriter together? or write over and through one another's drafts? However, from the larger historical pattern of their collaboration we can surmise that Halliwell's hand is guiding *Lord Cucumber* and Orton's hand is guiding *The Boy Hairdresser*, and thus the publication of these two works back to back allows us to theorize some differences between two writers who, in real life as in fiction, often presented themselves as speaking with exactly the same voice. [1]

Lord Cucumber details the life of poor orphaned Helen Hagg, Lord Cucumber's young secretary, and her love for and eventual marriage to Richard, Lord Cucumber's heir and son. Like Geraldine in *What the Butler Saw*, like the young Orton himself in fact, Helen is armed against a cruel, class-stratified world with only her typing and shorthand skills, and must face a considerable number of difficulties before finally bagging her man and literally walking off with him into the sunset.

The novel satirizes literature's obsession with the aristocracy, and specifically engages with the reader's desire for a worthy but poor heroine to claim her rightful (moral) place among the (idealized) upper classes. As with so much of their work, Jane Austen is a starting point. Halliwell and Orton also take specific potshots at genres where a naive class-lust reoccurs, such as Hollywood movies, the British murder mystery (*Death on the Nile* seems to be referenced particularly), and Mills and Boon novels. All of this is overlaid with a hefty dose of Firbankian camp. As Brigid Brophy notes in *Prancing Novelist: A Defence of Fiction in the form of a Critical Biography of Ronald Firbank*, 'Firbank is perhaps the inventor, certainly the fixer, of modern camp. Popes, cardinals, choirboys, nuns, flagellants, queens (both senses): all the classic camp dramatis personae are his.' Halliwell and Orton update and modernize these characters, giving us Helen Hagg, Lord and Lady Cucumber, Olive de Pineapple, Consuela – Duchess of Sodamint, Langley Fundament, Mrs. St. Cuckoo and a host of others. Halliwell and Orton also adopt Firbank's vivid, fashion-conscious, language ('She wore a bottle-green raincoat and carried a crimson umbrella striped with black') and his coy narrative elisions ('[*Lord Cucumber*] shut himself up in his study with Helen Hagg in attendance. The result pleased him more than ever, and at the end of two hours, when he stopped and Helen was gathering up her notes, she turned round to find him studying her'). Most importantly, each of the characters seems to be, as in Firbank, covertly pursuing a member of the same sex even as they overtly pursue more suitable mates. So we see that Helen is infatuated with Lady Thomyris just as Mrs. Mitylene is interested in Helen, and the novel's villains are, like Wilde's Lady Bracknell, society matrons who exert pressure on the characters to select socially appropriate matches regardless of personal desire.

These borrowings are not accidental, unintentional, or unconscious; rather, I believe that Halliwell and

Orton know exactly what they're doing. They are, quite simply, consciously trying to write a distinctly gay novel set within a larger gay literary tradition. Halliwell, the former classics scholar, gives the game away in the second half of the novel, in which all the main characters leave the world of the British country house and take a luxury cruise. But this is no ordinary cruise: it is selected by one of the novel's heroines, Lady Thomyris,[2] who wants to see all the old, legendary places:

> She wanted to study old civilizations, and for that purpose she joined this particular ship. No other trip would do. This one took in the places that she wanted to see – Troy, Ismarus, the Cyclops land, Laestrygonia, Circe's Island, Scylla and Charybdis, and Ogygia – finishing up in the land of the Phaecians.[3]

The places on this tour are all Homeric references; in other words, Halliwell and Orton's camp country house characters are touring through the geography of ancient Greek literature and myth. In the 1950s, there were two primary discourses for signifying homosexuality: classical literature and camp. In *Lord Cucumber*, Halliwell and Orton marry the two by sending Ronald Firbank's 'classic camp dramatis personae' back to tour the ancient Greek world – to discover their ancestors as it were. The characters sightsee at the tomb of Achilles, admire Priam's taste in architecture, ogle suggestive Greek sculpture, and listen to lectures on the Rites of Eleusis:[4] 'Helen Hagg became so excited that she dropped her handbag down a crevice.' By placing them in such a highly overdetermined homosexual milieu,[5] Halliwell and Orton 'out' the classic stereotypes of early twentieth-century genre literature. Today, Agatha Christie's 1952 play *The Mousetrap* (old-fashioned even when it was first produced) is performed in London with tongue firmly in cheek; today both cast and audience are well aware that that 'wild-looking neurotic young man' Christopher Wren is gay, and that Miss Casewell, 'a young woman of a manly type' is a lesbian – even though the text refuses to admit that overtly. In *Lord Cucumber*, written at about the same time as Christie's play, Halliwell and Orton explode the facade. The Vicar has run off with Lord Cucumber's copy of *Such a Little Queen*; Mrs. Mitylene, the hearty, adventurous middle-aged woman who saves our heroine, prefers clothes that are 'hard-wearing and warm' and is delighted that Helen Hagg has been so finely educated at St. Sappho's. In *The Mousetrap*, Christie uses implied homosexuality to suggest mental illness in her characters, and thus their potential for murderousness; sadly, this was, in fact, the liberal view of the time. But in *Lord Cucumber*, implied homosexuality is, as in Firbank's works, playfully ubiquitous, an unacknowledged fact of life which begs neither questions nor judgments.

The many literary references embedded in this novel suggest that Kenneth Halliwell was guiding the style of the project. Halliwell had a strong sense of literary and queer history, and from *The Protagonist* onward, his aim was to express and legitimize his more subversive meanings within the context of that history. Even after his partner became successful as 'Joe

Orton', Kenneth Halliwell continued to encourage him to broaden his literary boundaries, to extend his frame of reference. In his mature diary, Orton records how Halliwell directed his literary career:

> I had the idea that the play I intend to write set in prison, *Where Love Lies Bleeding*, should be, in the main, a satire on Genet using much of the story of *Querelle of Brest*. K.H. said, 'You must use all Genet's subjects – beautiful young murderers, buggery, treachery, bent and brutal policemen and theft.'

And Halliwell continually pushed Orton to connect his work back to the ancient Greeks, the starting point of any gay male tradition. As Orton noted in his diary:

> I've finished typing *What the Butler Saw*. Yesterday Kenneth read the script and was enthusiastic – he made several important suggestions which I'm carrying out. He was impressed by the way in which, using the context of a farce, I'd managed to produce a *Golden Bough* subtext – even (he pointed out) the castration of Sir Winston Churchill (the father-figure) and the descent of the god at the end – Sergeant Match, drugged and dressed in a woman's gown. It was only to be expected that Kenneth would get these references to classical literature. Whether anyone else will spot them is another matter. 'You must get a director who, while making it funny, brings out the subtext,' Kenneth said. He suggests that the dress Match wears should be of something suggestive of leopard skin – this would make it funny when Nick wears it and get the right 'image' for the Euripidean ending when Match wears it.

On the surface, Orton is praising Halliwell for 'recognizing' his classical literary allusions; however, the parenthetical '(he pointed out)' shows Orton admitting that something more complex was happening. The passage – which is quite different from Orton's normal way of discussing his writing – has the tone of a student quickly reviewing notes given by an admired teacher. Kenneth Halliwell was not simply 'getting' Orton's themes, but discovering them, or even creating them and, by doing so, helping to knit Orton into the greater literary tradition.

While Halliwell had a firmer grip on the literary past, John Orton had his eye on the literary future. While Halliwell tended to situate himself and his work historically, Orton's early solo work shows that he was interested in and paying attention to trends in contemporary writing. If Orton's second phase work shows us anything, it shows a writer who was interested in experimentation. While Kenneth Halliwell continued to write in the style of Firbank, producing *Priapus in the Shrubbery* in 1959, John Orton experimented with the popular new styles and forms. In the second, more independent phase of his career, Orton wrote a diary novel (*Between Us Girls*), a Swiftian satiric fable (*The Vision of Gombold Proval*), and two startlingly different plays: *Fred and Madge* and *The Visitors*.

Orton was also clearly intrigued by the spate of 'angry young man' novels that became popular after 1956. These works featured new, edgier, antiheroic protagonists, and Orton put a character of this type into his 1957 novel *Between Us Girls*. He is called Bob Kennedy, and he is the first character in any work who is firmly rooted in the fifties. When Kennedy is first introduced into *Between Us Girls* he is drunk and has a black eye. He is surly, pouting, and sexually ambiguous – a typical man-child such as Brando or James Dean would play on film: 'He peeled the cigarette stump he was smoking away from his lip and ground it into an ashtray. Behind the baby face, far down, there lay a deep nihilism.' Bob Kennedy is almost out of place in *Between Us Girls* – it is practically impossible to imagine him coexisting in the same universe as bubbly Susan Hope, the novel's protagonist, let alone marrying her, as he does at the story's conclusion.

But even after *Between Us Girls*'s rejection by publishers, Orton seemed reluctant to let the character go. Instead Orton recycled the Bob Kennedy scenes (and only those scenes) for his next novel, *The Boy Hairdresser*, and invited Kenneth Halliwell back on board to co-write it. In *The Boy Hairdresser*, Kennedy is expanded and developed into Donelly, and a key scene where Kennedy walks Susan Hope home is lifted nearly word for word. Now, however, it is set in a more appropriate universe: the scene is rainy, urban, North London, and Donelly walks a young factory worker named Jean home from an arcade:

He peeled the cigarette from his mouth. As they passed a wall, he brought out the piece of chalk and wrote Ban American Atom Bases. Jean sniffled to herself . . .

They walked on for a time. He didn't speak; he was trying to imagine her disappointment when she didn't see him again. They stopped in the shadow of a block of flats and he saw her lips waiting. He drew her close, pretending desire; she was naked under her sweater and he could feel her breasts through the wool. He put his hands up and made a slight movement: she didn't appear to notice even when he found the nipple. She was so passive her helplessness made him long to kick. Feeling a prick of unwilling excitement, he drew his hand down: he wasn't going to be caught giving pleasure to any little half-wit. They walked on.

'Don't you get sick of all this?' he said.

'All what?'

'Life, living.'

She looked surprised. 'No,' she said.

'Women never seem to.'

The thought irritated him. When they reached the flats where she lived and were waiting for the lift, he chalked up on the door an indecent rhyme: 'Is it true what they say about Eton . . . ?'

In an anger which took him by surprise she snatched the chalk and scribbled out what he'd written. There was a scuffle, and she threw the chalk into the street.

Donelly swore, kicked her hard on the ankle, and walked away across the threadbare turf whistling a Gershwin tune.

While Kennedy eventually marries Susan Hope in *Between Us Girls*, Donelly is clearly not going to marry Jean ('Getting married is fine if you go to the club to escape the bitch,' Donelly explains. 'Where we are it's different.') Rather, the object of Donelly's desire is a young man named Peterson, the boy hairdresser of the title.

In his analysis of *The Boy Hairdresser* in *Prick Up Your Ears*, John Lahr reads the book as autobiography: Donelly is Halliwell, Peterson is Orton.[6] One can make a good case for such a reading. For example, Donelly's offer to Peterson – 'Come and share my flat. Save money.' – is the same offer that Kenneth Halliwell made to John Kingsley Orton at RADA. Two years before Halliwell and Orton were caught by the Islington Public Library, Donelly and Peterson are boasting of their book thefts. Donelly explains:

> 'We're public benefactors in a way. We steal – the shops order more – the publishers are pleased – everyone is happy. We finance literature. We are a sort of Maecenas.'
> He kept his malice under control.
> 'You wouldn't even begin to understand the real reasons why we do these things.'

There are also passages that have a ring of emotional truth to them, that seem clues to something real in Halliwell and Orton's relationship.

> Peterson put down the pen. 'Why bother about me?' he said, 'I'm all wrong for you.'
> 'I'll be the judge of when to throw in the towel.'
> 'What must I do to deserve it?'
> Donelly laughed. 'I'll stick to you like glue. It's not easy to break a habit.'
> 'Let's get away from here – ' Peterson held out the bait half seriously. 'Those girls I pick up, they don't mean a thing. Wouldn't that be best?'

Throughout *The Boy Hairdresser*, Peterson is having affairs with young girls, just as Orton enjoyed being promiscuous with young men. Stress is placed on the age of the girls:

'Who is she?'
'A tart I met.' Peterson took down the snapshot, grinned, and put it back again.
'How old is she?'
'Only fourteen.'
'You do take risks, don't you?'

Later in the novel, Peterson kisses another young girl and muses: 'It was astonishing to think he could be jailed.' In his later diaries, Joe Orton moved from astonishment to rage:

Here and there were a number of nearly-naked young boys. This made me unhappy. After passing a fifteen-year-old youth lying face downward, wearing red bathing drawers, I said, in a rage, 'England is intolerable. I'd be able to fuck that in an Arab country. I could take him home and stick my cock up him!' 'This is verbal exhibitionism!' Kenneth said, glancing at a number of evil-faced old women in a shelter. 'Look at them – crouching like Norns or the spirit of fucking British civilisation,' I said. 'I hate this tight arsed civilisation.'

But if Peterson illustrates Orton's lust, he also expresses Orton's respect and regard for Donelly/Halliwell; he openly admits to being Donelly's 'boyfriend', and, about to seduce one of his young girlfriends, Peterson is suddenly struck by his affection for Donelly, and 'the idea of taking this girl to bed seemed to dwindle in importance.'

However, the main reason that Lahr reads *The Boy Hairdresser* as autobiographical is due to Donelly's incipient psychopathy and murderousness, which Lahr believes foreshadows Kenneth Halliwell's eventual murder of Joe Orton in 1967 and his subsequent suicide. The plot of *The Boy Hairdresser*, can, in the roughest sense, be summarized as 'Boy meets boy, boy loses boy, boy opens fire on a busy street.' Donelly meets Peterson; they try to survive in the mean streets of North London; Peterson is run down and killed by a hit man hired by someone he has been trying to blackmail; Donelly, in grief, decides to take this opportunity to resolve the question that has been nagging at him throughout the novel: to live or die.

> One day he would shoot himself, he was living already in the future: the hole in his temple blackened by burning . . . An idea started to form in his brain. When he went, he'd take others with him: five or six at least. Something for the Sunday papers to talk about. You could shoot five people down before they'd recovered their wandering senses. Perspiration ran on his shoulders in drops. The idea staggered. Why not cure the population problem by even so small an amount?

Early in *The Boy Hairdresser*, the timer on the ticking bomb that is Donelly is set: 'If Peterson were dead,' Donelly thinks, 'he could end it now.' After Peterson's death, Donelly opens fire, but the only person hurt is Donelly himself; the gun explodes in his hand and takes off two of his fingers.

Kenneth Halliwell *did* murder Joe Orton in 1967, and *The Boy Hairdresser* is a novel about incipient psychopathy. But they may or may not be related. Certainly, however, there is more going on in *The Boy Hairdresser* than a preview of Halliwell's eventual breakdown. That view seems to me to ignore three crucial facts; first, that Donelly is the hero of the novel; second, that the novel's primary writer was Orton himself; and third, that the late fifties and early sixties produced an entire body of literature with heroes equally psychotic. I would like to comment on each of these points in turn.

Donelly is clearly the (anti)hero of *The Boy Hairdresser*, and to the extent that Donelly can be seen as a stand-in for Halliwell, the book becomes a celebration of Halliwell's anarchic spirit. In *Prick Up Your Ears*, John Lahr notes that 'Orton and Halliwell were dropouts before the fall-out of Beat literature in the fifties filtered down through English society and made it modish. They questioned the culture's values but absorbed its literary traditions.' Lahr claims this of 'Orton and Halliwell', but to the extent that we can read *The Boy Hairdresser* as autobiography it shows that this stance was more true of Kenneth Halliwell than of John Kingsley Orton. Donelly, in *The Boy Hairdresser*, is a writer: 'You're one of those people who measure success by the number of copies sold,' said Donelly, 'It would surprise you, wouldn't it, that there are some writers too good to be published?' Donelly is given all the great anti-capitalist sentiments – 'He wondered why the world was permitted to carry on. Why didn't God scrap it and begin again. He might love thieves and adulterers, but how could even God love the wives of stockbrokers and the pigs who run and are run by materialism?' And it is Donelly who is the militant homosexual: at Peterson's funeral, for example, Donelly aggressively makes the nature of their relationship clear to the curate:

> Donelly said, 'His dealings with the army were not precisely – Do you understand? A love passing that of woman. You know the book of Kings?'
> The curate coughed, throwing a little phlegm into his throat.
> 'Of course.'
> 'It's my vade-mecum. We used to read it together.'
> He paused; the curate could not mistake his meaning . . .

In fact, while Peterson is portrayed as charming, he is also an ideological waffler:[7] one character refers to him as a 'crypto-beat, a fraudulent rebel, a man whose anger was not strictly on the level.' Peterson is torn between conventional values ('I know it sounds stupid,' said Peterson, 'but I don't want to drift . . . I'd like to put down roots before it's too late. I can't go on in this way forever') and a more rebellious life with Donelly. Later in the text, Peterson muses: 'If only I could get hold of the money, I could have the best of both worlds.'

Wanting Orton/Peterson to be the rebellious hero of *The Boy Hairdresser*, John Lahr inadvertently misquotes from the novel. In *Prick Up Your Ears*, we find the following: 'They had been stealing for a year from bookshops. Peterson had a great enthusiasm for anarchy' (*Prick Up Your Ears*, p. 144). But in *The Boy Hairdresser*, Orton and Halliwell wrote, 'They had been stealing for a year from bookshops. Donelly had a great enthusiasm for anarchy.' It is Donelly, not Peterson, who is enthusiastic about anarchy; Peterson's values are more fluid. If we read it as autobiography, the book privileges Donelly/Halliwell over Peterson/Orton.

But *The Boy Hairdresser* was written largely by *Orton;* as I noted above, it is the first of their collaborations where Orton's name rises above Halliwell's on the title page, out of alphabetical order or order of seniority or experience. As such, we have to see *The Boy Hairdresser* as a major turning point. The rebellious Donelly is Orton's creation. In trying to flesh out Bob Kennedy, the angry young man of *Between Us Girls*, Orton turns to Halliwell as a model of rebelliousness and subversion.

If Halliwell had the characteristics of a rebel, it was Orton who saw the literary value of such characteristics. After years of watching Kenneth Halliwell canon-build, developing a queer literature by citing and negotiating with other texts, it was Orton who suddenly realized that how he and Halliwell were living – who he and Kenneth Halliwell *were* – was itself socially relevant and interesting literature. It was Orton who had the crucial revelation: that the queer canon that Halliwell had been constructing led directly to them.

Orton was paying attention to the contemporary writing of the late fifties, or at least to the media frenzy surrounding the writers of contemporary literature. *The Boy Hairdresser* is consciously aware of the works of 'angry young men'; its characters discuss

Colin Wilson's *The Outsider;* it stops to take social-realist snapshots of North London and to complain about Americanism and the new mass-culture that bothered Richard Hoggart; it is seedy with a knowledge that seediness is hip. Donelly is consciously written in the mode of what Kenneth Allsop called 'the delink' in 1958's *The Angry Decade: a Survey of the Cultural Revolt of the Fifties.* Allsop claims that the term 'delink' – from the American delinquent – 'can usefully be broadened and extended in meaning to apply to the creative artist who has allowed himself to be pushed beyond the far reach of despair to severe personality disorder':

> Lucky Jim, in his most thick-ear emanation (and caricature versions of Lucky Jim dot the new novels like daisies in May) is a cheerful delink . . . The extreme delink has resigned, opted out, withdrawn to the narcissistic twilight in which Samuel Beckett's dustbin creatures exist. The heroes of some novels – Thomas Hinde's *Happy as Larry*, William Camp's *Prospects of Love* – have gone through the process of disengagement and emerged at the further end into medical schizophrenia (Allsop, p. 29–30).

By 1958, these kinds of characters were, as Allsop says, as common as daisies in May. Donelly's pseudo-psychopathic feelings may point to a realistic picture of Kenneth Halliwell the man, but it is more likely that they may also simply indicate that Orton the writer is using what was at the time a very common literary trope.

Perhaps most importantly, it was Orton who recognized the erotic potential in the world's sudden preoccupation with 'angry young men'. Britain in the late fifties and early sixties was fascinated with working-class masculinity – social realist films were in the cinemas, kitchen-sink dramas were on the stage, and the Beatles would soon come to dominate the airwaves. Was British culture's current obsession with working-class men really so different from Orton and Halliwell's own homoerotic tastes? When exactly does the homosocial blur into the homosexual? At a certain point, one could argue that an infatuation with men was an infatuation with men, even if the contexts for the infatuation were different.

This was the moment of Orton, and Orton took advantage of it to create a new kind of homosexual representation. Kennedy, Donelly, and Peterson are just the first of the young, beautiful and bisexual hooligans who populate Orton's works; thereafter come such characters as Wilson, Sloane, Hal, Dennis, Caufield and Nick. But Orton also took advantage of the cultural moment in creating his own public persona: Joe Orton the young, male, working-class, ex-convict, rebel playwright fell into an acceptable niche by the early sixties, but those adjectives had yet to be paired with *queer* in the popular imagination. In fact, they were almost the antithesis of queer.

In literature and in life, Joe Orton renegotiated the relationship between class and sexuality. Consider the complexities of the following Joe Orton statement, given in an interview with the *Evening Standard*:

I didn't suffer or anything the way Oscar Wilde did from being in prison, but then Wilde was flabby and self-indulgent. There is this complete myth about writers being sensitive plants. They're not. It's a silly nineteenth-century idea, but I'm sure Aristophanes was not sensitive. I mean, there's absolutely no reason why a writer shouldn't be as tough as a bricklayer.

Orton draws a distinction between himself and Oscar Wilde in class terms, positing his working-class toughness against Wilde's upper-class flabbiness in the evoked arena of prison. This comparison is then more generally extended in literary terms – why can't a writer be as tough as a bricklayer? – why are writers always thought to be refined upper-class types like Wilde? Orton is here showing himself to be a card-carrying member of the new classless Britain; he is an advocate of working-class authorship. But there's another reading here if you substitute the word 'homosexual' for the word 'writer', as the references to Wilde and Aristophanes almost beg one to do. (The choice of the word 'sensitive' is also telling in this connection, since 'sensitive' was one of the primary euphemisms for 'homosexual' in the fifties and sixties[8] – the other was, ironically, 'artistic'.) Read in this context, Orton's statement then loosely translates: 'All homosexuals are not like Oscar Wilde. Homosexuals are not by nature weak, sensitive, and effeminate. The Greeks, who we all know were homosexual, do not conform to current homosexual stereotype. Why can't a homosexual be tough? or working-class? like me?'

Orton also developed this kind of complex ambiguity in his image. Young, attractive and photogenic, Joe Orton was a poster boy for the new British arts, and pictures of him – the playwright in T-shirt and leather jacket, arms crossed, pouting into the camera against the background of a seedy London street – often accompanied newspaper reviews of his plays. He worked out, and boasted to his agent that he would be 'the most perfectly developed of modern playwrights if nothing else.' Proud of his physique, he had himself drawn nude by the artist Patrick Procktor for the programme of his play *The Erpingham Camp*, and posed for a series of photographs in 1965 wearing nothing but small black briefs. After the publication of the nude drawing in the theatre programme, a magazine called *Town and Around* challenged Orton, with much hostility, to explain the gimmick of representing himself naked. Orton responded innocently, 'There are many people who might like a nude picture of me, I'm not unattractive, you know.' Orton blurred the line between working-class poster boy and homosexual pin up, and showed the two were identical unless differentiated by context.

Ultimately Kenneth Halliwell's boyfriend John Kingsley Orton would successfully challenge both class and sexual stereotype in the 1960s. By creating a Joe Orton persona that fitted the accepted description of a working-class writer, John Kingsley Orton put his talent at the service of the new classless Britain, in which he honestly believed and which he always publicly supported. While Orton presented himself as a working-class tough, his plays had, thanks to Halliwell's instruction and his own diligent effort, visibly literary roots and a sophisticated tone, which caused some of the more astute critics to note with astonishment that the working-class tough sounded a lot like Jane Austen, and seemed to be referencing Sophocles. Ironically, Orton's hard-won education and sophistication would have been taken for granted if they had been coming from the thirty-one-year-old homosexual writer John Kingsley Orton (since the stereotype held that all homosexuals were cultured and artistic anyway) – but as the product of the overtly working-class Orton persona, they impressed. Thus Orton smashed two different stereotypes simultaneously; on the one hand showing that working-class men could be intellectual, educated, and high-brow, and on the other hand illustrating that homosexuals could be tough, detached, and deeply masculine.

The cultural impact of this double explosion is still being felt today. It was a victory for Orton, and a victory for his mentor Kenneth Halliwell, despite the later problems in their relationship, despite the tragic events of August 1967. The career of Joe Orton was the final, successful culmination of the collaborative work of these two writers; the novels in this volume document some of the stages in their decade-long struggle to have precisely this sort of impact.

FRANCESCA COPPA

Francesca Coppa is Assistant Professor of English at Muhlenberg College, where she specialises in British drama and cultural studies. She has published and lectured widely on Orton both in Britain and the United States.

Notes

1. In Orton's biography *Prick Up Your Ears*, John Lahr notes that Orton and Halliwell were said to sound exactly alike. Halliwell, in fact, could and often did convincingly pretend to be Orton over the telephone.

2. Lady Thomyris's name suggests Thamyris, a legendary (male) Greek bard, who 'is regarded by some as the first to love another male, with Hyacinthus or Hymenaeus (both of whom Apollo loved too) as the objects of his passion.' Quoted from Joseph Pequigney's article 'Myth' in *The Gay and Lesbian Literary History*, edited by Claude J. Summers (New York: Henry Holt, 1995, p. 511).

3. More specifically, these particular references are from *The Odyssey*; more specifically still, all can be found in the 29th chapter of *Bulfinch's Mythology*, a favourite book of Halliwell and Orton's.

4. The Rites of Eleusis is a reference to the myth of Demeter and her daughter Proserpine. The latter is forcibly taken to the underworld kingdom as a bride by the god Pluto; her mother searches desperately for her, and eventually it is agreed that Proserpine will spend six months above ground with her mother, and six months underground as bride to Pluto. The myth became the basis for fertility rituals; Proserpine is like a planted seed, which disappears into the ground and then emerges, blooming, in the spring. She is also a young woman seized from her mother for marriage. Note that the deal that Demeter and Pluto make to share Proserpine is strikingly similar to the concluding arrangement of Orton's 1964 play *Entertaining Mr. Sloane*. Presumably Helen Hagg is excited either by the idea of being carried off for sex, or by the idea of equally dividing her life between a man and a woman. (Orton and Halliwell stress Hagg's infatuation with Thomyris and other women.)

5. And if the homosexual atmosphere was not clear enough from the classics or the camp, people and things in the novel are routinely labelled 'gay' or 'queer': Mr. Richard is a 'gay young man'; Lady Thomyris's home, Slaughter St. Wilfred, is 'a gay place and no mistake'; Helen Hagg's taste for the country is 'queer' and so on.

6. Donelly's anger against Eton in the scene with Jean quoted above is further proof that Donelly is at least partly based on Kenneth Halliwell; Eton continued to be subject to Halliwell's scorn. In his mature diaries, Orton records that Halliwell bought an old Etonian tie and wore it, as a satiric gesture, to a party given by Peter Willes. Willes did not appreciate the joke, and called Halliwell, famously, 'a middle-aged nonentity.' Halliwell was deeply hurt by the remark, and Orton took umbrage on his partner's behalf. Certainly this event, which occurred a mere two weeks before Halliwell murdered Orton, was partly responsible for Halliwell's escalating depression; various sources including Orton reported that he was unable to banish the vicious slur from his mind.

7. Both Peterson's charm and his amorality link him not only with Orton himself, but also with Orton's most famous protagonist: Mr Sloane. Like Sloane, Peterson is hired as a chauffeur by an older man; like Sloane, he tries to take advantage of the situation; like Sloane, Peterson gets rather more than he bargained for from his employer, who is not nearly as harmless as he first seems.

8. Orton uses 'sensitive' in this context in *Entertaining Mr Sloane*. Ed defiantly tells Sloane that he's 'seen birds all shapes and sizes and I'm most certainly not ... um ... ah ... sensitive.'

Joe Orton: a Chronology

1933   *1 January:* John Kingsley Orton born in Leicester
1944   Orton fails his eleven-plus exam
1945-47 Orton attends Clark's College
1949   Orton begins writing his juvenile diary
1950   *April:* Orton takes elocution lessons
            November: Orton applies to the Royal Academy of
            Dramatic Art (RADA) in London
1951   *May:* Orton starts at RADA
            June: Orton moves in with Kenneth Halliwell at
            161 West End Lane, London
            June: Orton stops writing juvenile diary
1953   *April:* Orton and Halliwell graduate from RADA
            April–July: Orton works as assistant stage manager
            at Ipswich Rep in Suffolk
            Halliwell and Orton begin collaborating on novels
            Halliwell and Orton write *The Silver Bucket* (novel,
            now lost)
1954   Halliwell and Orton write *Lord Cucumber* (novel)
1955   Halliwell and Orton write *The Mechanical Womb*
            (novel, now lost)
            Halliwell and Orton write *The Last Days of Sodom*
            (novel, now lost)
1956   Halliwell and Orton write *The Boy Hairdresser*
            (a novel in verse, now lost)
1957   *June:* Orton announces in a letter to the publisher
            Charles Monteith that he and Kenneth Halliwell
            have begun to write separately
            Orton writes *Between Us Girls* (novel)
1959   Orton and Halliwell move to 25 Noel Road,
            Islington, London
            Orton writes *Fred and Madge* (play)
            Kenneth Halliwell writes *Priapus in the Shrubbery*
            (novel, now lost)
            Orton and Halliwell begin stealing and 'creatively
            re-arranging' the jackets of books borrowed from
            the Islington Library

1960   Orton and Halliwell write *The Boy Hairdresser* (novel)

1961   Orton writes *The Vision of Gombold Proval* (novel, published 1971 as *Head to Toe*)
Orton writes *The Visitors* (play)

1962   *April:* Orton and Halliwell arrested for stealing and defacing library books
May–September: Orton gaoled at H.M. Prison Eastchurch, in Kent, and Halliwell gaoled at H.M. Prison Ford, in Sussex, for stealing and defacing library books

1963   Orton writes *The Boy Hairdresser* (play); revised title: *The Ruffian on the Stair*
Orton writes *Entertaining Mr Sloane*

1964   John Kingsley Orton becomes Joe Orton
6 May: Entertaining Mr Sloane produced at Arts Theatre Club, London
June: Orton writes *The Good and Faithful Servant*
29 June: Entertaining Mr Sloane transfers to Wyndham's Theatre
31 August: The Ruffian on the Stair broadcast on the BBC Third Programme

1964-66 Orton writes *Loot*

1965   Orton writes *The Erpingham Camp*
February: first (failed) production of *Loot*

1966   Orton writes *Funeral Games*
September: second (successful) production of *Loot*
December: Orton begins writing mature *Diaries*

1967   *11 January*: Orton wins *Evening Standard* Award for Best Play of 1966. On the same day, Orton receives a letter informing him that he has also won the *Plays and Players* Award for Best Play of 1966
Orton writes *What the Butler Saw*
Orton writes *Up Against It* (Beatles screenplay)
June: under the title *Crimes of Passion*, Orton's one-act plays *The Ruffian on the Stair* and *The Erpingham Camp* are produced at the Royal Court Theatre
9 August: Orton murdered by Kenneth Halliwell, who then commits suicide

F.C.

A Note on the Text

All punctuation and the spelling of character and place names are as in Orton and Halliwell's typescripts for authenticity's sake.

LORD CUCUMBER

a novel
by
Kenneth Halliwell
and
John Orton

PART ONE

I

'I should be much obliged,' said Lord Cucumber, looking at his son, 'if you would devote a little, just a little, Richard, of your spare time to the business of earning a living.'

His son, who was perched on the arm of a leather chair by the fireplace, swung round to smile indistinctly at Lord Cucumber. Many thoughts seethed in his brain, thoughts not uncommon in only sons when they contemplate their fathers who have succeeded in commerce. Lord Cucumber was a fair-dealing man, firm and practical, whose character was a mixture of simplicity and astuteness. The family business was his pride, for he had built it up step by step, and he took pleasure in the thought that it and he were important. He had indeed given in too much to Lady Cucumber, who had social ambitions, and it was she who had insisted on Richard's going first to Eton and then to Magdalen, where he had received no education worth mentioning and had developed into a cultivated loafer.

'Don't be unfair, Dad,' sighed Richard, swinging his leg and looking sulky. 'I stayed at the Liverpool office for nearly a month.'

'What a concession!' said Lord Cucumber. 'I wonder it didn't kill you.'

'It nearly did,' said Richard amiably. 'I must say it was pretty foul.'

'It was what I did, year in year out, when I was your age.'

'What a life!' Richard Cucumber gazed into the yellow and gold-brown tones of the sunlight. 'And one only has one life to live.'

'Your own would have been considerably different if I hadn't kept my nose to the books,' said his father, drily.

A knock came at the door. Discreet and diffident, a secretary appeared.

'I beg your pardon, Lord Cucumber, but you told me to let you know when Miss Hagg came.'

'Miss Hagg. Oh yes, I'll see her at once.'

'Who's Miss Hagg?' said Richard, glad of the interruption.

'She's come about a job, wants a post as secretary and typist,' said Lord Cucumber. 'You know Miss Offjenkin is getting married, so there really is a vacancy, and if this girl is possible I'm going to try her.'

There was a knock at the door, and the secretary returned with a young woman. Richard, who had meant to go, took a look at her and thought better of it.

Lord Cucumber shook hands, introduced his son, and asked the girl to sit down; but while he talked he was subjecting his prospective secretary to sharp scrutiny. She had a little white face, fine eyes and dark lashes. She wore a bottle-green raincoat and carried a crimson umbrella striped with black. A little bit of a thing to be out in the world alone, thought Lord Cucumber: he liked studying faces, and believed that he could detect in hers character and courage.

'I knew your father well, Miss Hagg. We went to the same school and were always friends.'

Helen Hagg gave him an odd look and smiled. Her fingers hovered over her heart. She was rather nervous, he noticed, but that was natural. She looked extraordinarily young, almost too young. If she hadn't been Ralph's daughter he would never have thought of engaging her. Yes, she was like Ralph, he decided, she was small and very slight. Her hands and feet were slender. But it was his experience that the smallest people were usually the most determined. Her voice, when she spoke, was soft and well-controlled, and that impressed him. Lord Cucumber was susceptible to voices. Miss Offjenkin's had been shrill, and his wife, Lady Cucumber's, was metallic.

'Abercromby tells me that your father died out of England?'

'Yes.'

'Then you didn't live with him?'

'Off and on.'

Lord Cucumber smiled. 'I understand you know several languages?'

'I know nineteen,' said Miss Hagg, with dignity. 'I pick them up very quickly.'

'French, German, Spanish, and a little Italian – that will be quite enough for me,' said Lord Cucumber anxiously, and added, 'You see, you would come to me as private secretary and have nothing to do in the

5

office at present. I have other interests besides my business, as I think you know.'

'Is that why you want somebody who is good at Spanish?'

Lord Cucumber nodded. 'I should require you with me at the week-ends, so you would start at Hummingbird – my place in the country. I suppose you would like to come?

'Very much – more than anything,' said Miss Hagg.

'Then that is settled.' Lord Cucumber rose. 'I think I should like you to begin on Monday. When could you come down?'

'At once, if you like, Lord Cucumber. The Rabbits have asked me to stay with them, and I could go there tomorrow and come in when you want me.'

'That's excellent. I shan't be down, but I shall send instructions. My secretary will give you all the details,' said Lord Cucumber and shook hands.

Miss Hagg thanked him. Richard had been a silent witness of the interview, faintly amused, slightly interested.

'Not much like your usual secretaries,' he remarked when the door had closed behind Miss Hagg. 'She looks as though she ought to be still at school.'

'A bit young,' said his father, 'still she seemed a nice, quiet girl. I don't imagine poor Ralph left her a bean,' he added, dismissing Miss Hagg from his mind, and returning to more important affairs.

'Nice? Quiet? I wonder!' reflected Richard Cucumber. His short, masculine fingers stroked the faint line of moustache on his upper lip.

II

Meanwhile Helen Hagg, who was lunching in the
nearest A.B.C., felt giddy with elation. She ate her
poached egg slowly, and pondered on her good luck.
To be secretary to Lord Cucumber! It would be
wonderful. What made it better was that she would
live at Hummingbird. That meant good food, comfort,
and a country life, which she liked. She thought,
rather wistfully, that it would be lovely to have a
home; for Helen Hagg was peculiarly alone in the
world. Except for Herbert Rabbit, her father's cousin,
she had no relations, and both Herbert and his wife
evidently regarded her as an embarrassment.

Up till half an hour ago life had been a desolate
affair, her future had been uncertain. But now, thought
Helen, adding a cup of coffee to her order, the world
had taken on a different aspect. She felt sure that she
would enjoy her work, and she was attracted to Lord
Cucumber. He looked so kind, as well as clever. She
would do her utmost to please him!

Helen now gave her mind to clothes – a very
serious matter. She possessed at the moment only one
evening dress, and even that was not presentable.
Something had to be done, and her entire capital
amounted to little over fifty pounds. Nervous, but
excited, she spent the afternoon gazing into shop
windows. At the end of the day she had bought a light
summer mantle of sheer linen, a snug-fitting bonnet
made of white coque feathers, and an evening gown

of black embroidered with wasps. She had enjoyed herself, for with her shopping was an event.

The following day she travelled down to Huguenot Malherbe to stay with Herbert and Irene Rabbit. Her mood of elation vanished during the crowded railway journey. When she saw Herbert waiting for her with the Morris, she was filled with dread, for both her cousins disliked her intensely. Mrs Rabbit indeed had said on occasion that she had no intention of giving a home to the daughter of a man whom she had despised, and Helen had a consciousness that under their roof she could do nothing right.

However she was determined to behave nicely. She would not allow herself to think that Herbert had come to meet her, anxious only to hear the result of her interview with Lord Cucumber. Try as she would, the knowledge that Cousin Irene would impress Lord Cucumber's kindness on her the moment she arrived took the edge off her gratitude.

Herbert Rabbit was middle-aged. He had a white moustache, a confiding manner, and a habit of standing with his legs apart. He lived in a small drab villa with a large drab wife. Helen wondered whether he had ever loved Cousin Irene, or whether they had just fixed it up in a business-like way? One could never tell, and meanwhile Herbert was driving her down the main street and through the suburbs of Huguenot Malherbe. He was a nervous driver and did not care to talk in traffic, but when they turned off the main road towards the village of Ponceplural, where he lived, he burst out with the question that was uppermost in his mind.

'Well, what did Lord Cucumber say? Was anything fixed up?'

Helen, whom experience of not being wanted had rendered clairvoyant, knew that the outcome of the interview had been discussed night and day in the Rabbits' home. She could guess at the oft-repeated words. Now she hastened to put Herbert out of his suspense.

'Lord Cucumber,' she said, 'has engaged me. I begin on Monday morning.'

'I am glad,' said Herbert heartily. 'It will give you a start.'

'I hope it will give me more than a start,' said Helen gaily.

They had pulled up at Fairy Cottage. Inside Mrs Rabbit waited, equally anxious for the verdict. Helen's heart sank as she walked into the hall. Although she had been there seldom, it had imprinted itself on her memory, for she had always loathed it – the wallpaper heavy with yellow trumpet-shaped blossoms, blue carpets, gold dragons and porcelain vases. It was awe-inspiring, crude, and tasteless. Cousin Irene waited to receive her, her welcome even colder than the tea.

'How do you do, Helen Hagg?'

Mrs Rabbit presented her cheek to be kissed.

'Be careful of the cakestand,' she added, sharply, as Helen moved.

Herbert, who had been taking off his coat, hurried in.

'She's got it,' he said.

'I am glad to hear it,' said Mrs Rabbit. 'You were fortunate, Helen. Many girls have to make their way without any interest to help them. I hope you realise that your Cousin Herbert used his influence with Lord Cucumber?'

'I am very grateful,' said Helen.

'It is a wonderful opportunity,' went on Irene. 'I only hope you will do us justice. You owe us a great deal.'

An odd view, thought Helen Hagg, masticating a dry bun. Because really the Rabbits had done as little as they could, and the only time she had gone to them for the school holidays she had been charged with board and lodging. Irene Rabbit's face grew gloomier and gloomier during the evening, and her manner throughout Sunday made Helen count the hours until Monday morning, when her visit ended.

III

'If you please, Lady Cucumber, where do you wish his lordship's new secretary to have her meals?'

Lady Cucumber was in her sitting-room, not a very comfortable place. The three ornaments the room contained were queer. Only one picture was permitted, and Lord Cucumber said he would never sit in the same room with it. The walls were a filigree of shadows, but tall copper lamps cast a warm glow over the melon-pink ceiling. On a divan sat Laura Cucumber in a dressing-gown of brown silk shot with yellow flowers, turning over the pages of the Tatler.

She was a fair-fluffy woman, her fingers were like thin ivory sticks loaded with jewels. Her dark eyes were raised upwards at the corners, and her lips, a double curve of dusky crimson, were parted like the mouth of a tragic mask, as she looked up at Miss Poklewski-Koziazell – a troubled woman harassed by wrestling with servants and supplying the needs of Lady Cucumber's guests late at night.

'The new secretary?' Laura Cucumber wrinkled her forehead. 'I'd forgotten there was one. When is she coming?'

'She *came* early this morning, your ladyship.'

'Oh, really. Well, what's the difficulty? She'll have her meals with you, I suppose. Didn't Miss Offjenkin?'

'Yes, but I understood that Miss Hagg was the daughter of an old friend of Lord Cucumber's.'

Lady Cucumber pondered. 'Yes, I think Frederick did mention it. But it won't make any difference. What is she like?'

'Very young,' said Miss Poklewski-Koziazell.

'Indeed!' Lady Cucumber narrowed her eyes speculatively and put a monogrammed cigarette between her lips.

'She's some relation of Mr and Mrs Rabbit, I believe.'

Lady Cucumber looked relieved. 'Perhaps I'd better see her a minute,' she said. 'Any relation of the Rabbits should belong to a type that gives no trouble in a house. I visualise an angular young woman with big feet and watery eyes.'

A moment later Miss Poklewski-Koziazell returned with Helen Hagg, and one glance made Lady Cucumber decide that her husband had been a fool.

'How do you do?' she said. 'Won't you sit down.' She studied the girl and then passed the remark which always made Helen anxious, 'You look very young to be a secretary.'

'I left school over a year ago,' said Helen Hagg, her colour coming and going through her fear of making the wrong impression, 'and since then I have been learning.'

'My husband's secretary is a responsible position.'

'I know.'

'However, I never interfere with his work,' went on Lady Cucumber, airily. 'I expect Miss Poklewski-Koziazell has shown you your room and explained everything. I hope you will be happy here.'

'I know I shall,' said Helen Hagg, her nipples straining against her dress. 'I love my room.'

'I am glad of that,' said Lady Cucumber. 'I feared you might find it dull at Hummingbird.'

'No,' said Helen, 'I don't think so. I like the country.'

'A queer taste,' said Lady Cucumber, adding – 'My husband will not be down for a few days. I don't know if he has left you anything to do?'

'Yes, thank you. I think I understand what he wants.'

'Then that is all right,' said Lady Cucumber, and getting up signified that the interview was at an end.

At first Miss Poklewski-Koziazell was inclined to share Lady Cucumber's view, and to think Lord Cucumber unwise to embark on a girl of Helen's age, but as the days passed she changed her opinion. Helen Hagg turned out to be not only blissfully happy, but unexpectedly submissive.

IV

'Have some more of this. Mrs O'Bottom makes it very well,' said Miss Poklewski-Koziazell, relaxing after a hard day.

It was the night before a 'week-end'. A 'week-end' in Miss Poklewski-Koziazell's phraseology was quite distinct from the end of a week. All day she had been supervising bedroom arrangements, seeing that pen-nibs, soap and bath-salts were correct, and that every possible emergency was foreseen. Nothing could be left to chance. On these occasions Miss Poklewski-Koziazell did not dare to go to bed for fear of anything unexpected, and then had to get up early to see that all was in order of Lord Cucumber's requirements.

'Is this week's party specially important?' asked Helen, conscious that there had been more tension than usual.

'It is in a way,' said Miss Poklewski-Koziazell, a faint twinkle lighting up the sombreness of her eyes. 'Lady Cucumber always wants it to go well when Mr Richard comes.'

'Lady Cucumber is very fond of him, I suppose?'

'Dotes on him.'

'Is Lord Cucumber like that as well?'

Miss Poklewski-Koziazell lowered her voice. 'Not so much. I often think he's a trifle disappointed – would like his son to be more like himself. But Lady Cucumber doesn't care.'

'I wonder why,' said Helen.

14

'Lady Cucumber's a climber,' said Miss Poklewski-Koziazell savagely. 'She adores old families and titles, and means her son to marry one. There should be no difficulty about that, but he's rather a gay young man, and she's simply terrified that somebody will catch him.'

'Is Lord Cucumber like that?'

'Bless you, no! He'd like him to get hold of a nice girl and settle down.'

'Is anyone special coming this week-end?' asked Helen Hagg, making her voice very low and confidential.

There was a pause while Miss Poklweski-Koziazell looked at a china bull-dog on the mantelpiece.

'Yes,' she said at last. 'And I can see that Lady Cucumber hopes something will come of it. She's had one after another of these society girls down, and sometimes Master Richard nibbles, and then he gets shy. But this time she thinks he's hooked, though as to *that* I have my doubts.'

'Who is it? Dear Miss Poklewski-Koziazell, do tell me.'

'I mustn't sit here gossiping,' said Miss Poklewski-Koziazell. 'I must make a note about the flowers. Lady Cucumber said malmaisons for the dinner table.'

'But do tell me,' said Helen Hagg, her face clouding.

Miss Poklewski-Koziazell considered her plate with a supercilious air. 'Well, it's Lady Thomyris Dagobert, or the 'Tigress' as she is called. I dare say you have heard of her?'

Helen had. So had most people who read the illustrated weekly papers. From the moment of leaving her finishing school, Lady Thomyris had been acclaimed, and her reputation was now established beyond question. Constant rumours appeared in the papers of her engagement, but so far no actual announcement had been made.

'Lady Cucumber has set her heart on the match,' said Miss Poklewski-Koziazell. 'Of course it's one of the oldest families in England, and the women have always been famous for their looks. Consuela, Duchess of Sodamint, that's Lady Thomyris's mother, was a beauty too, so she gets it from both sides. I know all about them, for I come from near their place at Slaughter St Wilfred, and when I was a young girl it was a gay place and no mistake.'

'I've seen lots of pictures of Lady Thomyris,' said Helen Hagg.

'Bless you, that's just advertisement, so to speak.' Miss Poklewski-Koziazell leaned forward a little in her chair, her face vague and indistinct in the twilight. 'The Duchess of Sodamint spends quite a bit because she wants her to get married. But I hear privately, as my sister knows the governess of Lady Pasiphae and Lady Phedre (those are the two younger ones), that the duchess of Sodamint is pretty cross because she hasn't achieved a husband already. There have been several men *crazy* about her, but she doesn't seem to care for them.'

'Why should she marry if she doesn't want to?' said Helen Hagg.

Miss Poklewski-Koziazell brushed her chin with a napkin.

'Because of the other two. Lady Pasiphae is due to

be presented in May, and Lady Phedre is only a year younger.'

'Then she wouldn't object if Lady Thomyris married Richard Cucumber?'

'No, it would suit her very well.'

'I wonder if Mr Cucumber is in love with her,' mused Helen.

Miss Poklewski-Koziazell shrugged.

'I wonder too,' she said, as she walked away.

That evening some of the guests arrived, and Lord Cucumber returned from London. It was understood that the house-party was never to interfere with him, and he shut himself up in his study with Helen Hagg in attendance. The result pleased him more than ever, and at the end of two hours, when he stopped and Helen was gathering up her notes, she turned round to find him studying her.

'You are unusually good at translation, Miss Hagg, you must have worked hard,' he said.

Helen flushed with pleasure.

'I hope you like being here,' he went on.

'Oh, very much, Lord Cucumber – and I love the work.'

Her sincerity was apparent, and he looked pleased.

But, he thought as he went up to dress for dinner, it must be a dull life for a girl of her age. The idea persisted, and he went to his wife's room. He found her dressed and ready to go downstairs. She was in an amiable mood, for she was pleased with her new gown by Quasi Constantine. Oxblood suited her, and it went well with her fine necklace of garnets. In spite of constant trouble with her figure, Laura Cucumber was still a fine-looking woman, and her husband was very proud of her.

'Do you like my dress, Frederick?'

'It's remarkable,' he said, kissing her.

'Well, we'd better go down,' said Laura – 'or did you want to speak to me?'

'Yes. I suppose it wouldn't be possible to give Miss Hagg a little gaiety now and then?'

Lady Cucumber stiffened. 'Your secretary? I don't quite understand.'

'She's rather different from most secretaries.'

'Really, Frederick, I don't think it's a good thing to change her status. She wouldn't mix with our friends. And I'm sure she doesn't expect anything like that.'

'I only meant now and then,' said Lord Cucumber, drawing his eyebrows together.

Lady Cucumber walked across the wide yellow carpet strewn with blue tulips.

'I think that would be very difficult, Frederick. If one did it all the time she'd get to expect it, and if one only did it occasionally she'd feel hurt.'

'I don't think Helen Hagg is a bit like that,' said Lord Cucumber.

'In any case she wouldn't have the right clothes,' laughed Laura, picking up her evening bag. 'No, my dear, the girl's quite content as she is, and it's better to leave things.'

So saying, she inhaled the scent of roses mingled with cigarette smoke and went downstairs.

Helen Hagg was at work in Lord Cucumber's study the next morning when he broke off in the middle of a paragraph.

'That's my son now and Lady Thomyris. I think we'll stop now, Miss Hagg.'

He went out and Helen, feeling her curiosity stir, watched discreetly from the window, and as she watched she gave a sigh of pleasure. Thomyris Dagobert was one of those people who come up to expectations. She was wearing a marigold sweater and grey striped trousers. She was really lovely as she stood there, slim, charming and smiling, her short hair had a metallic gleam in its blackness. Her sculpted silver hat sprouted ears of jade-green wood. She looked like a fairy princess, thought the little secretary enthusiastically. Helen glanced at the fortunate young man by her side. He was tall and broad-shouldered, and had a gay, pleasant face as he smiled to greet his father. He was evidently pleased with himself and the world. Ramsrape, the butler, hovered in the doorway. Lady Cucumber's borzois, long-nosed, graceful, superbly elegant, waddled to meet them. The picture of a prosperous young man returning home with his bride-elect was complete.

That afternoon and the following morning Helen caught glimpses of Lady Thomyris, and each one deepened her admiration. That evening when the young people danced in the big hall, she and Miss Poklewski-Koziazell crept into the gallery to watch, and were enthusiastic about Lady Thomyris, who was wearing a white percale dress with mameluke sleeves. As Helen Hagg looked at them, her eyes shone with excitement. To her it was like a glimpse into another world.

It was not until the next afternoon that Helen came into contact with the object of her admiration. Lord

Cucumber had told her to bring her things into the conservatory. Around her as she typed, tendrils and tropical blossoms swelled, obtruded, and convoluted. Pearly-grey leaves suffused with purple, reddish flowers with pea-like bodies, lemon flowers with a dark green stripe, nodded and bobbed. Presently she heard a footstep behind her and looked round. Lady Thomyris had come in and paused to watch.

'I should love to do that,' she said, smiling and coming up to the table. 'Would you let me try?'

Helen put in a new sheet of paper. Lady Thomyris sat down, exclaiming when she hit the wrong letters.

'It's fascinating!' She glanced up, and met Helen Hagg's look of admiration. 'But I'm wasting your time.'

'You're not wasting my time,' said Miss Hagg.

Lady Thomyris rivetted her with curious, lime-coloured eyes.

'Can you do short-hand as well?' she said. 'Where did you learn?'

Helen told her.

'I should like to do that.' Lady Thomyris paused and went on tapping out words.

'Hullo! Is Miss Hagg giving you a lesson?'

Lord Cucumber had come in and stood looking at them. Lady Thomyris opened her eyes to their fullest extent.

'Yes, but I'm being very foolish. May I try again some time?' she smiled at Helen. 'Thanks most awfully for showing me.'

'Oh, Thomyris, dear, I was looking for you,' said Lady Cucumber from the doorway. She came towards them, moving her equine face into a controlled expression. 'I wondered if you were out with Richard.'

'I was, but we got back some time ago. I managed to get some fairly decent books from the library. Amy de With, no one can write short stories like her! and Arthur Stunt. I had an idea that I ought not to read the latter, but when I asked Father about it in the confessional, I learned that all was well, and that one of his favourite books was Stunt's *Muriel and the Spartan General*.'

'I say,' said Lord Cucumber, 'that sounds a bit high-brow to me.'

'It isn't at all high-brow.'

'I remember,' said Lady Cucumber, 'after reading his *Every Little Girl Can Teach Me Something New*, lying in the long grass and sobbing as though I had lost everything that was dear to me.'

'Never lend books to the vicar, by the way,' said Lord Cucumber. 'He has run off with my copy of *Such a Little Queen*.'

'You will never see it again!'

Lady Cucumber gave a fleeting smile, signifying that Miss Hagg might leave them. When she had gone, she turned to her husband.

'Well, Frederick,' she said, 'are you going on working?'

'Not for the moment.'

'Let's stop here,' said Lady Thomyris, sniffing a creeper. 'This smells heavenly. Do you know, I've never been to any of the places where these things grow.'

'You will,' answered Lord Cucumber. 'You have plenty of time.'

'It doesn't always depend on time.'

'Marry a rich man and you can go where you like,' said Lady Cucumber inexorably.

'Where do you want to go? Egypt, Greece, South America?'

Lady Thomyris smiled into the zebra-striped dusk.

'Nowhere like that. I want to see all the old, legendary places. If I were a man I'd be an archeologist.'

'Would you? That's a rather dusty job.' Lord Cucumber was surprised; secretly he thought her too statuesque. 'You like the lands of myth and fancy best?'

Lady Thomyris nodded. 'Yes, I feel the present world is rather squalid, don't you?'

'Not a bit,' said Lady Cucumber, laughing. 'The modern world offers a great deal, my dear.'

'What I want most desperately,' confided Lady Thomyris, 'is to go on a cruise. My godfather may arrange it – but that's a secret.'

'A cruise.' Lady Cucumber was thoughtful. 'One has to be careful of one's company.'

'One can always see the passenger lists.'

'I suppose lots of people are doing that.' Lady Cucumber had an idea and was turning it over in her mind.

'Well, I must return to my work,' said her husband.

'Which means that he wants to get rid of us.' And Lady Cucumber crushed a flower absent-mindedly between her fingers.

V

The weather was now very cold with a hard frost. There was another dance the next night and a lot of talk about slippery roads as there had been a slight fall of snow. But the snow stopped, and the following day the lake was declared fit for skating. Helen Hagg was pleased at the prospect. She had her skates, and was an expert, for she had spent two winters in Switzerland with her father.

Lord Cucumber saw her looking wistfully after some of the guests who were going down the hill to the lake.

'Do you skate, my dear?'

'Like a bird,' she answered.

'Then mind that you do it,' he said. 'I've got to go back to town tonight, and you are looking pale. Take some time off and make the most of the ice while it lasts.'

So Helen extracted an old skating costume from the bottom of her trunk, though it was years since she had worn it. Then she made her way down to the lake.

'Who's the girl doing all the stunts?' said Captain Delacroix, putting up his eyeglass.

Richard Cucumber glanced up carelessly. 'It's my father's secretary, Miss Hagg,' he said.

Other people admired the skill of the small figure in the marmalade-coloured skating dress. Lady Cucumber, who was asked about her several times, began to wonder if secretaries should skate. But

23

Helen Hagg was not conscious of being admired, although she was certainly the most noticeable figure on the ice. Lady Cucumber herself did not skate, and walked up and down to keep warm. In this way she failed to observe her son cross the ice in order to join Helen.

But Helen Hagg was not easy to join. When she saw him approaching she skated away until she came to that part of the ice where Lady Thomyris stood unsteadily. At that moment, Lady Thomyris staggered, slipped up, and Helen, after helping her to her feet, asked diffidently if she would like to try holding hands. The two girls skated away, Helen Hagg teaching. Presently Richard joined them, but he did not get what he wanted. His annoyance was not diminished by the arrival of Lady Thomyris's mother, who had come down to look on. Consuela, Duchess of Sodamint, a person of determination, observed the groups on the ice, saw that her daughter was not acquitting herself well, and that Richard, who should have been supporting her, was watching a small figure in a marmalade-coloured dress, who was demonstrating an intricate figure.

'Who's that?' she barked at Lady Cucumber, who stood huddled in sables looking miserable.

'It's Miss Hagg. My husband's secretary.'

'Frederick seems to have a pretty taste in secretaries,' said the Duchess of Sodamint. 'Don't you think it might lead to complications?'

'It already has,' said Lady Cucumber with asperity. And unable to withstand the cold a moment longer, she turned and walked towards the house.

The next day it was proposed that the house party should go to the theatre in Huguenot Malherbe. The news was communicated to Miss Poklewski-Koziazell at lunch time.

'Just as dinner was all fixed,' she lamented to Helen. 'Now they want a sort of high tea, as they leave at seven, and Mrs O'Bottom hates alterations.'

Helen sympathised and hurried off to skate. She meant to avoid the guests, and so went to the far end of the lake, which was hidden from the rest by an island.

Meanwhile her absence had been noted by Richard Cucumber. He took off his skates and walked up to the house. As he was going through the hall he met Ramsrape.

'Do you know where Miss Hagg is?' he said.

'I think she is skating, sir. I saw her go about two o'clock.'

'Which way?'

'Towards the waterfall.'

Helen Hagg had been at the other end of the lake all the time. Richard Cucumber swore, went to the garage and got out his car. It was already dusk and in a few minutes she would be coming in. The road ran close to the lake, and as Richard walked across the rough grass, Helen was standing with her back to him.

'So there you are,' he said crossly.

She had not heard him coming, and at the sound of his voice she turned quickly and caught her foot on a hummock, and fell, twisting her ankle.

'Have you hurt yourself,' he said, slipping an arm round her waist.

'Only a little,' said Helen Hagg, but she was white with pain.

'Let me help you to the car.'

She hobbled towards it, leaning on his arm. He tucked her up in the rug.

'I'll drive you back.' Richard leaned forward and passed his tongue over his lips.

'Don't bother. I shall be able to walk in a minute.'

'Don't be silly.'

They started to move slowly in the opposite direction from the house. As they gathered speed, turning to the left instead of the right as they should have done, Helen, who was occupied with the pain in her ankle, hardly realised it. At last she became attentive to the scenery.

'Which way are we going?'

'I thought we might go for a run,' said Richard, lolling over the steering wheel indolently.

'I want to get back,' said Helen Hagg. 'I have work to do.'

'Never mind that.'

'But I do. And I want my tea.'

'You shall have your tea, all in good time,' said Richard, and he accelerated. They were now doing over sixty.

Richard Cucumber was in an ugly mood. For two days he had been denied the thing he wanted. So he drove on faster, not answering Helen who continued to remonstrate. Plunging through twisting lanes, they came away from the villages and onto the downs.

'I think you are behaving hatefully,' said Helen Hagg.

'Don't be tiresome,' said Richard, stretching out his arm and pulling her to him.

'It's you who are tiresome,' said Helen, laying her hand on the door.

Richard Cucumber put his arm round her and pulled her back roughly.

'Don't be a little fool,' he said, as the car swerved into a tree.

There was a grinding of brakes, a crash, the windscreen splintered in all directions, the car slid to a halt. By a miracle neither Richard nor Helen were hurt, but it was clear that nothing more could be expected that evening.

The short winter twilight was fading, range upon range of blue-grey clouds mottled the sky. Frozen puddles stood out in the road before them like cameo portraits; the moon was just rising, and through the pine-fronds its light took on the texture of old lace. Richard tried to switch on his headlamps, but they had gone.

'I say, I'm frightfully sorry.'

Helen Hagg peered into the darkness. 'What are we to do?'

She was frightened and did not attempt to hide it.

Richard Cucumber stroked his moustache slowly with one finger. 'There must be somewhere,' he said, trying to sound more hopeful than he felt. 'I'd better go and have a look.'

'I'll come with you.'

'Take my arm.'

'No, thank you,' said Helen Hagg, distantly, and stumbled into the rough lane.

She was not only angry but she was worried. There was no sign of human habitation at the top of the hill. Richard had a recollection of some farm, but there was not a glimmer of light to show its existence. As they struggled on down the lane, it was clear that Helen's ankle hurt, though she made no complaint. At last they saw windows like three orange trees peering out of the gloom. The door was opened by a woman with black looped hair, a mask-like countenance, and claw-like hands. It appeared that she was Mrs Smith, and this was her farm. No, she had no telephone. She offered, however, to get them tea while they waited.

Richard Cucumber and Helen ate and drank in silence.

'I wonder what they'll think about me,' said Helen Hagg anxiously.

'I'll explain that,' said Richard, and tried to put his arm around her.

'Please don't! I'd rather you didn't!'

It was close on nine o'clock when they reached Ponceplural. Their arrival at Hummingbird was unfortunately timed, as it coincided with the return of the theatre party, and everyone saw that Richard was not alone. There was a compression about Lady Cucumber's lips that showed that she was really angry.

'I thought that you had had an accident on the ice,' she said with pursed lips, as she took off her hat.

'I thought that you had eloped,' smiled Penelope Pantagruel, an irrepressible young woman.

'With the young lady in the marmalade-coloured skating outfit,' said someone else, indiscreetly.

'I thought that Miss Hagg would also be missing,' said the Duchess of Sodamint, drily.

But Lady Cucumber appeared not to hear. She was seething with fury. It looked to her like an intrigue. And what a moment to choose, with Consuela as watchful as an old vulture. She was ominously silent. She had had a dreadful evening, and felt positively vicious when Richard followed her in and began his excuses.

'I'm frightfully sorry, mother, but we – '

'We?' said Lady Cucumber, in a terrible voice.

'Miss Hagg. She was walking over the rough grass by the lake, and turned her ankle. I was giving her a lift back.'

Lady Cucumber's teeth showed white in a brief smile.

'Back *where*?' she thundered.

'Back to the house.'

'Dear me!'

'I was making a detour, and then I ran into a tree.'

'Where was this?' enquired Consuela, Duchess of Sodamint.

'Oh, some miles from Cowcurse Priory.'

'Cowcurse Priory?' said the Duchess, intent as a terrier following a rat. 'But that must be fourteen miles away.'

'Not quite so much,' said Richard sulkily.

'It must be at least thirteen. I used to hunt with the Tong, and have a memory for distances.'

At this they all laughed, and presently, being sleepy after their late nights, they went off to bed.

'My dear,' said the Duchess of Sodamint as she

bade her hostess goodnight, 'just one piece of advice. GET RID OF THAT SECRETARY!'

VI

'She takes after her father, I'm afraid,' said Irene Rabbit, shaking her head. 'I should not like the responsibility of taking her.'

'I cannot see why you should be asked to,' said Lady Cucumber, studying the polish on her nails.

'I understand that she was doing her work all right?'

'As to that I am no judge,' said Lady Cucumber. 'Honestly I was not considering her work, but . . . what happened with my son.'

Irene Rabbit became faintly asthmatic. 'Helen Hagg has certainly behaved very badly.'

'You understand, Mrs Rabbit, till now my husband's secretaries have always been on a business footing. I am not blaming Miss Hagg. She is young, and it is natural that she should want to join in what is going on. But such behaviour does not fit in here.' Lady Cucumber gave a tragic sigh. 'I should not like to risk the recurrence of such an incident.'

Irene Rabbit was torn by conflicting emotions. That Helen Hagg was being dismissed without a character satisfied her spite, but there were other considerations. Mechanically she murmured that Helen had abused Lady Cucumber's kindness.

'It was not the first time that she and my son had been out together,' said Lady Cucumber. 'I have made enquiries. There is no harm in it, perhaps, but it is unsuitable and it caused a lot of comment.'

31

'When will you wish her to leave?'

'As soon as she can do so,' said Lady Cucumber, and there was a hard glint in her eye.

For different reasons both she and Mrs Rabbit decided that it would be undesirable for Helen Hagg to remain in the neighbourhood. Richard Cucumber, as well as his father, would be furious if ever he heard the truth.

'I am sure you understand, dear Mrs Rabbit. My son is kind-hearted . . . it would increase the difficulties.'

'Quite,' said Irene Rabbit.

Lady Cucumber drew her eyebrows together. 'The girl may be relying on living with you when she leaves here – '

'She won't when she has talked to me!'

Mrs Rabbit was taken at once to Lord Cucumber's study. Helen Hagg was typing feverishly, trying not to think for fear of breaking down. Her sense of security had been shattered. She had slept little, and looked white and apprehensive. The work she had loved was to be taken from her. She could hardly believe it. As the door opened, she glanced up and encountered Irene Rabbit's gaze. The malice of it was undisguised.

'So it's you, Cousin Irene,' she said, taking her hands off the typewriter.

'Yes, it's me.' Mrs Rabbit's voice revealed the venom of her mind.

Helen sat still.

'I've come to hear what you have to say for yourself. Not that I haven't heard all about it already.

I can't say that I'm surprised, but poor Herbert will feel the disgrace.'

'It sounds as if you had been listening to lies,' said Helen. She had a fiery temperament, and was aching with resentment.

'Isn't a dismissal a disgrace?' went on Irene Rabbit.

'If it is just.'

Irene Rabbit snorted. 'Did you expect Lady Cucumber to keep you on after your behaviour?'

'I think it would be better,' said Helen, 'if I were to tell you exactly what happened.'

'I don't want your account,' said Irene Rabbit, rudely.

'But you must have it. Please sit down.'

The pre-emptory tone so startled Mrs Rabbit that she complied, and Helen, in a voice full of vibrant emotion, gave a clear statement of what had happened.

'And now you have heard the truth,' she ended.

'Do you expect me to believe all that?'

'I do.'

Irene Rabbit laughed disagreeably.

'Then you must invent something more probable. It is obvious that you have been running after Richard Cucumber. I do not care to discuss how it happened. The fact is that it *did* happen.'

'But listen – ,' said Helen Hagg, flushing scarlet with fury.

'And now you have lost your job,' went on Irene Rabbit with relish. 'Where will you find another? And we have no money to spare for charity.'

'Did I suggest coming to you?'

33

'No, but it's obvious that you'll want to.'

Helen Hagg gave a proud toss of her head.

'As if we hadn't done enough already!' continued Irene.

'What have you done exactly?' asked Helen.

'You are a very ungrateful girl to ask such a question,' gobbled Mrs Rabbit. 'Didn't we take you into our house upon several occasions? Didn't Herbert attend to your education?

'I went to your house twice as a paying guest, and my education was paid for out of the money my mother left me.'

'And what about this job?' barked Irene Rabbit.

'Lord Cucumber was an old friend of my father's .'

'Well, I hope it's taught him the truth. Like father, like daughter. Your father was a waster too.'

She shrank back, as Helen Hagg ran round the typing table and stood over her.

'I forbid you to speak like that of my father. You resent his memory,' said Helen, tensely, 'because he once told you that you were a common-minded woman. But don't worry. I'd rather starve than come inside your house.' She opened the door. 'And now you will go. I am finishing work for Lord Cucumber, and you are wasting his time as well as mine.'

Shaking with fury, Mrs Rabbit scrambled to her feet.

'I never – I never – ' she stuttered.

'Probably not,' said Helen Hagg, 'but if more people had told you the truth about yourself, you might be a better woman. As it is, it makes me sick to be in the same room as you!'

Something impelled Mrs Rabbit across the threshold, and before she could collect her wits the door had closed, and she heard Helen Hagg turn the key.

PART TWO

VII

Helen Hagg sat on a bench in Trafalgar Square. The droop of her shoulders showed her condition. She had had nothing but bad luck since leaving the Cucumbers; she had explored every avenue without result. She had tried one thing and then another, but she was severely handicapped. She had no friends in London. The few she had made had gone right away. She had not a soul to whom she could tell her troubles, and loneliness enveloped her like a dark cloud.

She sat trying to think of a possible opening. She had tramped from place to place, interviewing employers in offices, trying to get taken on in the chorus of musical comedies, and also in innumerable shops. She had only had a cup of coffee since morning, and no supper the night before, and as she watched pigeons pecking up crumbs, she tried to decide whether to have a midday meal or wait until evening.

On one point she was determined. Nothing should make her write for assistance to either the Rabbits or the Cucumbers, for the thought filled her with burning resentment. In a way she was suffering from mental shock. Helen Hagg knew she had given of her best, and her ejection had inflicted a wound from which she would be slow to recover. Until that morning she had refused to give way to the fear that lurked in the background of her mind, but now as she sat shivering it came out and gibbered at her. What was the use of going on? There was, after all, not a soul to whom it would matter if Helen Hagg plunged in the river and ended it all.

But at this point Helen took herself in hand. Getting up, she dispersed these gloomy thoughts by movement, moving briskly through the streets, trying to find comfort in the sight of the human beings that thronged there. Her way led up the Haymarket, and she came to a standstill before the windows of a travel agency, for she was attracted by the brilliantly coloured advertisements.

These were of ivory mountains against a copper-coloured sky, blazing red streamers pendant from cyclamen trees, globes of orange and blue-striped fruit, misty continents and red-gold oceans. They were gay and crude, and Helen stood entranced as she remembered her happy days of wandering, when laughter and companionship were hers. If only a miracle could happen. She stood wishing this with such an intensity that several passers-by glanced at her curiously.

The ways of fate are strange, for it was then that Helen Hagg had a chance encounter that was to change her future.

Mrs Brenda Mitylene was walking towards Piccadilly trying to decide where she would lunch. She had little use for people who were indifferent to one of the most solid pleasures of middle age. She looked an extremely prosperous widow of fifty, and this is what she was. She was neat in dress, leisurely in movement, and rather stout. No one who met her casually would have supposed that she had been a successful member of the Secret Service.

As she wandered on, wondering if her club or the Grill-room at the Berkeley should supply her lunch, she turned to look at a picture in a shop, and collided with a girl. She was a collector of old coaching prints and apologised absent-mindedly, for this was a rare one. She was recalled to realities, however, by the sound of her name being spoken in a low, vibrant voice, and she turned.

Helen Hagg was a little anxious, as she had had one or two nasty experiences, and yet was certain that it was Mrs Mitylene, though she had not seen her for several years. It had been when she was with her father in Yokohama. Brenda Mitylene had put on weight, but Helen was sure it was she.

'It is Mrs Mitylene, isn't it?' Her voice shook a little as she spoke. 'You won't remember me, but I'm Helen Hagg.'

But Brenda had been trained to remember faces. She had not approved of Ralph Hagg, but she had been amused by him.

'But I do, perfectly,' she said, her eyes shining like polished jet. 'This is very nice. How kind of you to stop me in the street.'

Helen Hagg gave a trill of deprecatory laughter. After weeks of indifferent faces, it was pleasant to get a welcome of any form.

A pretty girl, thought Mrs Mitylene, who was susceptible, and she flushed bright pink with excitement.

'And what are you doing these days?' she said. 'I heard about your poor father's sudden and unexpected accident. Poor Ralph! As a companion, he was hard to beat. An excellent fellow!'

The Rabbits would hardly have agreed with this verdict, but it enchanted Helen.

'I'm living in lodgings,' she said.

'Dear me! But I know young girls do that now.'

There was a blast of chilly wind, and Mrs Mitylene shivered.

'Devilish cold standing here. Where are you lunching? What about coming and having a spot with me?'

It is needless to say that Helen Hagg thought well of the suggestion, and in a few minutes they were seated at a small table in the Ladies' Room of Brenda Mitylene's club.

'I hope you are hungry. Most girls are on diets, and do nothing but peck nowadays.'

Helen Hagg reassured her, and Mrs Mitylene regarded her approvingly. The colour began to come back into Helen's cheeks as they talked about old times. Since her retirement from the Secret Service, Mrs Mitylene had become the director of a shipping line.

'Of course shipping has been a dead loss for years,' she said, watching Helen with vague, veiled eyes. 'So we run educational cruises, it pays better.'

'I looked at some of the advertisements as I came by just now,' said Helen.

Mrs Mitylene coughed.

'All right if you strike good weather. We have one starting next week. An awfully brainy business, with countless professors lecturing day and night. Highbrow, you know, but I like it. I may go along myself. In fact I may tell you in confidence that I am going along.'

'Oh, Mrs Mitylene,' said Helen, her heart beginning to pound, 'do you think it would be possible to find a job for me on board?'

'A job! What sort of a job?'

'Anything,' said Helen with a high, unnatural laugh. 'A stewardess.'

'But my dear girl, that's ridiculous. How could you be a stewardess?'

'I'm a good sailor, and I'm sure I could do anything, and I do desperately need it,' said Helen Hagg, suddenly crimson, for she hated asking for favours.

Mrs Mitylene appeared to be thinking deeply. She looked at Helen with faint amusement, noted the signs of poverty, and sighed.

'Have a coffee, and tell me about it,' she said.

Helen Hagg told her the whole story, not omitting anything. She found that Mrs Mitylene knew the Cucumbers, liked him, and detested her. However as she listened attentively, she could not help seeing Lady Cucumber's point of view. Helen was far too good-looking to have with a grown-up son about. She fell into silence.

'Please, oh *please* – ' began Helen.

Mrs Mitylene assumed an aspect of deepest gloom. 'It would be too rough, Helen Hagg, for most of the crew are foreign.'

'As if I cared!' said Helen, drinking some coffee in an agitated manner. 'Oh, Mrs Mitylene, you don't know what it's like to wander up and down the streets. Truly I could do any amount of work, and I'm strong.'

Mrs Mitylene's eyelids drooped heavily over her eyes.

'Well,' she said, 'we might go to the office, but it's late in the day. Everything will be arranged.'

In the offices of the company, two efficient ladies were sitting at big desks. Mrs Mitylene took the elder lady aside, and for some moments there was a whispered colloquy. The elderly lady took one glance at Helen and shook her head.

'Far too young, Mrs Mitylene.'

'What about the office?'

'That is absolutely full. We have Mrs Duckspawn and Lottie Teapot.'

'Is there no hole, no corner?'

'I'm terribly sorry but I'm afraid not.'

'This is the daughter of an old friend of mine . . . '

Presently Mrs Mitylene came to tell Helen of the verdict which she had already half suspected. She blinked hard as they came out of the warm office to keep back her tears. However she thanked Mrs Mitylene very charmingly for all the trouble she had taken. She had begun to say goodbye when Mrs Mitylene turned a pair of prominent eyes upon her.

'Of course you know, Helen dear, I'm in a fix. It's about my maid, Lucy Schliemnann. Little hussy, she's gone soft at the last moment; says she won't go. She's been reading about shipwrecks, and when I told her passage was taken, she cried all day and said she'd be drowned. You may say why not cancel the girl's passage and go without her; and so I would, but my brother Bernard is making a fuss because of my heart and asthma. He won't let me go alone.'

'Oh Mrs Mitylene,' said Helen, in an imploring voice, 'won't you take me?'

'You!' said Mrs Mitylene blankly.

'Yes.' Helen's eyes were like coals. Her face suffused with a blush. 'I know I could be a good maid. I sew and pack well, and I've learnt some dressmaking. I have my V.A.D. certificates, and have done a little nursing.'

She gazed at Mrs Mitylene, her voice sinking to an unsteady whisper, and Brenda Mitylene stared back, appraising her.

'If only you would,' breathed Helen.

'You can't expect me to jump at you like a fish at a fly,' said Mrs Mitylene severely. She paused and considered. 'I must have time to think. Look here, meet me in the restaurant at Zouch, Finit, and Dromes' at half past four and have tea. Just by the lift. I'll tell you then.'

She nodded dismissal, and watched Helen Hagg walk away.

At half past four Helen was waiting by the lift as she had been told. Her expression was that of a stray dog that had been ill-treated, and any doubts which Mrs Mitylene may have felt vanished.

'I've thought it over, and I'll take you,' she said, gruffly, and turned away to give her order, pretending not to see the tears of relief that came into Helen Hagg's eyes.

'Mind you,' said Mrs Mitylene, as she poured out. 'You may find me a bit sharp now and then, and by the end of the voyage we'll probably have had enough of one another, but it's worth a trial. After all, I needn't engage you beyond the voyage, and whoever I get now will be a stranger. It isn't the right job for you with your education. But you look capable, and I've paid for the passage. Where did you go to school by the way?'

'St Sappho's.'

'Quite a good place as schools go,' said Mrs Mitylene. 'You probably owe more to your father than you think. Well, we must talk business: have you got your passport? Good. I shall be in London on Monday evening, and you can join me at the hotel and we'll start next day. We'll stop a night in Byzantium and join the ship there.'

Mrs Mitylene's fingers played with the clasp of her handbag, and she gave a lascivious forward tilt to her pelvis.

VIII

Lady Cucumber told the steward where to put her chair, and sat at ease watching a fine sunset over Byzantium. The sunset was so coagulate that it seemed as though tangerines, apples, and melons were being pulped on the skyline. The sea was blue flecked with amethyst and damson. A group of champagne-coloured stars suddenly appeared low down in the sky.

Lady Cucumber was amused by the commotion caused by new passengers coming on board. It was a lively scene. Shouts resounded, motor boats and sampans, kayaks and gondolas plied to and fro; stewards ran backwards and forwards across her field of vision with bags, suitcases and trunks. Lady Cucumber felt content, for the cruise not only promised to be pleasant, but ought to bring about something definite between her son and Lady Thomyris. A series of fortunate events had made it possible that they should be passengers on the same ship. It seemed almost as if it was 'meant', as she had said to Lord Cucumber. She herself had had a bronchial cold, and a well-trained doctor had said that a cruise would be beneficial. Then the Duchess of Sodamint told them that Lady Thomyris had been given £300 by her godfather so that she could travel.

But Lady Thomyris had views, very definite ones. She wasn't going to embark on a luxury cruise without an object. She wanted to study old civilisations, and for that purpose she joined this particular ship. No other trip would do. This one took in the places she wanted to see – Troy, Ismarus, the Cyclops land, Laestrygonia, Circe's island, Scylla and Charybdis, and Ogygia – finishing up in the land of the Phaecians. If Lady Thomyris had a fault, thought Lady Cucumber, it was that she was a high-brow.

At that moment Richard Cucumber and Lady Thomyris came back with a list of passengers. Quickly they read through the A's – Lady Abdomen, Mr Antigonus, and many others. Lady Cucumber stopped abruptly at the G's.

'Miss Hannah Gammon. That odious woman!'

'Who's she?' said Richard.

'Oh, a woman I used to know. She lived near us when I was a girl.' Lady Cucumber's eyes darted upwards. 'And here in the M's is Brenda Mitylene. That dreadful woman!'

'I don't suppose she will bother us,' said Richard.

His mother agreed, and they went on looking at the list. Lady Thomyris, who had another copy, was reading the names of the lecturers. Richard looked over her shoulder.

I don't think I know anyone except the Warden of St Asp's,' he said. 'I met him at Oxford. Do you?'

'There's this one. I know him.'

'Langley Fundament. 'Greco-Phoenician Sculpture'. What's the old boy like?'

'He's not old,' said Lady Thomyris, briefly.

Richard strolled along the deck with her. Lady Cucumber, who was lazy, remained where she was, sometimes looking at the list she held, and sometimes at the sea, which was glittering with colours like crushed jewels. A motor boat was approaching with more passengers, and as it drew up at the foot of the ship's ladder a squat, pyknic figure rose up, wearing a mannish hat and a large cape, and Lady Cucumber recognised Mrs Mitylene. No one else would come on board dressed like that. How the clothes expressed the woman! Lady Cucumber glanced down complacently at her own charming spinach-coloured dress, her fine nylon stockings, and grey suede shoes.

Mrs Mitylene began to mount the ladder slowly. She looked ill. Behind her came a slight figure, carrying a hat-box. The girl's face was not visible, but there was something familiar about her. Lady Cucumber had an uneasy feeling. She knew that it couldn't be – and yet – They reached the top and she gave a start of recognition as the girl spoke.

'Do come and rest, Mrs Mitylene, and I'll make all arrangements.'

She turned and the horrid doubt in Lady Cucumber's mind was confirmed. It was Helen Hagg!

Helen Hagg met Lady Cucumber's gaze, inimical and dismayed. Two dark spots of colour appeared in each cheek; no greeting was exchanged, but it was as though swords had been clashed. Mrs Mitylene, who was in the throes of one of her heart and asthma attacks, had not seen Lady Cucumber, and went on slowly.

Although the meeting had been a shock, Helen Hagg had little time to think about it. For the next two hours she was busy administering to Mrs Mitylene's comfort. Fortunately she was a born nurse and did not get flustered. Mrs Mitylene had a cabin to herself, and in a short time she was installed in her berth, with extra pillows and a hot-water bottle at her feet, and Helen doing everything necessary. The passports were shown, the seats at table secured, and Mrs Mitylene found that she could relax. It was an immense comfort, and she lay back relieved.

Helen was kept very busy. At last, for the first time she let her mind dwell on Lady Cucumber. She wondered who was with her. It might be Richard.

At this Helen Hagg paused in her unpacking, and an angry colour came into her cheeks. Well, she would soon know. She went in to dinner, and glanced round apprehensively. At a table some distance off she observed Lady Cucumber next to a figure in a gown of black meshed with copper. Beyond was an empty place. Helen Hagg knew instinctively who would occupy it, and was prepared when a big fair-haired young man lounged across the saloon and sat down next to Lady Thomyris.

So! the party was complete. A fury of which she would not have believed herself capable surged up in Helen Hagg, roused by the sight of Richard Cucumber. It was caused by the recollection of dreadful weeks of misery and disappointment. And now this carefree young man ate his dinner serenely, unaware of her presence. She saw him smile at Lady Thomyris, and she remembered Lady Cucumber's contemptuous glance. She hurried over her dinner and returned to Mrs Mitylene, whom she found much better and studying the passenger list. She had discovered the presence on board of the Cucumbers.

'Yes, I saw Lady Cucumber as we came on board,' said Helen.

'Did you, dear?'

'Yes, and she looked right through me!'

'Did she, now,' said Mrs Mitylene thoughtfully. 'By the way, my dear, I'm going to call you my companion.'

'You are very good to me,' said Helen Hagg, keeping her face half averted.

'I shouldn't wonder if I get quite fond of that child,' reflected Mrs Mitylene, adding to herself, 'She's thoughtful and clever, and does things without being told.'

And with a contented sigh she went to sleep.

A cruise is pictured as a pleasant progress over smooth waters, but often it is nothing of the kind, and so the passengers found. The wind rose almost to gale-force from the north; land and sea alike were covered in a canopy of cloud. The ship went steadily and slowly to avoid unnecessary motion, but Lady Cucumber, who was a poor sailor, felt sick as she lay wondering what to do about Helen Hagg.

IX

The next morning Lady Cucumber sent Rocket, her maid, to ask Richard to come and speak with her as soon as he had finished his breakfast. The ship, which ought to have arrived at Kum Kalessi, was three hours late owing to the weather. The only thing Lady Cucumber could hope was that her son would not catch sight of Helen Hagg before she tackled him. As it happened, he had had a puzzling glimpse of Helen's back, but she had disappeared and he could not be sure. So before Lady Cucumber could introduce the subject, he brought it in himself.

'Mother, there is a girl on board who is very like Miss Hagg.'

'It *is* Miss Hagg,' said Lady Cucumber.

'How did she get here?'

'She seems to be with that horrid old woman – Brenda Mitylene.'

'Then she has left Father?'

'Yes, I meant to tell you but I forgot.' Lady Cucumber smoothed her pale gold hair with one hand. 'We found her unsatisfactory.'

Richard Cucumber showed surprise. 'I thought Father was pleased with her.'

'He was at first, but then she got flighty. A girl of that age can't be trusted.'

'But she seemed tremendously keen?'

'She was,' said Lady Cucumber, with a deep, liquid sigh, ' – in words!'

'And that was all it amounted to?' Richard pondered. 'When was all this?'

'Oh, a while ago. I don't remember the date. In any case,' said Lady Cucumber, firmly, 'I mean to avoid her, and Brenda Mitylene, and I hope you will do too. Miss Hagg was very impertinent to me before leaving, and Brenda is a nasty old woman. Don't get mixed up with either of them, Richard. There are plenty of other people on this ship, Heaven knows.'

'Well,' objected Richard, 'one must be civil.'

'You need only say good morning. That is quite sufficient.'

But Richard Cucumber made no promise, and wandered away leaving his mother rather unsatisfied.

At twelve o'clock there was a considerable bustle as everyone had to get lunch before landing at Kum Kalessi. Her duties with Mrs Mitylene interested Helen Hagg, for she liked trying her hand at new things. She also liked Mrs Mitylene, but she could not repress a wish that the clothes she had to handle were more alluring. Mrs Mitylene had a cult for that which was hard-wearing and warm. It was easier to be interested in the kind of clothes Lady Thomyris wore. Her warm admiration for the Duchess of Sodamint's daughter had not been diminished by her connection with the Cucumbers, and as she went up on deck she came face to face with her at the top of the stairs.

'Why, it's Miss Hagg!' said Lady Thomyris. 'The Cucumbers didn't tell me that you were coming.'

'I'm not with Lord Cucumber now,' said Helen, flushing. 'I'm here with Mrs Mitylene.'

Lady Thomyris looked slightly puzzled.

'I haven't met Mrs Mitylene yet,' she said, 'but she looks . . . interesting.'

'She is very good to me.'

'Didn't you like your work with Lord Cucumber?'

'Very much, but I couldn't hear of a job, and I'm lucky to get this.'

Lady Thomyris was astonished, for she remembered Lord Cucumber's eulogies. She would have liked to ask more, but was naturally discreet.

'Well, I must go and get ready to land. We'll meet often, I hope,' and with a smile that charmed all admirers, she went down to her cabin, leaving Helen Hagg enchanted.

How lovely Lady Thomyris had looked in that rose-red jumper suit with the cap to match! The shepherd's plaid coat that went with it was just right. Helen sighed, but it was with pleasure and not envy. Her own wardrobe was as limited as it could be, but she loved to look at charming frocks on other women, and this pleasure was certainly hers as far as Lady Thomyris and Laura Cucumber were concerned.

The landing was unpleasant. It had to be made in motor boats that heaved and bobbed beneath them as they went down the ladder. Professor Paganpash, the chief lecturer, went ashore with the first party. The wind was keen, and the mackintoshes of elderly ladies athirst for knowledge billowed like balloons. The professor had a commanding manner and a sonorous voice, but whilst the others crowded round to hear him give a resumé of the Trojan war, Lady Thomyris stepped aside with Langley Fundament. Lady

Cucumber gave this young man an inquisitive glance, for she had seen his look of rapturous admiration, and it had struck her as slightly unsuitable. He would have been good-looking if he had not worn glasses and a ginger wig, and he was pointing out the beauties of a statue of a Pancratist.

Lady Cucumber drifted away, trying to disassociate herself from the scrum, and yet hear what was being said, two things that were difficult to combine. In due course they reached and inspected the tomb of Achilles, and then everyone wandered about looking at the things that pleased them. Richard Cucumber, who hated improving information, walked up to get a view of the back of a gigantic statue of Patroclus, and in doing so came face to face with Helen Hagg.

'Hullo!' he said, and stopped.

'Hullo,' said Helen Hagg, coldly, appearing not to notice his outstretched hand.

She turned away, her head held high. It was odd, but she conveyed the impression that she did not want to talk to him. Instantly she hurried off to join the group which surrounded Professor Paganpash, amongst whom was Mrs Mitylene.

With almost miraculous speed she had thrown off her indisposition. She admired Priam's taste in architecture, and as she had not heard all that Professor Paganpash said about it she plied him with questions, to which he replied rather petulantly.

'A wonderful place, Troy,' said Mrs Mitylene, 'far too good for the old rip that built it.'

A sentiment which the professor did not consider merited a reply, and he moved away.

Mrs Mitylene was annoyed to find that her exploration of Hecuba's turkish baths must be curtailed on account of their late arrival. She insisted on poking about in the narrow excavations for some time, and it was with difficulty that Helen Hagg got her back to the quay, where they found the last boat waiting. In it sat the Cucumber party, which had been delayed by the enthusiastic researches of Lady Thomyris and Langley Fundament. The sailor who helped Mrs Mitylene in seated her next to Lady Cucumber, and, thus placed, the two ladies were forced to speak.

'We haven't met for ages, Laura. How are you?'

'Quite well.'

Lady Cucumber's eyes strayed to Helen Hagg. Thomyris had moved up to make room for her, and this placed her next to Richard.

'How is Lord Cucumber?' said Mrs Mitylene, continuing the conversation.

'Very well, thank you.'

And Lady Cucumber turned away to discourage talk. They were now in a trough of the waves, spray broke over them; Laura Cucumber's smart hat was ruined, and her coat soaked. On reaching the ship she hurried down to her cabin to repair the damage.

The rest of the evening did not improve her temper. The big saloon was occupied by one of the lecturers giving an address on Mycenean burial customs, and the smoking and writing rooms were provided with amplifiers. This made it difficult to escape receiving instruction, and feeling cross, Lady Cucumber decided to have a look round, and determine with whom she could play bridge during the rest of the voyage. Her eyes fell on two women seated at a table having their coffee.

One of them had a dull, white face and chestnut hair, and wore a black bandeau sparkling with pale blue beads. Her companion was attracting much attention by the violence of her gestures. Both women were well-dressed, they were smart, they looked as if they would be worth cultivating. Their dresses were so arranged as to heighten each other: white, with ecclesiastical purple, and royal blue.

They too seemed as though they would not want to spend their evenings listening to lectures.

The next morning the ship anchored off San Vincenzo di Cartignano. Lady Cucumber, Thomyris, Richard, and Langley Fundament managed to get the best of the dilapidated collection of cars, and Laura insisted on having it closed. She was justified as it turned out, for snow showers soon obscured the wonderful view. Lady Thomyris was the only one of the party who enjoyed it. The grim landscape and the absence of human habitation appealed to her, and she talked with animation to Langley Fundament. Lady Cucumber hated the interminable drive, and said so plaintively.

'And I cannot imagine why we have brought a packed lunch with us. Surely a hot lunch at the hotel would have been better?'

The first sight of the hotel changed her opinion. As they drove up to the Grand Hotel, they realised how extremely primitive was the capital of the Lotus-Eaters. Stiff with cold they went into a big room with bare boards. There were a few tables without cloths, and the cruise passengers sat on benches each with a paper bag containing sandwiches. They were met with the news that the coffee had given out. It seemed like a malignant fate, thought Lady Cucumber, for they must either stand, or sit at a table where Helen Hagg and Mrs Mitylene were seated already.

'I think you know my companion, Miss Hagg,' said Mrs Mitylene.

Lady Cucumber nodded frigidly. Mrs Mitylene was not pleased at her attitude, she was determined that Helen should not be cut with impunity.

'I've known Lady Cucumber since she was ten,' she explained to the assembled company. 'Dear me, Laura, what a funny little girl you used to be.'

'Did I?' said Lady Cucumber, languidly, and she yawned.

'It's a long time ago,' said Mrs Mitylene. 'Nearly forty years.'

'Not nearly as long as that,' snapped Lady Cucumber, aroused from her apathy.

'It must be. Lady Cucumber's father was our local doctor,' she explained. 'I remember, Laura, when you were born. We didn't see much of one another, though, after you married and went to Manchester. I remember calling on you one day, and you had to do your own cooking and burnt the chops.'

'What fun!' said Lady Thomyris.

'Is that bottle of wine never coming?' said Lady Cucumber.

Richard went off in search of a scurrying waiter.

Lady Cucumber drank some wine, and then went to the window to get away from Mrs Mitylene. A fine snow was falling, and there was nothing to see in the land of the Lotus-Eaters, and nothing to buy but picture postcards.

'I hope you won't mind my changing, but I'd rather go back in an open car,' said Lady Thomyris, coming up behind her. 'I want to see more of the country, and Miss Hagg says there are some vacant seats in their char-a-banc.'

'You'll catch a chill. It really is most unwise.'

But Lady Thomyris was obstinate. And then Richard said he would come too, and left Lady Cucumber to follow in the closed car. As she put her foot on the step she heard a voice behind her:

'I wonder if you would mind our coming in your car. We drove up in an open one, and got nearly frozen.'

Lady Cucumber turned and, seeing the two women she had picked out the night before, assented. She made a few polite remarks, and met with responsive smiles, and then an unpleasant slither at the bend of the frozen road, and a horrifying glimpse of sheer rock and the valley fifteen hundred feet beneath caused her to grasp the older stranger familiarly by the knee. There were apologies, laughter, and they grew friendly.

The stranger introduced herself. She was Olive de Pineapple, and this was her sister, Mrs St. Cuckoo. Both spoke admiringly of Lady Thomyris's beauty, and Olive de Pineapple confessed to having taken a dislike to Helen Hagg. Altogether they were very congenial, disliking lectures and displaying a taste for bridge and poker.

'It really is an extraordinary thing,' said Lady Cucumber, crossly, 'that Brenda Mitylene should foist her maid on us. That's what the young person is called on the passenger list.'

She harped on and on about Helen Hagg.

'I must really speak to dear Thomyris. I am sure the Duchess of Sodamint would not like her consorting with people of that stamp.'

'That's the worst of cruises. They are so very mixed,' said Olive de Pineapple, shaking her head.

But Mrs St. Cuckoo found Lady Cucumber's voice disagreeable.

'Naturally,' she said, suddenly opening her eyes very wide. 'And why not? Those who wish to be exclusive had better charter a yacht – if they can afford it.'

Lady Cucumber did not trouble to answer.

'She was once in our service, as a sort of typist,' she murmured bitterly.

'I thought she looked nice,' said Mrs St. Cuckoo, aggressively, ' – a decided cut above many of the passengers.'

Lady Cucumber felt antagonism stir within her. 'Indeed, Mrs St. Cuckoo, you are mistaken,' she said. 'We were obliged to get rid of her in a hurry.'

Mrs St. Cuckoo merely yawned.

'They gave us a very good sweet at dinner last night,' she said. 'I must ask for the recipe.'

She was a gluttonous woman, and after any meal liked her nap. Her eyes closed, and Lady Cucumber gave it up.

X

Richard Cucumber was pacing the deck. Helen Hagg was nowhere in sight. As he mounted to the top deck, however, he caught sight of a solitary figure looking at the coast-line.

He went forward full of affability.

'Ah, there you are. I've been looking for you everywhere.'

Helen Hagg turned, and no one could have construed the glance she gave him as a welcome.

'Why?' she asked, disconcertingly.

'What a funny question!' Richard Cucumber laughed.

Helen Hagg flushed a deep cherry colour.

'What's come over you, Helen Hagg? You used to be so friendly.'

This went home, and Helen Hagg bit her lip as if she had been struck a brutal blow.

'Now, my dear, ' went on Richard Cucumber, 'have a heart. You can't deny you're avoiding me.'

Helen said nothing for a moment. She seemed to be considering the coast.

'I don't deny it, ' she said.

'But why?' pleaded Richard Cucumber.

'I think it better.'

'What a silly thought.'

He remembered that afternoon on the downs, and slipped his arm round her shoulders. She twisted herself away.

'Please leave me alone,' she said.

'I'm sorry.' Richard Cucumber's tone was good-tempered, but held a note of surprise. 'Still, you might tell me why you're unkind.'

'I'm not unkind.'

'Yes, you are, and capricious. Aren't we friends?'

'No.'

'But I like you so much.'

'I don't like you.'

'That's horrid of you. You used to be different.'

'I didn't know you so well then.'

'What do you mean?'

'Just what I say. And I'll be clearer still,' said Helen Hagg, the whites of her eyes glittering faintly in the declining light. 'I'd much rather you didn't follow me around.'

Richard Cucumber staggered back a pace or two.

'You are very clear indeed, Helen Hagg.'

'It is best that there shouldn't be any misunderstanding,' said Helen Hagg, in a voice more thrilling than a scream.

Richard Cucumber laughed suddenly.

'I don't believe you mean it,' he said.

His tone lashed her to a fury.

'Listen,' she said. 'I'll give you just one of the reasons I don't want you. If your mother were here you wouldn't be talking to me, and I don't like your doing so when you think she's out of the way. For one thing it's insulting.'

'That's absolute tosh. You didn't talk like this down at Hummingbird.'

This silenced Helen for a moment.

'Well, I've finished with Hummingbird,' she said, repressing a sob which rose in her throat.

'Helen!'

'And don't call me Helen.' Her heart was beating quickly, and tears of distress and anxiety filled her eyes. 'Only friends do that.'

'I thought I was one,' said Richard Cucumber, perseveringly.

'You were wrong.'

'My dear, why be so abusive?'

'I don't intend to provide amusement for a rich, spoilt young man. There is only one person in your family that I respect,' went on Helen Hagg viciously, 'and that's your father.'

'You're being damnably rude!'

'It's time you heard the truth.'

'Is there anything more you want to say to me?' enquired Richard Cucumber, ominously.

'Oh, you think you have only to smile to put a girl into a flutter,' said Helen Hagg. 'Go down onto the next deck, and let me enjoy the sunset.'

XI

Shipboard friendships are notoriously rapid. Lady Cucumber, who always needed an audience, had found an ideal one in Olive de Pineapple. And she was an excellent card-player – perhaps too excellent, reflected Laura Cucumber ruefully, calculating her losses of the past two evenings.

'I always love your clothes,' Olive de Pineapple was saying as they paced up and down. 'That colour shows up your garnets so wonderfully. How wise you are to wear them constantly. Sea air is supposed to be good for them.'

'I wish you would say that to Lord Cucumber,' said Laura, with a brief glitter of laughter. 'He didn't want me to bring them.'

'Why ever not?'

Lady Cucumber stared at the sea. 'He thinks it silly to pay the extra insurance. Frederick is odd.'

'Aren't most men?'

'No doubt.'

Olive de Pineapple narrowed her eyes and looked at the horizon.

'And after all,' went on Lady Cucumber, 'what is the use of having them and not wearing them?'

'None.'

'And I'm sure there's very little risk on a cruise of this kind.'

'I should hope not indeed!'

In the course of their perambulations, they passed Lady Thomyris, whose head was close to Langley Fundament's, she like a nymph by Praxiteles, he, red-haired, golden-armed and slim, like a faun at day-break. Lady Cucumber looked at them with disapproval.

'Have you seen Richard?' she said, sharply.

But Lady Thomyris hadn't.

'I don't understand,' said Lady Cucumber, crossly, as she walked on, 'what a girl like that wants with all this high-brow talk about architecture and lost civilisations. It would be more natural if she occupied herself with thoughts of getting a husband.'

'Doesn't she?' said Olive de Pineapple.

'Not at all,' declared Lady Cucumber, sharply. 'Oh dear, no, Lady Thomyris is overwhelmed with education, and Mr Fundament is a means to an end. I don't suppose she thinks of him as a man.'

'He'd be rather nice-looking if it weren't for those glasses,' said Olive de Pineapple.

'That doesn't weigh with Thomyris a bit.'

On their next turn round they met Richard coming down from the upper deck. He looked flushed and cross, and though he joined them he hardly spoke. He caught Olive de Pineapple's amused glance, and realised that this lady did not let much escape her. Nor was the reason for his rage lost on Lady Cucumber. All her suspicions were aroused. That odious little serpent of a girl was trying to get hold of Richard again. And what had she been saying?

With a mumbled excuse about having left his book somewhere, Richard Cucumber left them.

'That detestable Helen Hagg,' broke out Lady Cucumber. 'I wish she was anywhere but here! She spoils the whole voyage.'

'Surely, dear Lady Cucumber, she is hardly worth thinking of.'

With a curious forced smile, which altogether vanished, leaving her face strangely pale, Lady Cucumber said 'Absolutely – but wherever she goes there is trouble.'

'Perhaps you would rather not tell me . . . ?'

'You'd never repeat it, dear?'

'Of course not.'

'Well it was . . . you can imagine my horror. Because . . . men are stupid – oh! well, I am sure you know what I mean.'

Olive de Pineapple nodded. And as she listened to the outpourings of Lady Cucumber's hopes and fears, her mind was busy. Was Helen Hagg an adventuress? If so, she was a clever one . . .

The next morning all was excitement and bustle. They had reached the Piraeus, and a fleet of taxis was waiting to take them to Athens. Lady Cucumber and her party as usual secured the best and largest. Mrs Mitylene and Helen Hagg got one without springs, but the discomfort was not sufficient to impair their sense of joyous anticipation.

It was a busy morning. Professor Paganpash led the way with his usual agility, his enthusiastic followers swarming after him like bees after a queen. Lady Cucumber was one of the few who did not enjoy it. It was, as she remarked to Olive de Pineapple, not much of a town for shops, nothing but bead necklaces, sponges, and postcards. She had not studied the itinerary and was shocked by the long list on the afternoon's programme. That day was worse than usual. They trudged from one point of interest to another, and she was worn out by lunchtime. Then, before she had time for a comfortable cigarette, they set off for the Museum.

After the long day Mrs Mitylene was tired, and when they reached the ship Helen Hagg made her lie down. Every day convinced Brenda Mitylene that she had been lucky to get the girl. Helen Hagg now performed the duties of secretary and companion as well as maid.

The Traveller's Club, who had planned the tour, did not allow time to be wasted. The passengers were again lectured before going to bed and rose early to drive to Eleusis. The wind was keen, and upon arrival they grouped themselves, shivering, around Professor Paganpash to listen to his famous account of the Rites. Helen Hagg became so excited that she dropped her handbag down a crevice. As they all moved to another part of the precincts, a young man scrambled down to retrieve it, and as she thanked him she heard Lady Cucumber, who had seen the incident, say to Olive de Pineapple:

'Rather an old dodge for striking up an acquaintance.'

With fury in her heart Helen Hagg watched them move away. Why was the woman so persistently odious? How she hated the Cucumbers! Purse proud snobs! She was glad she had told Richard Cucumber what she thought of him. And yet – -- – she couldn't forget the strange expression upon his face, angry but also hurt.

She and the young man reached Professor Paganpash's group after the new part of his lecture had begun. He was a fine lecturer and inspired the imagination of his audience. Helen Hagg went to help Mrs Mitylene, and her new acquaintance joined them. He introduced himself as Dracula Jones, and told them he was travelling alone. Mrs Mitylene liked him, and was pleased when he joined them later at lunch.

An important thing had happened to Dracula Jones when he scrambled down the crevice to recover Helen Hagg's handbag. From that moment he was convinced that this girl was different from all the others he had met, and this impression deepened in the intimacy of ship-life. The days at sea gave her little to do, and she had time to join in the games, while Dracula Jones now considered himself a permanent member of their party. Helen Hagg, however, tried to stop him from getting too serious. There were signs of this the afternoon before they reached the Cyclops' land, and Helen had slipped away to a sheltered corner where she sat making a pyjama case for Mrs Mitylene. She had not been there long when Lady Thomyris joined her.

Helen Hagg interested Thomyris. Her fancy for her was as strong as the antagonism which she felt for Olive de Pineapple. Thomyris was more observant than most people supposed, and she liked the way Helen identified herself with the interests of whoever employed her. There was a pause while Helen Hagg sewed.

'How neat you are!' exclaimed Lady Thomyris.

'I learned at a convent school in France,' said Helen Hagg, selecting a skein of vermillion silk. 'I find that it soothes me.'

'It has just the opposite effect on me,' said Lady Thomyris, her hands fluttering aimlessly. 'I tore my dress last night, and – '

'Why don't you give it to me to do?'

'You wouldn't!'

'Really I would. I'd love to do anything for you,' said Helen Hagg, simply.

Lady Thomyris jumped up.

'Come down to my cabin.'

The two girls hurried below, and the dress was produced.

'You're very clever at things,' said Lady Thomyris, as Helen Hagg set to work on it. 'And what pretty hands you have.'

'You say such lovely things,' said Helen.

Praise from Lady Thomyris Dagobert was praise indeed. She herself was especially dowered with beauty that day. She was wearing white, and the sea-air suited her.

'I speak the truth,' she continued. 'I envy you.'

'Oh, I am only useful because I must be.'

'I think it is *wonderful* to be useful.'

Usually reserved, she found something in Helen Hagg that made her easy to talk to, and she began to voice her longings for an unconventional life, with interests outside society. She told of her wish to excavate.

'Somewhere like Gomorrah,' she said, 'or Antino-opolis. The idea simply thrills me.'

Helen Hagg listened as she sewed. She could not imagine Richard excavating. With a sudden catch of her breath, she switched from thoughts that startled her, and concentrated on what Lady Thomyris was saying.

'I wonder if you would do something to please me,' said Lady Thomyris, suddenly.

'Of course – if I can.'

'I want you to take this dress of water-green striped with silver, and this ribboned black hat, and this small black lace fan. You are not offended, are you?'

Helen Hagg looked up, tears in her eyes.

'It is wonderful of you to think of it.'

'They are a bit small for me.' Lady Thomyris shook her ear-rings kittenishly. 'Let's slip them on now.'

She overcame Helen Hagg's real reluctance, and the result surprised both of them. Pleasure gave her a becoming flush. Lady Thomyris waxed enthusiastic.

'What did I tell you?' she cried. 'You are really charming with all those natural curls and those big eyes.'

Helen began to see herself in a new light. Something seemed to have snapped inside her.

'Now,' went on Lady Thomyris, with an intimate glance, 'we must see to your hair. I shall show you the way Madame Moloch does mine.'

Blissfully Helen Hagg resigned herself, and Lady Thomyris snipped with a pair of nail scissors, parted and rearranged until finally she stood back and pronounced herself satisfied. Helen began to stammer her thanks, but Lady Thomyris cut them short by kissing her.

'And now,' she said, 'I may call you Helen; and please will you call me Thomyris.'

'There is only one thing I can do in return,' said Helen Hagg. 'Will you let me keep your clothes straight and mended? That's what I'd love to do.'

'It's what I'd love too,' laughed Lady Thomyris, as they went out mutually satisfied.

The change in Helen Hagg's appearance did not pass unnoticed. Mrs Mitylene observed it with a chuckle. The men on board reacted to it without recognising the cause. Lady Cucumber put up her lorgnettes and stared.

'Thomyris, how remarkable! That Hagg girl has a frock just like the one you wore.'

'It is,' said Lady Thomyris. 'I gave it to her.'

'You *did*!'

'We are friends,' said Lady Thomyris, indistinctly.

'Friends! That seems hardly the right word. With Mrs Mitylene's maid . . . Dear child,' declared Lady Cucumber with a grave and meditative air, 'do you think that your mother – ?'

'I am old enough to make my own friends,' said Thomyris.

'Girls are infuriating,' confided Lady Cucumber to Olive de Pineapple, later. 'I can't imagine what attracts them about that common little minx.'

'Possibly you should rub it in a little less often,' said Mrs de Pineapple, smiling to soften her opposition. 'Young people incline to take the view you tell them to avoid.'

'Young people,' said Lady Cucumber, 'are damned fools!'

XII

'I've been thinking about what you said to me the other day,' said Richard Cucumber.

He had come upon Helen Hagg by accident in a sheltered corner of the deck. She gave him the impression of being in a kinder mood, and he lingered, hardly knowing why he did so.

In reply to his first awkward approaches, Helen Hagg grew scarlet.

'I was terribly rude,' she said. 'I'm afraid I lost my temper.'

Richard Cucumber stroked his forehead and looked at her with faint amusement.

'You're not in a temper now, are you?'

'No,' declared Helen, her flush deepening.

'And do you think me conceited? I want to know.'

'Well – just a little,' stammered Helen Hagg. She gave him a half smile.

'Still,' said Richard Cucumber, 'that wasn't your principal reason for being so angry with me – '

Helen was silent.

'Was it?'

'Perhaps not.'

'One day you're as gay – you're as as gay as a pigeon,' said Richard, aggrieved, 'and the next you're a regular little crocodile. You make it impossible to be friends.'

'We cannot be friends,' said Helen Hagg, with a bitter laugh.

'Why not?'

'Ask your mother.'

Richard Cucumber wanted to go on arguing, and would have done so had Mrs Mitylene not come on deck. She had heard that the Cyclopean authorities had finished looking at the passports, and they could land.

The remembrance of her conversation with Richard Cucumber made Helen Hagg less intelligent than usual over the sightseeing, though she listened while Mrs Mitylene exclaimed with delight at the beauty of the mosques, domes, and minarets of that city.

'Come and see what I think is the most wonderful thing here,' cried Langley Fundament, joining the party.

'What's that?' snapped Lady Cucumber, who was infuriated by the length of the sightseeing programme.

'The Cyclops' cave.'

'I fail to see what's interesting about a cave,' said Olive de Pineapple, snubbingly.

'Wait,' said Langley Fundament and, smiling, he led the way down a flight of steps.

Even Lady Cucumber was surprised into an involuntary exclamation of admiration.

They appeared to be standing at the entrance of a vast Gothic cathedral. The place was lit by electricity, and hundreds of tall black rocks like spires produced an impression which it was difficult to forget. The unique loveliness made them wish to linger, but the inexorable guide said they had already exceeded their time and would be late for lunch.

The meal, at a large hotel, was a noisy affair as a band of Cyclopians played and sang with surprising verve. Lady Cucumber found that it made her head ache, and led the way into the lounge, followed by Olive de Pineapple and Mrs St. Cuckoo. Miss Bumdockdousse, who was head mistress of a girls' school in the north of England, had made friends with Mrs Mitylene and was sitting at her table with Dracula Jones and Helen Hagg.

'Young Mr Cucumber and Lady Thomyris make a charming pair,' she said. 'Somebody told me they were engaged. Is it true?'

'They don't act as if they were,' commented Dracula Jones, critically.

'It would be suitable,' said Mrs Mitylene. 'She is lovely, and he has money.'

A trivial conversation, and all three of them turned to a more important subject. Miss Bumdockdousse, who had been to Cyclopolis before, told them things about the centuries of violence and vice which had left of it a derelict city. Helen Hagg sat motionless and did not hear a word. Those casual remarks had aroused in her an almost unbelievable intensity of feeling. She knew that her efforts of the past weeks were useless. She loved Richard Cucumber more than ever.

The moment of self-revelation had left her pale, so that Dracula Jones asked anxiously if the room were too hot for her. Helen Hagg smiled, and forced herself to listen to the discussion of the afternoon's programme.

The afternoon was less enjoyable than the morning. It had become cold and everyone was tired. Mrs Mitylene prevented Helen Hagg from buying a stick of mint rock, as she had deep doubts as to the processes by which it was made, and they came away with nothing more distinctive than a pleated gold turban which could have been purchased at half the price in London.

During the night there was a commotion on B Deck, and it was rumoured that Mrs St. Cuckoo was seriously ill. Olive de Pineapple, in a lovely dressing gown which swept the floor like a wizard's robe, bustled about arousing doctors and stewardesses. Her skirts flashed blood-red down the grey vaulted corridors of the ship, and her hair fell in serpentine coils round her neck. Doctor Sturmunddrang diagnosed appendicitis. Voices rose, and so did the patient's temperature. Olive de Pineapple intervened. The Orient Express, she believed, was passing through Cyclopolis that day. Why not get a sleeper and go through to Vienna. The groaning patient agreed.

'Do you know much about nursing, Mrs de Pineapple?' asked the doctor.

'I? Not a thing.' Olive de Pineapple looked surprised.

'Mrs St. Cuckoo is not in a fit state to travel alone,' said the doctor firmly.

'Then you must get a nurse,' said Olive de Pineapple, displaying a most unsisterly indifference.

Later in the morning Mrs Mitylene was standing in a large crowd waiting to go ashore. The only person missing was Helen Hagg, and Dracula Jones was looking for her anxiously.

'She's sure to be here in a minute,' said Mrs Mitylene, and as she spoke Helen came hurrying along manoeuvring her way through the crowd.

'There's your coat, you silly child!'

'Oh Mrs Mitylene, may I stay behind?' cried Helen Hagg.

'But I thought you were so keen to see the tomb of Polyphemus?'

Helen Hagg's grey eyes had a troubled look.

'It's Mrs St. Cuckoo,' she said. 'I heard her groaning and I went in; she keeps begging me to go with her to the hotel.'

'Surely she will have her sister with her?' said Mrs Mitylene, moving towards the gangway.

'She doesn't seem to want her sister.'

'Well, do as you like,' said Mrs Mitylene, crossly, 'but remember the ship sails at three.'

Helen Hagg busied herself packing bags in Mrs St. Cuckoo's cabin. Soothed by her efficiency, Mrs St. Cuckoo lay still and watched. The pain was easier, but she still looked ghastly. Presently Olive de Pineapple opened the door, and paused at the sight of Helen Hagg.

'I see you've collected a ministering angel, Ivy,' she said.

'She is coming with me to the hotel,' said Mrs St. Cuckoo, faintly. 'I wish she would come to Vienna.'

Helen Hagg shook her head.

'I'm sorry, but I couldn't leave Mrs Mitylene in the lurch.'

'Since Miss Hagg is doing everything so beautifully, I'll make myself scarce,' said Olive de Pineapple.

Mrs St. Cuckoo waited till the sound of her footsteps had died away, then put her hand under the pillow and pulled out a leather case.

'I want you to take charge of this,' she said with a mysterious glance. 'Don't give it to Mrs de Pineapple on any account.'

Helen Hagg was bewildered by this strange attitude of one sister to another, but Mrs St. Cuckoo was in no state to explain, and she put the case in her handbag. This seemed to quiet the sick woman.

'Stay with me as long as you can,' she whispered.

Helen Hagg said she would, and helped her to dress, then made her lie down again. They waited till Mrs de Pineapple reappeared.

'The doctor says he will be ready to take you, Ivy, in a few minutes,' she declared, touching her chin with a long, glittering fingernail. 'And if you don't mind, Miss Hagg, I too will get ready.'

Although this remark seemed to cause Mrs St. Cuckoo uneasiness, Helen Hagg felt she could hardly remain. She went out, and Olive de Pineapple shut the door after her. Helen could hear voices in the cabin which seemed to be raised in altercation, and all her nursing instincts were aroused. Whatever cause for annoyance Olive de Pineapple might have, she must not be allowed to vent it on anyone in Mrs St. Cuckoo's condition. But the angry voice went on. There was a sound of movement, and suddenly Mrs St. Cuckoo called out sharply: 'Miss Hagg! Miss Hagg!'

Helen Hagg opened the door, and then stopped amazed. Mrs St. Cuckoo was sitting on the side of her berth, her face was ashen, her eyes glittered with fever. Olive de Pineapple stood over her threateningly. The dressing-case which Helen had just packed was open, and the contents lay strewn all over the floor. Mrs de Pineapple turned a furious face in her direction.

'I thought I heard Mrs St. Cuckoo call,' said Helen Hagg.

'I did call,' said Mrs St. Cuckoo.

'Ivy fancied that she had forgotten something, and I was looking for it,' said Olive de Pineapple, smoothly.

'Don't leave me again,' cried Mrs St. Cuckoo, and caught at Helen Hagg's hand.

'All right. I'll stay,' said Helen soothingly. 'I only left while your sister put on her things.'

'She's not my sister!' said Mrs St. Cuckoo, her voice becoming weird and ominous.

After her repudiation of Olive de Pineapple, the pale and haggard figure of Mrs St. Cuckoo lay back exhausted with closed eyes, and what Mrs de Pineapple might have replied was never known as the doctor arrived to help his patient ashore.

'I have been lucky, Mrs St. Cuckoo,' he said, 'for I have heard of an Englishwoman, a Nurse Nutshell, who is travelling on the express. She will share your compartment and look after you. I hope your journey won't be too bad.'

'It is very good of you to take all this trouble,' said Mrs St. Cuckoo, graciously.

Dr Sturmunddrang looked at Olive de Pineapple.

'Somebody had to do it,' he said, pointedly.

On reaching the hotel they were shown into a gloomy bedroom. Dr Sturmunddrang settled his patient, and said he would go down to wait for Nurse Nutshell, and give her drugs for the journey.

'Stop with me,' muttered Mrs St. Cuckoo to Helen Hagg.

Presently Olive de Pineapple leant forward.

'I want to speak to my sister alone, Miss Hagg,' she declared, a sinister note entering her voice.

'She says she's not your sister,' said Helen Hagg. Some instinct made her distrust Olive de Pineapple and stand by the sick woman.

'She's light-headed,' said Mrs de Pineapple.

'She asked me not to leave her.'

'Don't you think that you take a great deal on yourself?'

Helen Hagg drooped her head and the hot blood rushed to her face.

'I can't help it; I promised her.'

'I can hardly discuss my private affairs in front of a stranger,' said Olive de Pineapple, her full lips curling in a contemptuous smile.

'Mrs St. Cuckoo,' said Helen, 'is not fit to discuss anything.'

Olive de Pineapple gave Helen Hagg an odd look. Irritation flickered between her eyebrows. She tapped her knee with a glove.

'Will you leave us?' she almost shouted.

'No, I will not.'

Mrs St. Cuckoo opened her eyes.

'Don't let her persuade you, Miss Hagg,' she said, weakly. 'She only wants my money.'

'She's raving!' cried Olive de Pineapple, white with rage. 'Ivy, what have you done with those papers?'

'I shan't tell you,' said Mrs St. Cuckoo, with a faint but peculiar smile.

This enraged Mrs de Pineapple. In a fury she snatched Mrs St. Cuckoo's handbag from the bed, opened it and turned over the contents. Next she picked up a coat and searched the pockets. Having drawn a blank, she turned towards Helen Hagg with a very evil expression.

'I expect she gave it to you to look after.'

Replying to the menace in her tone rather than the words, Helen Hagg picked up the telephone that was by the bedside and called for Dr Sturmunddrang.

'What the devil did you do that for?'

Olive de Pineapple's voice shook with rage. Mrs St. Cuckoo once more closed her eyes. It seemed to Helen a long time before the doctor came, but it was actually only a few seconds. He was followed by a stout motherly-looking woman. He looked enquiringly at Helen Hagg.

'I thought Mrs St. Cuckoo was getting over-excited,' she explained.

The doctor gave a brief glance at Mrs de Pineapple and nodded. Then he went over and felt his patient's pulse.

'Will you say goodbye now, Mrs de Pineapple, and go down with Miss Hagg,' he said. 'It is time we started; I want to give your sister an injection before we leave. I will join you in the hall in a moment.'

Olive de Pineapple went toward the bed.

'Goodbye, Ivy dear.'

Mrs St. Cuckoo shrank back.

'Goodbye,' she said, and looked towards Helen Hagg. 'Have you got it,' she whispered.

Helen nodded and took the case out of the bag she had in her hand. Mrs St. Cuckoo's fingers closed round it, and she gave a smile of satisfaction.

'Thank you for that, and for the rest,' she said.

Dr Sturmunddrang opened the door, and Olive de Pineapple went out, followed by Helen, who was apprehensive, for she expected a scene. It looked, however, as if Olive de Pineapple had accepted the inevitable. They had gone down a flight of stairs before she spoke.

'It is dangerous, Miss Hagg,' she said, 'to interfere in other people's affairs.'

And her voice was as caustic as nitrate of silver.

XIII

Helen Hagg, Olive de Pineapple, Miss Bumdockdousse and Dracula Jones had come on board
together, and paused to read the typewritten sheet of
news that was pinned outside the purser's office. The
information supplied to passengers was an odd med-
ley. Today it set forth a resolution of the United
Nations, American views on disarmament, announced
the fall of the French government, the deaths of a peer
and a dramatist, and ended with the engagement of
Lady Thomyris Dagobert to Mr Richard Cucumber.

XIV

They had come in for a spell of fine weather. It was warm, and the ship moved in smooth waters with views of islands, lovely in outline. Helen Hagg leaned her head against the rail, feeling sick with misery.

Beauty, new places, and life itself no longer mattered.

It was like this when they anchored about midday at Ogygia, and the passengers prepared to go ashore in small boats. Mrs Mitylene, who had been ill in bed, leaned on Dracula Jones' arm with Miss Bumdockdousse by her side, and Helen Hagg came a little behind. As they straggled over the rough ground, clambering among some ruins with a carpet of wild flowers growing among the stones, Helen stopped to pick some. When she heard footsteps she did not turn to see who it was, and her heart gave a jump when Richard Cucumber spoke.

'How do you like this island? Don't you remember telling me you had been named after it?'

For her name was Helen Ogygia Hagg.

She pressed her fingers together in an agony of mad longing, for his words conjured up the smell of damp beech leaves and the glow of the setting sun between bare trees. She tried not to think of these things. She strove to make her voice sound casual.

'How wonderful of you to remember that!'

Richard Cucumber picked some flowers to add to her bunch, and Helen Hagg began to feel desperate.

Why didn't he go away and leave her alone, she thought, with wild wet eyes and quivering lips. She turned very pale, then, controlling the rapid beating of her heart by a strong effort, she forced a careless smile.

'I haven't congratulated you,' she began – 'But I do. I think that Lady Thomyris is lovely in every way, and I'm sure that you'll be very happy.'

'Thank you,' said Richard Cucumber, a faint trace of embarrassment in his manner.

Lady Thomyris could now be seen some distance ahead with Professor Paganpash, leaping with incredible agility from boulder to boulder.

'Helen,' said Richard Cucumber, impulsively, and taking her arm he drew her from the main path, and together they came to a curious shrine, sacred to pilgrims but now deserted.

Helen Hagg edged away a little from his arm, which showed an unmistakable tendency to circle her waist. She began playing with the trinkets on her bracelet, endeavouring to feign the most absolute unconcern, but her pulse had begun to pound and a million hammer blows struck at her heart.

'Helen,' he repeated, impulsively, 'why did you leave Hummingbird? Weren't you happy?'

A choking sob rose in her throat, but she repressed it.

'Didn't you know? I was sent away.'

Richard Cucumber started back; a strange bewildered horror passed over his face.

'But why?' he demanded.

'It was because of . . . that evening.'

'When we had the accident! You don't mean – ?'

He flushed darkly, and his eyes glittered with a

82

lustre she had not seen before.

'Surely you knew?' she demanded, a pained, puzzled air filling her grave eyes.

'Of course I didn't. Who sent you away?'

'Your mother.'

'Good Lord!'

Richard Cucumber's eyes gleamed and flashed with a fierce, unholy fire.

'So I went to London to get a job,' went on Helen Hagg, almost inaudibly.

'And found Mrs Mitylene?'

'It wasn't as easy as that,' she said, a chilling pride blossoming in her sea grey eyes. 'People without references don't pick up jobs in a hurry.'

'Without references? You don't mean – ?'

Richard Cucumber's disturbance was plain, he was not going to let the matter rest till he had further details. Helen Hagg did not rest on Lady Cucumber's behaviour, but gave her full opinion of Irene Rabbit.

'Beastly people, the Rabbits,' said Richard. 'I always hated them. Oh, my dear, I'm terribly sorry. How you must have hated me!'

'Not really,' said Helen Hagg, gently, in a voice that trembled just a little.

'Can you ever forgive me, Helen Hagg?'

'Of course,' she said, with a quick, dazzling rapier-thrust of laughter.

'How you must have suffered. I shall talk to mother directly!'

'Your father was always good to me,' said Helen Hagg, hastily, 'but your mother wouldn't understand.'

'Oh Helen, we all treated you abominably.'

'You were a little inconsiderate, but – but – '

She shook her head. For a moment she was off her guard, and her expression startled him.

'I've been a damned fool,' he said, remorsefully. And he gave way to a mad longing to hold her in his arms.

'Helen!' he exclaimed.

But their solitude was at an end. The rest of the passengers came scrambling towards the shrine. Richard joined Lady Thomyris and walked down the glen to see some ruined villas. Miss Bumdockdousse got Dracula Jones to come and help her take some photographs, and Helen Hagg persuaded Mrs Mitylene to sit and rest, for the steep climb had been too much for her.

'I like to think of this place when it was alive with nymphs and satyrs,' said Mrs Mitylene. 'I'm sure it was a happy place.'

They sat silent for a while. Helen Hagg leaned her back against a pillar, unconscious that Mrs Mitylene was studying her face.

'Helen,' said Mrs Mitylene, abruptly, 'sometimes I wonder if you are enjoying all this as much as you expected.'

'Don't you know it is the most wonderful thing that ever happened to me!'

She spoke with conviction. Even if it brought unhappiness, this voyage had given her something she would never lose.

Mrs Mitylene said no more. She felt sure that Richard Cucumber's engagement had hurt Helen. If only the tiresome girl would get interested in Dracula Jones; but love and reason are seldom in harmony.

For some time the passengers had been making their way back towards the shore in twos and threes, and Helen suggested that they should follow. Mrs Mitylene was strangely disinclined. When at last she consented to make a start, she grew faint and said she must wait. Helen began to be alarmed; she could not see the sea from where she stood, and there were no signs of the others. Mrs Mitylene had now grown so blue about the mouth that it was unsafe to leave her, but as soon as she showed signs of recovery Helen Hagg ran as fast as she could to the water's edge. Her worst fears were confirmed. The smoke from the ship showed that she was getting up steam. The last boat had landed its passengers.

Helen Hagg took off her coat and began to wave vigorously.

PART THREE

XV

Richard Cucumber took out his glasses and focused them on Ogygia. He thought of his conversation there, of the way Helen Hagg had looked, of her soft voice, the sweep of her lashes on her cheek.

But he was not to be left in peace. Lady Cucumber joined him. Once more he directed his glasses upon Ogygia, and paused, interested.

'Look, Mother! I believe there's somebody signalling from the shore.'

'Well, what of it?' said Lady Cucumber, tranquilly.

'Isn't the place uninhabited?'

'No, There was a museum, and a small hotel where somebody said you could stay.'

'It may be a passenger left behind,' he said with a note of serious sympathy.

'I shouldn't think so,' said Lady Cucumber, ruthlessly. 'Anyway, the ship is due to start.'

Richard Cucumber gave one more look.

'It's Helen!' he exclaimed. 'I'm sure of it.'

'Helen?' said Lady Cucumber, frigidly.

'Helen Hagg! I must tell the captain.'

He raced off along the deck.

'Oh, if only he had been looking the other way, and

she had been left behind!' reflected Lady Cucumber. 'But it's just like that *awful* girl to do things to attract attention.'

There was confusion, noise, orders, and shouting. A boat as lowered, and Lady Cucumber, hot with indignation, saw Richard get into it with the crew. By this time some passengers who had finished tea came on deck and were full of interest.

'How clever of Richard to spot her,' said Lady Thomyris.

Lady Cucumber did not reply. Her thoughts had been busy. Why had her son called Helen Hagg by her Christian name. She didn't like it. She turned towards Lady Thomyris, and saw that she had walked off with Langley Fundament.

Langley Fundament's mind was in a turmoil. He had decided that it was time to wake from his dream. It had been like a soap-bubble, lovely, iridescent, fragile, and now it was shattered. But Lady Thomyris spoke to him, and his resolution wilted. He told her what she wanted to know about Circe's island, which they were to visit the next day, and described the excavations and reconstructions.

'You said you had been offered one of these jobs,' said Thomyris. 'How can you hesitate?'

'I shan't any longer,' said Langley Fundament.

'How lucky you are. I wish it was me.'

'But surely you will have a wonderful life – now,' he stammered.

'I suppose so,' said Lady Thomyris, dully.

Langley Fundament studied her face and wondered what she was thinking. He had a craving to tell her everything. Romance overwhelmed him like a flood, sweeping away the barriers of common sense and shyness. The worship in his eyes had made her colour faintly; he moved nearer.

'This part of the world can't have changed much,' she said suddenly, with lowered eyelids and a half-smile.

> 'I love the memory of those naked times
> Whose statued Phoebus gilt in happier climes.
> Both sexes took a carefree pleasure in
> Their litheness then, without a sense of sin – '

She broke off with a gay laugh.

'Baudelaire,' said Langley Fundament, opening his eyes wide in respectful wonderment. 'Do you know "The Vampire's Metamorphosis"?'

'Yes,' said Lady Thomyris, in a low suffocated voice.

> 'I'm so skilled, learned sir, in pleasure's charms,
> Entwining lovers in my dreaded arms,
> Or to their teeth abandoning my bust – '

'I who am shy and wanton, frail, robust,' finished Langley Fundament.

> 'That on these cushions swooning blissfully
> The impotent Angels would be damned for me!'

'Oh how I dislike crudity, realism, clashing discords, the machine-made world of every day. Here you can imagine Homer's people. Don't talk to me about England,' she added with a flash of passion. 'The present is pretty sordid. I want to forget all that now.'

'And do you suppose I want you to remember anything but this moment,' cried Langley Fundament, equally carried away.

It is clear that a conversation of this sort is inclined to be disturbing. Both realised this and returned to Aegean civilisation.

'Go on telling me about *Aegea*,' she said, for she was surprised at herself and ashamed at Langley Fundament's outburst.

'I can't tell you how glad I shall be to get home,' said Lady Cucumber, peevishly.

She sat on a stone and looked with distaste at Circe's island. She disliked it intensely. She had hated the drive from the beach through clouds of dust. The sun was hot, and she had gone up and down steps all morning. She had looked at the enchantress's Palace, her feet had swollen, and her heels were too high. Except that it had resulted in Richard's engagement, she had detested the cruise.

Even her only solace, bridge, had been unsatisfactory. It was true that since Mrs St. Cuckoo's departure she had lost less money, but Olive de Pineapple still held her I.O.U.s for some hundreds of pounds, and Lord Cucumber would be furious.

'Are you coming to Elpenor's tomb, Mother?' said Richard, suddenly appearing round one of the buildings.

'Certainly not. I've had enough – more than enough,' said Lady Cucumber.

'I think you're wise to sit and rest,' he said, and

went on. Lady Cucumber saw him catch up with Helen Hagg and the two walked together.

'That girl won't let him alone even now he's engaged,' she burst out.

'She certainly is persevering,' said Olive de Pineapple.

'I think I had better visit this tomb after all, to keep an eye on them.'

The two ladies rose and walked slowly down the slope.

'I think I shall die,' said Lady Cucumber.

They were sitting in an indescribably dreadful car. It had no springs and no cushions, and the passengers faced one another. As they lurched over enormous holes, Olive de Pineapple's energies were concentrated on trying to prevent her head from hitting the roof. Lady Cucumber thumped the glass at the back of the driver, but he took her signals as a wish to go faster, and accelerated.

She was the more incensed when a well-sprung car passed them, choking them with dust, and she saw that it contained her son and Helen Hagg.

'Look at them trying to get past everyone. That's Miss Hagg's doing,' said Olive de Pineapple.

'It's a disgrace to put us in a thing like this,' gasped Lady Cucumber. 'I shall complain to . . . how is it that . . . ' Her speech had to be delivered in a series of jumps and squeaks, and she desisted from exhaustion.

At this moment one wheel slithered down a grass slope, and the car nearly upset on the edge of a steep drop. Terrified, Lady Cucumber scrambled out. Presently her voice was raised in shrill protest and rebuke. She hated walking, and was nearly hysterical.

'We might have been killed,' she cried. 'I shan't stir from this spot.'

'I'll stay with you, dearest,' said Olive de Pineapple.

As Langley Fundament and Lady Thomyris talked, Richard Cucumber wandered towards the inner chamber of the great beehive tomb. At the entrance he saw Helen Hagg, and came close to her. The pressure of his fingers upon her arm sent a curious thrill through her body. She stumbled over a big stone, and would have fallen if he had not caught her.

'Take care, Helen Hagg!'

She had hardly recovered her balance, and for a moment he held her closely. It was a tumultuous moment for both of them. Touch is a mysterious thing, especially when it is unexpected. And Richard Cucumber's touch swept the barriers aside which had for so long parted them. But only for a second. They drew apart without a word and went back to the main party. Helen Hagg took photographs for Mrs Mitylene in the entrance, trying the while to keep her hands steady.

Considerable time had been allowed for lunch and a rest before they went on to visit the royal piggeries, and Mrs Mitylene decided to sit quietly with Miss Bumdockdousse. Helen Hagg found them a sheltered position, and was told to spend the next hour as she chose.

Helen Hagg had no doubt what she wanted. Slipping behind a big rock, she clambered onto a mountain path which took her right away from the others.

The ground was carpeted with scarlet anemones. Far away in the valley she saw a shepherd playing his pipes. It was the land of art and legend. Bunches of ivory cloud gathered on the horizon, clouds like trembling ballerinas against a hyacinth-blue sky, clouds like icebergs seen from the transparent depths of a polar sea. Helen was glad to be by herself, and particularly to avoid Dracula Jones.

Nothing should spoil her enjoyment of the beauty.

Even as she thought this, she heard a step. It was too late to escape, but she saw that it was not Dracula Jones but Richard Cucumber who had tracked her down. She stood still, her heart thudding. He came straight on, reached her, and without a word of explanation his arms went round her, and in a moment he was kissing her madly.

Overwhelmed by his directness, Helen Hagg made no resistance. The long fight to repress her feelings had weakened her, and it was heaven to find herself in his arms.

'Helen,' said Richard Cucumber, savagely, 'I adore you.'

But Helen Hagg remembered Lady Thomyris, who had been kind, and started to struggle.

'You must be mad,' she said, trying to push him away.

'Helen Hagg, don't you love me?'

'No,' she said, faintly.

His fresh sweet lips closed on hers with unaffected enjoyment.

'You little liar!'

'Please, let me go.'

He took no notice, but merely smiled down on her.

'What about Lady Thomyris?' said Helen Hagg, apprehensively.

Richard Cucumber's arms relaxed and he stepped back.

'I know,' he muttered.

Helen Hagg touched him. The slight pressure of her blossom-white hand made him cry almost aloud with anguish.

'We've behaved vilely,' she said. 'Lady Thomyris is sweet.'

'I know she's sweet,' said Richard Cucumber, 'but I can't help myself. I love you, Helen Hagg.'

Helen Hagg drew herself erect. Her lashes were wet and her cheeks were damp with tears.

'Not really love me,' she said, broodingly. 'If you did, *this* wouldn't have happened.'

'My dear, aren't you just a bit to blame?'

'It's no use reproaching me,' said Helen Hagg, interrupting him with a stately glance.

'Helen, don't talk like this. I'm mad about you.'

'I'm sorry,' said Helen Hagg, wearily, 'but it's really hopeless.'

'Nothing is ever hopeless,' declared Richard Cucumber, rubbing her rosy, velvet cheek against his moustache with tenderness.

'Oh yes, it is. Your engagement is widely known.'

'Blast it!'

Helen Hagg moved away. The bangles on her bracelet brushed briefly against the rock, making a musical murmur of sound. She could not but be thrilled by the words he had spoken. A curious liquid sensation ran through her. She was passionately in love, but she would not sacrifice Lady Thomyris Dagobert's happiness.

'She – Thomyris – has always been wonderful to me. I couldn't hurt her.'

'Would it hurt her?'

'It would,' said Helen Hagg.

She looked ravishingly beautiful, thought Richard, a curious smile shadowing rather than brightening her face. He gave her a rapid glance of wonder. Helen Hagg raised her glorious eyes to his.

'This will pass,' she said, sighing dispassionately. 'You will forget me.'

'No!'

Something in his tone struck her, and she looked up intently.

'You are the most maddening girl in the world,' he went on. 'Aren't engagements broken every day? Do you want to tie me to a girl I don't love? Oh, you're a perfect little fool. You're as cold-blooded as a fish.'

'It's no good,' said Helen Hagg, angrily, as he held her close showering kisses on her face.

He caught her by both arms and drew her more closely to him, but Helen Hagg stood rigid until he released her. She could bear it no longer, and turned away with a quivering lip.

'We must go back now,' she said, dully.

XVI

Mrs Mitylene's health gave Helen Hagg the excuse of staying behind when the others visited Scylla and Charybdis. She knew she was missing something beautiful, but for once she did not regret it. She felt too battered to risk another scene with Richard Cucumber, and she was certain he would not let her alone.

Mrs Mitylene had been observing Helen Hagg with keen eyes. Helen had been reading aloud, but Mrs Mitylene knew that her mind was far removed from 'Liaisons Dangereuses', and observed that her answers to comments were wandering.

'I think you've read enough,' she said, and as Helen Hagg was putting in the book-marker, she added abruptly – 'My dear, what's up between you and Richard Cucumber?'

'I don't know what you mean,' stammered Helen.

'You know perfectly well.'

'Yes, but I can't talk about it,' said Helen, shakily.

'He made love to you, didn't he?' said Mrs Mitylene, her bold bird-like eyes sparkling with amusement. 'I know he has always wanted to.'

The words were unexpected. Helen Hagg, to her own horror, responded by dropping her head in her hands and bursting into tears.

It was the culmination of all her emotions – love, happiness, anxiety, humiliation, and despair.

Mrs Mitylene contented herself by saying, 'There, there, my dear,' while she waited for the paroxysm to subside.

Helen Hagg raised a tear-stained face.

'Now tell me all about it.'

Helen Hagg did so.

Mrs Mitylene pondered and mused, and then fell into a reverie.

'Well, well, we shall see,' she said after a considerable pause, but refused to explain further. She told Helen she felt better for the rest and would get up.

Shortly after this the various parties returned. A sudden squall had sprung up, and most of the passengers had been drenched. Lady Cucumber, Olive de Pineapple and Lady Thomyris came dripping up the ladder. Lady Cucumber was furious, and Thomyris amused.

'I'm going straight off to change.'

'So am I.'

Lady Thomyris gave her clothes to a stewardess, and lay on her bunk with a book. She wanted to relax and distract her mind. It was an annoyance when she heard a knock on her door. She said 'Come in,' fearing Lady Cucumber. But to her surprise she saw Mrs Mitylene's weatherbeaten face in the doorway.

'Please don't get up. I've come to ask if I might have a little talk with you.'

'But of course,' said Lady Thomyris, politely.

Mrs Mitylene seated herself, and paused as if she were collecting her ideas, then looked suddenly at Lady Thomyris.

'I am going to say something to you which will be unpardonable. And when I have said it you will probably ask me to leave your cabin at once . . . '

Lady Cucumber, after changing her wet things, came up to the saloon for a late tea, and was joined as usual by Mrs de Pineapple.

'Dearest,' said Olive, in an over-effusive manner, 'I wonder if you would do me a favour.'

She laid a persuasive hand on Lady Cucumber's arm. An arch smile flickered across her face.

'What is it?' said Lady Cucumber.

'Do wear your lovely yellow chiffon evening dress tonight, with those wonderful beads you bought on Ogygia and the shrimp-coloured ear-rings. I have a fancy to see them together.'

'But I always wear my garnets,' objected Lady Cucumber.

'They'll be safe in your cabin for once,' said Olive de Pineapple, her eyes growing limpid, transparent almost. 'And, dear, though they are simply marvellous, I am getting just a teeny weeny bit tired of seeing you in nothing else . . . '

'My garnets have been taken out of my trunk,' screamed Lady Cucumber. ' – Out of my bag! Stolen! Here on your ship!'

She stood facing the First Officer, dressed in an apricot silk negligee with wide-flowing sleeves and a square neckline. Her maid, Rocket, stood in the background mopping her eyes.

'Milady, I am desolated. Have you searched everywhere?'

'Of course.'

Rocket dragged a large cabin trunk out and began to rummage in it.

'There is no need for that,' snapped Lady Cucumber. 'Last night before dinner I placed them in my dressing bag, and it was not locked properly by that fool of a maid.'

'But I did, my lady,' said Rocket. 'I remember doing so.'

'Nonsense! Obviously you didn't. It's the grossest carelessness. Well, don't gape.'

And after delivering a homily to Rocket on the subject of stupidity and neglect of duty, Lady Cucumber began to scream vituperations at the ship's officer.

'You do not think there can have been a mistake?' he said, weakly.

'Impossible.'

The First Officer looked harassed.

'Somebody must have got in,' he suggested.

'Obviously,' said Lady Cucumber.

'Were the boxes locked this morning?'

'The jewel case was.'

The First Officer did not know what to suggest, and was relieved when Richard, who had just been found, came in.

'Richard, I've been robbed!' Lady Cucumber gave way and burst into tears.

'Steady on, Mummy darling. Tell me what happened.'

'It's my garnets,' sobbed Lady Cucumber. 'What am I to do?'

'Try and be calm,' said Richard. 'We may get them back.'

'It was the first time I hadn't worn them,' said Lady Cucumber, a low gasping sigh quivering from her lips. 'I wanted to show Olive the necklace of shark's teeth that I got in Ogygia. After I dressed for dinner I didn't come back to my cabin till I went to bed.'

'But Rocket is here a good deal during the evening, aren't you, Rocket?'

'Yes, sir,' said Rocket, her face clouding. 'Though I did go on deck for a breath of fresh air.'

'And you saw no one?'

'Mrs de Pineapple came down to fetch something from her cabin, and Miss Hagg was passing and spoke to me.'

'Miss Hagg!' cried Lady Cucumber. 'What was she doing?'

'She mends Lady Thomyris's things, my lady, I believe.'

'Extraordinary!' said Lady Cucumber thoughtfully.

'Darling, I feel dreadfully to blame,' said Olive de Pineapple, over lunch.

'How *could* you know,' wailed Lady Cucumber.

'You say you had never been without them before?' enquired Richard.

'Never.'

'Who could have got in?' said Olive de Pineapple.

'Anyone,' said Lady Thomyris. 'A thief would be on the watch, and when Lady Cucumber was seen at dinner without her garnets, would have seized the opportunity. It must have happened while Rocket was at supper.'

'You can trust Rocket, I suppose?' said Olive de Pineapple.

'Absolutely. She has been with me for fifteen years,' said Lady Cucumber, 'and she always has charge of my jewellery.'

'Well, I'm out of it,' said Lady Thomyris. 'I stopped on deck till bedtime, and went down at the same time you did.'

'I went down to fetch my book,' said Olive de Pineapple. 'That was about nine, I think, and I stayed in my cabin for a little while.'

'Did you see anyone on C deck?'

'I saw Rocket – oh! and Miss Hagg.'

'Yes, that's just it. Miss Hagg,' said Lady Cucumber. 'Whereabouts was she?'

'She was talking to Rocket, close to Lady Thomyris's cabin.'

'Didn't you say the case was locked?' broke in Richard. 'It has a peculiar key.'

'Yes, Lord Cucumber had it specially designed.'

'That is certainly curious,' said Olive de Pineapple. 'Where do you keep the keys, darling?'

'On a small bunch – but I always carry it.'

'Where?'

'That all depends – sometimes on my garter. But last night it was in my evening bag.' Lady Cucumber stopped abruptly, staring in front of her.

'What's up, Mother?' said Richard.

'Do you know,' said Lady Cucumber excitedly. 'I lost my bag for several hours last night.'

'Do you mean you were without it for a time?' asked Lady Thomyris.

'Yes,' said Lady Cucumber, looking wildly about her.

'When did you miss it?'

'I didn't. That girl, Miss Hagg, brought it back to me. She said she'd picked it up in the writing room, but the odd thing is that I don't remember going there.'

'How *very* peculiar,' said Olive de Pineapple, reflectively.

'Does all this suggest anything to you?' said Lady Cucumber, looking from one to the other and lowering her voice mysteriously.

'What sort of thing?' said Lady Thomyris.

'Isn't there a connection? Miss Hagg was near my cabin. Later it was she who gave me back my bag.'

Richard Cucumber pushed back his chair. His face was flushed.

'Mother,' he said, 'this is a scandalous suggestion!'

Lady Cucumber looked from Lady Thomyris to Olive de Pineapple. Thomyris shook her head, but Olive nodded.

'She's very hard up,' she said.

'It's monstrous,' said Richard, furiously. 'Mother, you ought to be ashamed.'

'I'm sure you're mistaken,' said Lady Thomyris, hotly.

Lady Cucumber disregarded them.

'It all hangs together!'

Olive de Pineapple gave a low laugh of malice.

'It does rather look like it. After all what do you know about the girl? Dear Lady Thomyris, you haven't seen as much of the world as I have. A girl like that – '

'What do you mean by 'a girl like that'?' shouted Richard Cucumber.

'If you must defend her, Richard,' said his mother, 'I think I must quote her father's record.'

'I'd stake my life on her honesty!'

'So would I,' said Lady Thomyris.

'Dear me, what champions!' said Lady Cucumber, in a sudden access of passion. 'But if you'll excuse my saying so, Thomyris, Miss Hagg has had ample opportunity of learning our habits, and the time Rocket usually goes for supper. Richard, dear, will you pay? I don't want to sit here for ever.'

XVII

The idea once implanted grew like a weed in Lady Cucumber's mind.

Everything fitted in. And the day after tomorrow they would reach Phaeacia, and the depraved creature would be able to get away with the Hummingbird garnets. If they were to be recovered, action must be taken. Without telling Richard, she sent a note by Rocket asking if Mrs Mitylene and Miss Hagg would come to her cabin.

'What on earth does the woman want?' said Mrs Mitylene. 'Whatever it is she can wait. Come for a turn round the deck, Helen.'

Half an hour passed, and then a steward arrived to ask Mrs Mitylene and Miss Hagg to come to the Captain's cabin.

'You wanted to speak to us, Captain Fanny-johnson?'

'It is not I but Lady Cucumber.'

Mrs Mitylene turned. 'Yes?' she said.

'I thought it better to go into this matter before the Captain,' said Lady Cucumber. 'My garnets were stolen from my cabin last evening.'

'Were they?' Mrs Mitylene was full of sympathy. 'How do you think it happened?'

'That is what I am here to find out,' said Lady Cucumber, with meaning.

'But in what way can I help you? And how can Miss Hagg?'

'I have every reason to believe that Miss Hagg can,' said Lady Cucumber.

Mrs Mitylene raised a hand to her throat, attempting to stifle the sound of horror which was about to escape.

'But how?' she enquired.

'By giving them back,' said Lady Cucumber.

There was a deadly silence. Helen Hagg sank back upon her chair staring blankly into the distance. Her face grew paler, and her dark eyes dilated. At last she staggered unexpectedly to her feet, flaming with rage.

'You are a wicked woman, Lady Cucumber!'

'I believe you have them at this moment,' said Lady Cucumber, evenly, and her eyes were hard.

Folding her hands on the table in front of her, she stated in cold tones the reasons for her monstrous accusation. When she had finished, the fury in Helen Hagg's face made Mrs Mitylene put a restraining and protective arm round her.

'Now, Laura,' she said, 'I really sympathise with you in your loss, but I beg you to believe that this dear child had no part in it.'

Helen Hagg shot her a passionate look of gratitude.

'Your faith is remarkable,' said Lady Cucumber. 'But I'm afraid all the evidence is against her.'

It was at this moment that Richard and Lady Thomyris arrived on the scene.

'What's all this about, Mother?' said Richard, his eyes going to Helen Hagg, who sat, her eyes as calm as Heaven, regarding Lady Cucumber.

With a sublime gesture, she flashed a burning glance upon him and turned away.

'Your mother accuses me of stealing her garnets,' she declared.

'That's a pretty beastly thing to say, Mother.'

'I am afraid I have a low opinion of Miss Hagg,' said Lady Cucumber in a full, penetrating voice.

'I know she didn't do it,' said Lady Thomyris, suddenly.

'How do you know?' said Lady Cucumber.

'I just feel it.'

Lady Cucumber smiled unpleasantly.

'It would be difficult to persuade me that she didn't take them.'

'And I am as certain that she didn't,' said Richard. And he crossed over and stood by Helen Hagg.

'Milady, I am distracted,' said Captain Fanny-johnson. 'It is very difficult.'

Lady Cucumber cast her eyes up to Heaven beseechingly. 'Such incompetence!'

'What steps do you wish me to take?' said Captain Fannyjohnson, goaded beyond endurance.

'You must order a search of her belongings.'

'I am quite willing,' said Helen Hagg, promptly.

'Then you must search mine as well,' said Mrs Mitylene.

'And mine,' cried Richard.

'And mine.'

'My *dear* Thomyris, do you think that is really necessary!'

Lady Cucumber seemed to become aware of the general attitude of hostility.

'Everyone is against me,' she said, and pressed her handkerchief to her eyes.

There arose a scene of the utmost confusion. The contents of Helen Hagg's bags were emptied, then her trunk. The distracted Rocket, under Lady Cucumber's directions, hunted everywhere. She shook out dresses, turned bedding upside down, but in the end it was established beyond doubt that the garnets were not in her cabin. Then Helen Hagg was forced to submit to a personal search. Every cranny was examined; every imaginable hiding place was explored. Rocket toiled and Lady Cucumber helped, spurred on to further efforts by Mrs Mitylene's sarcastic smile.

After this it was Mrs Mitylene's turn. Last of all Lady Thomyris's possessions were explored, but all efforts failed to discover the garnets. Finally Mrs Mitylene spoke:

'I hope you realise you've made a perfect fool of yourself, Laura?'

'I realise that someone is cleverer than I thought,' almost hissed Lady Cucumber.

'How about apologising?'

'Apologising!'

Lady Cucumber's face flushed, and her hands grasped at the air convulsively.

'All the same,' said Mrs Mitylene, 'I wonder who did take those garnets, Helen?'

They were in the throes of packing. Helen Hagg went on putting the clothes into heaps without replying. Resentment seethed within her. The scene in the Captain's cabin had left her feeling physically sick, and she did not want to talk about it.

'Will you have the Goblin-glen or the Mulberry cape?' she asked.

'The Mulberry cape,' said Mrs Mitylene, adding as soon as it had been packed – 'No, the Goblin-glen.'

Helen took the Goblin-glen when Mrs Mitylene said wouldn't it be better to land in it, and pack the fur coat, and at that moment there was a knock on the door. Helen Hagg, who was nearest, opened it.

'You!' she said in surprise.

'I came,' said Richard Cucumber, 'to ask you to marry me.'

'My dear boy!' said Mrs Mitylene. 'Aren't you engaged to Lady Thomyris?'

'We find that we made a mistake.'

'That was very sudden,' said Mrs Mitylene, weakly.

A sachet, on which was embroidered a strangely shaped cat, slipped from Helen Hagg's hands, and the handkerchiefs were scattered. Mrs Mitylene felt that the cabin was too small for the emotions that it contained, and walked out. Richard Cucumber, who had stooped to help recover the handkerchiefs, straightened up.

'What is your answer?' he said.

'It's too preposterous!'

'Why?'

'For one thing your mother thinks I'm a thief.'

'You won't be marrying my mother!'

She cast down her lustrous eyes and her cheeks took on a warmer shade. Vaguely awed by her quiescence, he gazed upon her enthralled and for the moment speechless.

'Richard, I think you're wonderful!'

'Helen Hagg, I adore you!'

Helen suddenly gave way. The shock of the past few hours found expression and she flung herself into his arms, sobbing from the revulsion of feeling. Richard Cucumber kissed her hair and soothed her. After a few minutes she drew away.

'Is it true about you and Thomyris?'

'She has broken it off.'

'Do you think she guessed about . . . us?'

Her radiant face grew warm with speechless eloquence.

'Even so,' she continued, 'there could never be any question of my marrying you until I'm cleared.'

'But how can we clear you?'

'Only by finding the garnets!'

'Impossible!'

'May I come in?' said Mrs Mitylene, meekly, from the doorway. 'Well, my dears, what have you settled?'

'Helen refuses to marry me until the garnets are found.'

'I think she is probably right. I also think,' said Mrs Mitylene, judicially, 'that the discovery of the thief is going to take us all our time. Now let's put our heads together . . . '

The tour might be considered over. It was the last day at sea. People were busy packing, playing games, and organising a fancy-dress dance.

Lady Cucumber, after a sleepless night, had decided to advertise her loss. There was naturally a lot of talk, though as she had not been popular with her

108

fellow passengers, the general feeling was one of hope that she would not get her garnets back. Lady Cucumber was feeling genuinely unwell from worry and lack of sleep. She had not got up, but lay brooding; then summoned Richard.

'I could never have believed,' she said, burying her head in the hollow of her arm and lying quite still, 'that a son of mine would take the part of thief against his own mother!'

'Helen Hagg is not a thief!'

'Don't be a fool!'

'She isn't.'

'All I know is that if she once gets ashore it will be the end of any chance of recovering them.'

'Please, don't go on repeating that, Mother!'

And Richard Cucumber turned to go. He was determined not to tell her that his engagement was broken until they reached Phaeacia, as he and Thomyris had agreed that it would be a shame to upset her further. A knock at the door gave him the excuse to open it, and he found a steward with a wireless message.

'Just one moment, Richard, while I see what it is.'

Lady Cucumber read it and threw it down with an exclamation of despair.

'This is the absolute limit! Your father is joining us in Phaeacia in two days time. What *am* I to say to him?'

She began to weep bitterly, waving Richard aside. He was much distressed, but finally went away. Lady Cucumber remained in tears until Olive de Pineapple arrived to see if she could be of any use.

'Darling Laura, don't go on like that,' she murmured.

She put eau-de-cologne on her friend's head, stroked it softly, and sympathised the while. Without her make up, and ravaged by tears, Lady Cucumber was a piteous sight.

'It's Lord Cucumber,' she cried. 'I don't know what I shall say to him. And I had meant to get a private detective to watch that girl. *You* don't doubt she's got them, do you, Olive?'

'If she hasn't, who has?' said Mrs de Pineapple.

XVIII

'My dear Lady Cucumber,' wrote Thomyris.

'I hope you will try to forgive me as Richard has done. He will have told you by this time of the end of our engagement, so by now you will understand why I could not come to your hotel in Phaeacia, nor travel back with you.

'But now I have decided not to return to England for some time. I am going to marry Langley Fundament, and we are going to the land of Nod, where he is to work on the excavations. You will be angry with me, but don't let it last. You have been so kind to me that I hate to feel I must annoy you.

'Your affectionate

'THOMYRIS.'

'Well, that is the last straw. Nothing more can happen now,' said Lady Cucumber, dramatically, but in this she was mistaken.

XIX

'Dear Miss Hagg,' said the letter, which had been sent from a nursing home in Vienna:

'This is the first letter I have been allowed to write, and I want to thank you.

'I've had a rotten time in hospital, and I have felt pretty bitter about Olive de Pineapple's treatment of me after a longish partnership. She thought I had had it, and if it hadn't been for you would have left me penniless. I shall give her a wide berth when I get about. She is too hard-boiled, even for me, and I want to tell you to keep your eyes skinned, for Olive does not forget an injury, and if she can she'll do you.

'Also you might give your friend Richard Cucumber a tip to look after his mother's garnets. Naturally I don't want her to know this, but I'd like to prove I'm not ungrateful for the way you stuck by me.

'Yours ever,

'IVY ST. CUCKOO.'

XX

'Well,' said Mrs Mitylene, pensively regarding the Grand Phaeacian Canal, 'we must get to work. I wonder what Lady Cucumber will have to say about it?'

She looked at her watch, for her interview with various persons had taken longer than she expected. There was no time to lose, and without further explanation she took Helen Hagg into a flower-shop where she selected a basket of crimson crab-orchids. To Helen's astonishment she asked for a card on which she wrote 'Hommages', and signed it 'Connie Walsingham', and had it wired onto the basket.

'I was not in the Secret Service for nothing,' she murmured, a slight smile dawning at the rigid corners of her mouth.

As soon as they reached the Hotel Putrideros, she had the flowers sent up to Mrs de Pineapple, with a message that the lady was waiting and would be glad if she would receive her. The page-boy returned to say that Mrs de Pineapple begged Miss Walsingham to come up to her sitting-room.

'Come along,' said Mrs Mitylene, and Helen Hagg followed completely mystified.

Olive de Pineapple's sitting-room was empty when they reached it, but Helen Hagg had hardly time to wonder what Mrs Mitylene meant to do before the door leading to the bedroom opened and Olive came in. The smile of welcome on her face quickly faded and gave place to a look of astonishment.

'There is some mistake,' she said, stiffly.

'No mistake, Mrs de Pineapple. We want to see you upon a little matter of business.'

'Really!' Olive de Pineapple gave a little flourish of brittle laughter. 'I am afraid I cannot attend to it now. I am expecting a friend, and I hear she has just arrived.'

Her eyes wandered to the basket of crab-orchids on the table.

'Connie Walsingham won't be here,' said Mrs Mitylene.

Olive de Pineapple stared.

'The boy brought me her name?'

'I'm afraid I borrowed it. I wanted to see you about the loss of Lady Cucumber's garnets.'

Olive de Pineapple's eyes glazed. She took out a cigarette and began to light it.

'It was a terrible thing to happen at the end of a charming trip,' she said, amiably. 'Won't you sit down?'

'I feel it would be better for us all to get to the bottom of this quickly,' said Mrs Mitylene.

'It would indeed.'

Olive de Pineapple's forehead puckered. She looked reflectively at Helen Hagg. She presented the picture of an agreeable woman of the world trying to help in the solution of a difficult problem. Mrs Mitylene's smile was triumphant and her voice even as she replied:

'I have every reason to think that you've got them in the next room.'

Olive de Pineapple's reaction to this was instantaneous. She turned very pale, a cold shiver ran through her, her face was contorted with a sudden spasm, but she endeavoured to smile.

'I'm curious to know what could have given you this amazing idea. Don't you know that Lady Cucumber is a great friend of mine?'

'That doesn't alter my opinion,' said Mrs Mitylene.

'I hope you won't force me to send for the manager.'

'I hope so too.'

'Or to appeal to the British Consul.'

'I shouldn't if I were you,' said Mrs Mitylene, viciously. 'There are certain informalities about your passport. The name you are using is not the one under which my friend, Don Theotocopuli, the chief of police, remembers you!'

'He is entirely mistaken.'

'No, no, you were calling yourself Lady Marjorie Melon. Enquiries should also prove you to have been in Puerto Plata that time when Mrs Elroy-Flecker lost her big moonstone, and at Nurmansk when Lord Emission of Semen was robbed of his monogrammed cigarette-case, and we should find that you were in the post office at Hyderabad when the Maharanee was deprived of her emerald cuff-links. All this might make the police suspicious!'

'What you say is preposterous!' said Olive de Pineapple, pressing her hands together and casting down her pale-coloured, treacherous eyes. 'You force yourself into my room and bully me because you think I am a woman alone.'

'I am not going to bully you,' said Mrs Mitylene. 'On the contrary I am going to make you an offer.

Hand over the garnets now, and not another word shall be said.'

There was a pause. Olive de Pineapple's complexion had gone a curious grey under her rouge.

'Lady Cucumber is not a person to be relied upon,' she said in a very low voice. 'She might insist upon prosecution.'

'I have thought all that out,' said Mrs Mitylene, her full brown eyes meeting the pale yellow ones with immeasurable scorn. 'Lady Cucumber has signed a letter completely exonerating whoever gives them back.'

'Where is it?'

'Here.'

'The name is not filled in.'

'It will be when I get the garnets,' said Mrs Mitylene.

Mrs de Pineapple, alias Marjorie Melon, alias Lady Grace Compost, alias Elizabeth Lambslettuce, better known as the Duchess of Bean, sat very still, while Mrs Mitylene waited. The clock on the mantelpiece ticked loudly. Helen Hagg felt she could hardly breathe so great was the suspense. The criminal's face was set like a mask. She seemed to be weighing her chances, trying to find a way out.

At last Olive de Pineapple got slowly to her feet, and went into the bedroom.

They could hear her moving about, and presently she returned holding a pair of stockings. These she unrolled, and spilled a pool of glittering fire on the table. Mrs Mitylene scribbled something on a sheet of paper, and handed it to Helen Hagg together with Lady Cucumber's letter.

'Now,' she said, briskly, 'take this to Laura, and ask her to fill in the name I have written. Her room is number 54. I will stay here.'

'Must I?' Helen Hagg looked at her pleadingly. An encounter with Lady Cucumber was the last thing she wanted.

Mrs Mitylene nodded impatiently.

'And be quick,' she snapped.

Lady Cucumber was lying on a sofa by a window overlooking the canal. She was dressed in champagne and tangerine, with a large black bangle on her ankle. Richard stood beside her.

'Miss Hagg!' exclaimed Lady Cucumber, a glance of great wonder and expectation flashing into her face.

'Mrs Mitylene sent me with this.'

Lady Cucumber's eyes lit up with hatred and triumph. So! The girl had been forced to confess. Her son would see now what sort of a creature she was.

'Do you want me to fill in your name, Miss Hagg!'

Her tone was ominously quiet. Helen Hagg broke into a low peal of laughter.

'Mine!' she said. 'I am sorry you misunderstood.'

Lady Cucumber snatched the paper, and gave a startled cry.

'Olive de Pineapple! I don't believe it! I can't! Olive!!! No, it's impossible.'

She leaned back with closed eyes, trying to grasp the idea. She remembered confidences exchanged, vows of friendship, and many pleasant moments. Her soul revolted at the treachery.

'I can't believe it,' she repeated.

'Why not ask her?' said Helen Hagg.

'I will,' declared Lady Cucumber, swinging her body round from the reclining position.

She marched ahead, along the corridor and up the stairs, her draperies billowing about her, her head high. Richard and Helen Hagg followed. When they reached the sitting-room, Olive de Pineapple and Mrs Mitylene sat facing one another, and Mrs De Pineapple was smoking a cigarette. Neither of them had touched the garnets which lay in a bloody streak on the light wood of the table. Lady Cucumber's eyes widened when she saw them.

'Then it's true!' she gasped.

Olive de Pineapple laughed, and her laugh was as chill as the gleam of light on the edge of a sword. She continued smoking. Her face was sphinx-like as her eyes went from one to the other.

At last Lady Cucumber gave way.

'You . . . adventuress!' she almost screamed, white with fury.

'Well, goodness me,' drawled Olive de Pineapple.

'If I ever see you again I shall hand you over to the police!'

'On what grounds?'

'Your impudence is unbelievable – or is it usual in people of your profession?'

'Profession!'

'Thieves,' hissed Lady Cucumber.

'Really,' said Olive de Pineapple, amiably, 'Haven't I got your letter thanking me for returning the garnets? I'm not sure I can't claim a reward!'

'You are quite the most dreadful woman I ever met,' said Lady Cucumber, and left the room without so much as a glance at the people who had helped her.

Mrs Mitylene, Richard, and Helen Hagg followed, and Olive de Pineapple went into her bedroom to pack. Richard went to his mother's room, where he found her stretched on the sofa with Rocket fluttering around her with smelling salts and aspirin.

'I am very glad you have got your garnets back,' he said, curtly.

'Yes,' said Lady Cucumber faintly.

'And I have come to ask you to be nice to Miss Hagg.'

Lady Cucumber sat up, startled at his uncompromising tone.

'It's important, you see,' went on Richard, unmoved, 'because I'm going to marry her.'

'What!' cried Lady Cucumber.

Everything that had gone before seemed insignificant in comparison with this supreme misfortune. Her face worked, her expression was piteous.

The sun was setting over the Grand Phaeacian Canal, as Richard Cucumber took Helen Hagg in his arms. Above them the sun spread a glittering crown of light, woven into intertwisted strands of glistening gold which cast prismatic reflections upon them. A circle of mystery, widening into rings of glory.

'Helen! I feel as if I've come to the end of a long trip,' said Richard Cucumber, holding her fondly to his breast, as if she were a precious fragile flower of which not one petal must be damaged.

Helen Hagg raised herself in his arms and gazed upon him with her bright, brilliant eyes. A mystic light that was not of the sunset seemed cast on her face.

'Oh, Richard,' she said, 'it seems that I've waited all my life for this moment. Now that I'm in your arms I feel that I've really come home!'

Half swooning with the force of his emotions, he suddenly grasped at her hand.

'You and I have found what we've been searching for all the days of our lives!!'

'How can you be so sure?' she said, the shadow of a smile on her lips deepening and softening.

Richard Cucumber laughed. 'My heart just told me so . . . and it's never lied yet.'

'Oh, darling!'

'Oh, Helen, I love you so! I'll always love you!'

'Don't ever stop saying that, Richard!'

She gazed upward – upward – far into the vistas of the setting sun. A dreamy, meditative smile parted her lips. In a sudden access of passion he seized both her arms and held them as in a vice.

'Darling,' he said, his voice pulsating with keenest desire, 'I've got a gondola waiting!'

Her cheeks grew dark with pleasure and surprise. The bronze-gold of the sunset seemed to melt in her hair; the blackness of night floated liquidly in her eyes. As they descended the steps of the Hotel Putrideros, serpentine twists of fiery vapour and forked tongues of brightness fell glimmeringly on the shining waters. Flecks of crimson like floating rose-petals drifted in the sky.

They walked in a path of roseate radiance, walking on steadily, never once looking back.

From her room on the first floor of the hotel, Lady Cucumber watched them, until their gondola became a black silhouette against the sunset, until it gradually diminished and disappeared. In a prophetic flash of vision she saw what her life would be like with Helen Hagg at Hummingbird. Tears rolled down her cheeks. Nothing, nothing would alter her defeat.

Breaking into a wild fit of delirious laughter, she flung her stole desperately across her mouth to stifle an agonised convulsion.

THE BOY HAIRDRESSER

a novel
by
John Orton
and
Kenneth Halliwell

1

For over an hour he had lain in the bath, a rubber pillow behind his head, watching the sunlight move across the wall.

Half a dozen beer bottles stood in the washbasin; the room smelt of stale cigarette smoke. The window rattled. The sound of children at play drifted in from the street.

Damn Peterson, damn him: he's late.

The water was getting cold. Reaching forward, his arms like an oarsman, he turned on the tap. With the increased heat sweat broke out on the backs of his hands. Sitting there with his knees thrust up he felt lonely. Reaching for a bottle he swallowed the beer the way Peterson had taught him. Applaud me: but no one applauded. Instead, in the silence, a child screamed.

Donelly hammered with one hand on the edge of the bath. He was bored and sullen. There was nothing to do except bite his nails or read.

He shuffled his bare toes against the taps. His eyes searched to the right and left. He slithered lower into the water. Nothing stirred. Silence.

And then he heard a voice.

He lay motionless. He waited; but saw no one. It was his own voice. He lay without breathing and the sound came again.

A guardsman in his underwear
In a vision once I saw;
Along the mountain tops he came,
His privy member all aflame,
Most horrid and unnatural.

He fell into a coma as he listened to his own voice.

His mind ran on to beasts and wars and fights, enormous spectacle and single combat, imagined or real.

He lay still.

There is no need to trace the cause of quarrel between the right buttocks and the left buttocks, to catalogue the conflicts which have scarred the whole area from groin to vertebrae, or to guess the extent of provocation on either side.

The thoughts slid past frothing and bubbling, white, ridge upon ridge, until he was almost asleep.

He lay, and his aloneness was vast about him. Very softly there came a sound. The noise faded. He closed his eyes and dreamed. He dreamed of his tongue, long, red and loose, of dipping it into a stoup of holy water. The end began to swell, a great bulge appeared on the end. This swelling increased until it formed a face. Red, weasel eyes stared at him, the tight mouth opened and spoke:

And so the gods distinction drew,
Good luck to art, a sod to you.

He floated a beer-bottle down the bath, towards the soap-dish, towards the sounds from the street, jumped out and dried himself.

Light from the backs of warehouses mixed with strangled sunbeams on the canal, both failing to pierce its opacity, the result of chemical waste tipped in by the ton. Here nothing lived, no fish, no weeds: no insect played on the surface. When stones were thrown, the sterile mud rose in geometric circles. Waves, when there were any, lapped on a littoral of broken bottles.

Donelly watched the pavement, watched the canal, then turned to watch his own face in the mirror vanishing with the steam. He spat the taste from his mouth, took another bottle and poured it into a toothglass.

He left it on the window-sill after scarcely reducing the foam.

Time was running short, Peterson was injured or dead: he had to sober up in order to identify the corpse. As he rubbed it across his shoulders, the towel chafed his skin. He gulped breaths of air, a recklessness gleamed in his eyes: he was almost happy. With remarkable veracity he saw all the dreary squalor which must one day be ended.

If Peterson were dead, he could end it now.

It crossed his mind to wonder whether Peterson would be altogether recognisable lying on a mortuary slab. No mistaking the irregularities of complexion, the discoloured patches under the eyes, the scar on his chin where he had cut himself bathing. But the truculence and charm – those things age can wither and custom infinitely stale – would be gone.

A knock came at the bathroom door.

His thoughts stopped.

Peterson made no excuse for his lateness.

'Aren't you out of the bath yet?'

'No.'

'Got a spare bottle?'

He knew his excuses wouldn't be believed. And why should they: he was a liar, unable to keep a grasp on the truth. No one refuted his excuses more powerfully than he, more effectively demolished the lies.

'Sorry I'm late.'

Donelly lifted his glass, studying the tracery of foam on its surface. 'What does it matter.'

'As a matter of fact I was late because – '

Donelly didn't listen. He watched Peterson gulp the beer down, thinking how he anticipated all the pointless lies, watching for any sign that this time he might tell the truth.

But Peterson was a good liar: nothing was to be read in that face, which bore no trace of experience beyond the classroom.

Peterson was in the bedroom rummaging in a drawer.

'What's this you've been reading? Can I borrow a tie? Book any good?' The questions were automatic.

'Not much.'

'You probably missed the point.'

'If I'd paid for it, I'd have wanted my money back.'

'What was it about?'

'An old man who lived in a derelict piss-house.'

'Sounds interesting.'

'It wasn't. As far as I could see all the sadness, the satire, were on the book-jacket.'

Peterson laughed and his fillings showed.

'I don't suppose there was any point to miss.'

Donelly nodded. He had proved to himself the pointlessness of so many things, so many virtues, so many vices, without purpose, leading nowhere.

'She was a Catholic.'

'Who was?'

'The woman who wrote this book.'

'Oh, her – ' Peterson posed before the mirror, throwing his chest out, contracting his waist, his good-natured gold-flecked eyes admiring their own reflection: Donelly noticed his neck needed washing.

'Such a sensation when she lapsed.'

'Did she? Why did she?'

'She found a currant in her communion wafer.'

He picked up the books scattered around, wondering which were stolen and which were loaned.

'They're very careless. A woman I know was given Stone's ginger wine on Christmas Eve.'

'It disillusioned her?'

'I expect so.'

He walked to the table, strewn with weekly papers. 'This place is a pigsty,' he said.

'Oh, I don't know.'

'You don't have to be polite with me.' He picked up a watch that had stopped, tried to tell the time, and put it down again. 'I've let the place go to pot lately.'

Outside a car backfired. They became aware of a silence, and then of footsteps in the hall. Donelly waited until they had gone away and began to question Peterson.

'How much money have you got?'

'None.'

'What about the books you were going to sell?'

'As a matter of fact,' said Peterson, posing against the bed, 'I didn't get much for them.'

'Why not?'

He shrugged.

They had been stealing for a year from bookshops. Donelly had a great enthusiasm for anarchy. The theft of toilet-rolls from public lavatories, pens from post offices; the obscene telephone calls, the cards inserted in Praed Street windows giving the addresses of vicars' aunts and aldermen's widows, and the time he had loosed a rat on a crowded dance floor.

These were rehearsals. One day he would show them. He could afford to wait.

He watched a fly crawl on the window without interest. It took off in a flash of silver and alighted on top of an illustrated Zurbarán, which had once cost five guineas.

'We can sell some of these,' he said, pointing.

'I know.'

'What are you going to do until then?'

'Something will turn up.'

The taste of beer returned to Donelly's mouth in a belch. When Peterson needed money it dropped from the sky. His optimism was remorseless and dangerous. Something could be sold, something pawned; a girl persuaded to part with a few pounds: for two quid he would screw a zebra.

'I'll lend you – '

'I won't scrounge.'

'It wouldn't be.'

'I'll pay you back.'

Donelly tried to smile. What a charmer he looks, with the light falling onto his hair: tough yet in a way weak: in need of protection. Tired, as though from climbing trees on a windy day; a schoolboy, red and buffeted from the playing fields and a shower. Peterson was as trapped as he was, and yet treated his cage as a playground, making the cage disappear, the bars melt.

'You can't go on like this,' said Donelly. 'Hart will give you a job.'

Peterson leaned on the wall with a hangdog insolence.

'No. That club he runs sounds fishy.'

'He won't ask for references, why should you?'

Peterson shook his head. 'I don't like things I can't understand.'

'There's nothing – '

'I don't want to get mixed up with that kind of thing.'

'What kind of thing?'

'I don't know.' Peterson caricatured a grin. 'Is it girls, or boys, or celluloid ducks, or dope?'

'What do you want? Security in your old age? I think I'm wasting my time.'

'You try too hard,' said Peterson.

There were times when he fathomed Donelly's reasoning only too well.

'You want a safe job? – get paid every Friday?'

'I've no quarrel with that world.' Peterson stood silhouetted by the lamplit window. 'I'll manage: I've three pounds.'

'Where from?'

'It isn't much but – '

Donelly slammed the door and they went downstairs.

' – there's always the Labour Exchange.'

'Hart will give you a job.'

'I don't want that kind of job.'

'You can give it up if you don't like it.' Donelly cut him short.

A thin drizzle was falling, blown eastwards across the slate and corrugated iron, misting the glossy reflective waters of the canal.

Hart looked over his shoulder.

No one followed him, but his fears and uncertainties were as clearly visible as electric cables connecting him to the ground. The man by the lamp-post, the housewife, the girl at the window, all seemed to take more interest in him than usual.

He looked over his shoulder again and then at his watch.

He was rich. He had scored over the boys he was at school with. He was afraid. They had no fears; they had no money. He wasn't doing five years like Greene; he smiled, thinking of Bryson his special tormentor, whose popularity rested upon having attempted to rape one of the charwomen. They had paid no attention to him, thought him not worth caring about. And now they were both inside.

And he was free.

And afraid.

He looked at the dome of the cinema where he had spent his afternoons when he should have been playing football. The width of the street divided him from a queue of children on the opposite pavement. It was easy to get lost between the school and the park; he had never been in the team; one boy more or less watching had not been noticed.

He felt a twinge of nostalgia for those afternoons, for the smell of lavender disinfectant, the air of expectancy when the screen lighted up. He had been born at the Roxy during a matinée performance of *Broadway Melody*. Three weeks premature, his mother had delivered him in the manager's office, while Dick Powell tapped his feet and Ruby Keeler sang.

In that place his ideas of good and evil were formed; his knowledge of man's place in the universe came from a projection box and its shimmering beam.

He pulled his dog to heel, touched, as a policeman passed, by a feeling of panic.

Peterson stared at himself in a window. A car's headlights illuminated his almost vanished reluctance. If he had not pawned or borrowed until there was nothing left, he could have refused the job.

Donelly looked at him. His glance held affection, and a quality that was lethal. Peterson's simplicity belonged in a flat with nappies drying; he should be a happy captive, an old man at thirty. There was no escape for him, ultimately.

'Hart will give you a job,' he said, opening his collar. The rain had made it warmer. I'm mad, and

God is on his side and fights for him and all the people like him. He felt a drop of rain run down inside his collar.

Peterson said, 'Let's call in at my place.'

'Why?'

'We won't be long.'

Donelly noticed the first buds on a tree. It would soon be Spring. Spring was traffic lights beaded with moisture, lamps shining on sodden macs, the rubbery smell of gardens, new window displays.

'I can't take this job,' Peterson said.

Some malice of memory caused him to bring to mind his other job: among the coloured bottles, the creams and hair restorers he had been conforming and happy.

'You've no choice,' Donelly said.

'You're sure it's alright?'

'It's a job.'

Peterson hunched his shoulders. 'I was happy, you know.'

Donelly flinched like a boy who has been caught out. 'Were you happy?' This was an accusation.

'Happier than I am now.'

'Now you're free.'

'Yes. Now I'm free.'

'You've got to choose a line of action,' said Donelly, 'and stick to it.'

'Well,' Peterson said, 'I've no regrets.'

The words floated out on a wave of denying laughter.

'It's no use looking back.'

Peterson avoided his eye. He licked his lips first one

way and then the other, examined the ground. Donelly recognised in his silence a quality of the unpredictable: the pause before victory or defeat.

'Here we are,' Peterson said. 'Here we are: home from home.'

He opened the door and hurried Donelly in, not wanting to meet his landlady. The house was unaired and stuffy. On the sofa a dog lay asleep with a patch of eczema behind its ears. The house was empty, the coast was clear.

'What's the time?'

'I don't know.' Peterson opened the door of his room. 'My watch is in hock.'

The door closed behind them with scarcely a click.

'You can get it back – soon.'

The room was little more than a cupboard lighted by an unshaded bulb: a chair covered in rexine, a cheap chest of drawers, a mirror. Donelly sniffed at the smell of stale Californian Poppy; a woman had been in the room recently, and it was disturbing – like being watched.

'What did we come for?'

'To pay the rent. She's kicking me out tonight if I don't.'

Donelly came to a halt in front of a photograph pinned to the mirror – a snapshot of a girl, obviously taken in this room, the bed was just visible. She was young – and yet it wasn't the immature breasts that surprised as the air of professionalism, of being at home in front of the camera. He felt an envy of the girl and her enjoyment.

'Who is she?'

'A tart I met.' Peterson took down the snapshot, grinned, and put it back again.

'How old is she?'

'Only fourteen.'

'You do take risks, don't you?'

Peterson's face crinkled into a smile. 'There are no risks.'

'No?'

'She's the kind who carries french letters around in her school-bag.'

'Is this her powder?'

'She hasn't been here; you can't risk letting them know where you live. We went to her house.'

'Often?'

'I used to meet her after school. I can't risk nosing about too much where she lives.'

'I thought there were no risks?'

'As a matter of fact,' said Peterson, 'this powder *is* hers – ' He told the truth so unexpectedly that Donelly was made a victim of the charm he despised. 'She has been here once or twice: she was here – '

'Today. That's why you were late?'

'Yes.'

Donelly knotted his fingers together. The rain ran down the gutter outside with a vomiting noise. He thought of the old whore to whom he'd once caught Peterson giving pleasure. A vein in his temple throbbed; he understood why men entered monasteries.

'Do you think Hart will give me a job?' said Peterson.

Donelly looked up. 'He's sure to.'

'I'm not much good at anything.'

'There's no need to tell me.'

'I know it sounds stupid,' said Peterson, 'but I don't want to drift.' He sat on the bed and lifted his shoe. 'I'd like to put down roots before it's too late. I can't go on in this way for ever.'

Donelly saw the stifled desires pushing their way to the surface: the pram in the hall, the modernistic wallpaper and dining-room suite, the furniture arranged in a jungle of wifely good taste; and Peterson in the complacent roundness of his conformity.

Peterson said, 'You can't reject all the values of society.'

He stared at the hole in his shoe and heard Donelly's voice, dimly, coming from a distance:

– the values of society? What values? The things we take seriously will be laughed at in fifty years. Who doesn't laugh at nineteenth-century attitudes? – and yet they imagined them to be the right ones.

– our morals will look silly before we die.

– why work in a factory for a lousy eight pounds a week?

Donelly paced up and down by the edge of the bed; Peterson sighed.

– you want to be a respectable member of society? There are none. They are the worst perverts of all. The more respectable, the more perversity. Take that Mrs Dale –

He swung round.

– I'll bet what she does in bed would shock her mother! These conformists give me a pain in the arse. They look down on so many things – and yet they have vices –

She sounds the biggest old prude unhung, people would think she'd never – and she must have –

– I'll bet she thinks of sex twenty-four hours a day. All the time she's talking to her mother and that haggy old char, I'll bet she's nearly going out of her mind with thinking about sex.

Ordinary respectable people are –

What is the difference between living off the earnings of one woman, or hundreds of women in a factory?

– Just pimps and super-pimps.

Men and women who work in shops, factories and offices are prostitutes slaving for a super-pimp.

– And you want to be one of them?

Peterson heard Donelly's voice come to a stop. He stared.

'I want – '

'You want a fortnight's holiday out of fifty-two, and a pension when it's over.'

'Oh, well – ' Whenever a discussion reached this point Peterson refused to follow it.

He fumbled in his pocket. 'I'll see what Hart has to offer.'

'It won't carry a pension.'

'He pays well?'

'You'll get your share.'

Peterson laughed. His fears tucked away, he lit a cigarette and smoothed out some notes.

'I'll pay the old bitch, and then we'll have a meal.'

'Tell her you're leaving,' said Donelly.

He was not lulled by this suspect bravado: he preferred Peterson wracked with hesitations, only at ease in a conspiratorial way, like a schoolboy with his own enjoyments.

'Come and share my flat. Save money.'

'Good idea,' said Peterson. 'Meet you in half an hour with my bags packed.'

'Usual place?'

'Yes.'

Donelly opened the door. A sullen woman in glasses leaned over the banister, a Woodbine hanging out of the corner of her mouth; somewhere above an accordion was playing.

2

The road was wet and shimmered under the street-lamps. Peterson walked quickly, trying to catch up with the girl ahead of him. From behind she looked older than she was – her buttocks thrust through the thin material of her skirt – carrying a book under her arm. Peterson came alongside as she was entering the café and gave her a smack on the bottom.

She turned. 'Oh, it's you.'

'Yes, it's me. Were you expecting anyone else?'

She pushed out her lip and pouted. 'I think it's a bit much – you *hurt* me.' A lock of hair fell over her face and trembled as she spoke.

'Did I?' said Peterson, pushing open the door.

'Yes.'

Over by the window a young man was reading; his glasses were held together at the bridge of the nose by a soiled piece of adhesive tape.

The chair opposite him had a coat draped over it. As Peterson came up, he was saying to the waitress:

'I've got a friend coming.'

'Hallo, Colin,' said the girl.

'It's alright, miss, this *is* my friend. You're looking pretty ravishing tonight, sweetie.'

He glanced in Peterson's direction.

' – to what do we owe the pleasure?'

'You don't mind if Steve joins us?'

'Not at all.' He beckoned the waitress. 'Plaice and chips for three.' He stared after the woman's retreating back. 'And how is the world with you?' he said to Peterson. 'Got a job yet?'

'I'm still one of the undeserving poor.'

'So the world is treating our friend here very nicely?' His eyes were traitors, showing dislike and scorn. 'Is that my book, sweetie?'

Fran poured sauce over her chips.

'I lent a book to Fran, though I don't believe she can read.'

Fran pouted. 'I don't like that, Col.'

'You don't like it? Well, I apologise. What did you think of it?' He smiled down at her in a superior way.

'It was – strange.'

'Ah, but did you understand it, Fran?'

'Well – '

' – That's the point. If I was to say to you, what's the point of it, could you tell me?'

She picked at her fish. 'It was about religion and – the way we think about each other, and things.'

Peterson stuffed his mouth with fish.

'Not bad,' said Crane, spreading his legs beneath the table, 'not bad. But did you get the message, did you understand the teaching?'

'It was depressing.'

'I thought you'd say that. It was depressing was it?'

'Yes, but you only gave me volume two and I wanted to know what happened in volume one.'

Crane raised his eyebrows. 'It isn't a love-story, sweetie; you can't expect anything to happen in Nietzsche.'

Fran looked uncomfortable. Somewhere faintly a clock struck the hour. For a moment no one spoke.

141

Peterson finished his fish and found his attention wandering. He heard Crane's voice through the clatter of cups, the hiss of rain on the window.

'I'm taking up writing again – well I thought I ought to because – a novel – it's *most* interesting.
The plot.
In the staff quarters of a famous hotel the old chef is dying. He knows and the management know that shortly they will elect his successor. Will it be one of the existing kitchen staff? Most likely candidates are –
Raymond, warm and sympathetic, but given to extravagant dishes, and
Bushell, a man with half Raymond's gifts, but shrewd, prosaic and reliable.
The struggle for mastership of a hotel kitchen serves as a paradigm of power politics – '

Peterson stared hard at a round smear of tomato ketchup on his plate; Crane nodded.

' – factions soon form. Arthurine Talbot is Raymond's partisan, and so is the desk-clerk, Mrs Glyn-Daniel. But the rival party is equally strong and –
A most interesting novel.
I expect it will be published – '

Peterson watched the steam rise slowly from the tea urn; noticed the waitress carrying a tray; the rain hissed on the window. His eyes met Fran's. He smiled.

There are many kinds of crucifixion; not all involving the use of wood and nails. Long before Donelly saw Peterson, he heard his voice and then his laugh. He experienced a feeling of nausea, knowing each careless phrase, each lie meant to win friendship: the threadbare tricks of a shallow mind.

Ten minutes on his own and Peterson had picked up somebody; he had found an audience: it was an enviable habit.

' – I was worried about being called as a witness, but they gave me protection.'

'How many years did you say he got, three?'

Donelly laughed a silent laugh as he reached the table, stood behind them for a moment pretending to look for someone.

'How long ago was this?'

'Eighteen months – no, it'll be two years in May.'

'Aren't you scared?'

'Why should I be?'

'Well, I mean, when he comes out . . . '

Peterson leaned back, his hair falling over his eyes. 'He won't try anything.'

'He may have it in for you.'

'I can settle anything he can manage. Oh, hallo,' he said, turning his head, some glib phrase dying upon his lips. For a minute he was unsure of himself. While the girl stared he remained speechless, finding it difficult to play a part in front of Donelly.

'Steve's been telling us how he was scarred,' said the girl.

'Who?'

'Steve.'

Donelly said maliciously, 'His name's Percy.'

'It isn't,' said Peterson. His face had lost its charm and began to twist with embarrassment.

It was hot in the café and he had taken off his tie; through the open neck of his shirt the flesh looked white and vulnerable.

Donelly felt a desire to say something unpleasant.

'When did you change it?'

'Steve is my second name; you know that.'

'I forgot.'

'What's in a name,' said the girl.

Donelly was reminded of an old woman made young by plastic surgery. She couldn't be more than fifteen yet her facial contours, her eye-sockets, and her bright mouth already contained an immeasurable hardness. She knew so much – and thought she knew so much more. From the way she looked at Peterson, it was obvious that she was falling for him. He pitied her, pitied the blotchy skin caked with make-up, the not quite straight nose, the smell of cheap scent. He remembered the spilled powder, the Californian Poppy: Peterson liked them young.

She opened her compact and gave her spots a deeper coating. 'I think they ought to have given Steve a medal.'

Donelly, watching with distaste, felt in need of a drink. 'They did want to, but his religious convictions wouldn't permit it.'

'I didn't know he was religious.'

'Didn't he tell you? – but then he's so modest.'

She looked at Crane for help. 'You can carry modesty too far.'

144

Peterson scowled, but didn't attempt to contradict.

'When shall I see you again, Steve?'

While Crane adjusted his hat in the mirror, smoothed the creases in his short mac, she goggled like a goldfish waiting for someone to throw her an ant's-egg. 'How about Monday at half past four?'

Peterson nodded; fidgeted with a salt-cellar.

' – I'll be there about half past,' said the girl, as she went through the door.

Donelly said, 'So you were knifed in a dance-hall?'

'If she believed me.'

'She believed you.'

Peterson smiled. 'I had to give them their money's worth; Crane was going to pay for the tea.'

He had as rigid and unimaginative a set of values as a shopkeeper.

'I've never had my money's worth.'

'You know me.'

'Too well.'

'You've had nothing to eat,' said Peterson.

'I'm not hungry.' Donelly stared at the plastic cruet, the ash-tray full of cigarette ends smeared with pink.

He stood up, giving way to a spurt of interior laughter at his own thoughts, at himself for being what he was. He buttoned his mac.

'Do you really think she believed me?'

'They all do.' He emptied the ashtray onto the floor and ground the mess into the tiles with his heel.

'Did you like her?'

'If it gives you pleasure. She's below the age of consent, isn't she?'

'She's got her head screwed on.'

'I hope you know what you're doing.'

Peterson laughed a fatuous laugh, his charm gone. 'All that technical bull,' he said, knotting his tie; 'she knows more about sex than my old woman'll know when she's sixty.'

Donelly watched the grin on his face, and saw, as though reflected in glass, the final situation from which he would be unable to squirm. He saw the familiar charm become sinister: what a nasty old man he'd become, all that dirtiness wriggling and repressed.

'I must have a drink,' he said.

'You've been knocking it back lately,' said Peterson, signalling to the barmaid.

'It's my own liver.' Donelly ran his eyes over the barmaid's hips. 'Have you taken your bags to the flat?'

'No.'

'Why not?'

'She's keeping them.'

'I see. How much do you owe her?'

Peterson simulated embarassment. 'Four pounds.'

'Pay her tomorrow – another drink?' He burped and signalled the barmaid.

'It isn't good to drink on an empty stomach.'

Donelly shrugged. 'It's my own stomach.'

For the best part of an hour they sat swilling beer, watching an occasional customer come through the doors. Behind them the barmaid opened bottles, piled sandwiches upon sprigs of parsley. Each time the door opened a smell of sooty rain drifted in.

'Another?' said Donelly. While Peterson fetched it, he went to the lavatory. Among the obscenities was scribbled Durex Gossamer Sensitol Lubricated Is The

Only Hope For India. When he got back to the bar, Peterson had his foot on the rail, leaning his elbow beside the barmaid.

'You're quite a wit,' she was saying; her swollen face glared in the light of the brasswork.

'You think so?'

'Yes, we get a lot of your sort in here.'

'Have a drink – or are you TT?'

Her mouth fell open, a bus rumbled by outside. 'What did you say, dear, I didn't quite catch?'

'You'll have to buy yourself a deaf-aid.'

'Your sort make me tired.' Her eyes slid back to her copy of *Woman's Realm*. 'We get a lot of your sort in here, I've met so many.'

'If those lips could only speak,' said Peterson: 'you ought to write your confessions for the Sunday papers, or are you scared they might deport you?'

'My conscience is clear.'

'I'd be surprised if there were many days you had your breakfast alone.'

'You surprise easy, don't you? What right have you to say a thing like that?' The manager glanced in from the other bar for a few moments. A gleam came into her eye.

'You hear a lot about barmaids,' Peterson said.

'I'm not that type.'

'You're not too old are you?'

'Too old for what?'

Over her head Donelly could see reflected in the large mirror an old woman in the corner talking to herself. Peterson watched her move away to serve another customer. 'Is it still raining?'

'Yes.'

'I thought it'd stopped.'

The place was almost empty, the light winked on unopened bottles.

'I'm thirty-two,' she said, coming back.

'Well, you want to pull yourself together, you look a hundred and ten.'

The woman in the corner had stopped talking to herself and was watching them, wondering if they were good for a drink. Her coat was too old for the material to be recognised – more like a canvas tarpaulin; her face had a kind of starved intensity, seeming to change shape as though in water. She began to sing to herself, then broke off and laughed with calculated madness. Somewhere a clock was striking. A hand went up to her mouth and she started to bite her nails, nipping each finger in turn.

'She ought to be put away,' said Peterson.

Donelly looked round. 'Why?' he said, 'She isn't doing you any harm.'

'She's mad.'

'She's not mad: I often sing to myself.'

'Not in *here*.'

Donelly measured the distance between themselves and the woman. 'Maybe she's happy, maybe she's had a win on the Pools.'

'She smells too.'

Donelly looked with interest at the woman, the hair escaping from under the old-fashioned hat. 'It's a pity if people can't smell without being thrown in an asylum.'

'I never said anything about an asylum.'

'Anyway,' said Donelly, putting his glass down, slopping beer on the counter, 'she's not potty. Some people would say we were potty; if they knew half the facts, they might say that Einstein was mad.'

'Biting her nails like that.'

'You used to bite yours.'

'That's beside the point.' Tears of fury pricked behind Peterson's eyelids.

'And what point would there be in locking her up?'

'I never said anything about locking her up – '

'Keeping her there, costing the taxpayer money.'

'You don't pay taxes.'

'I might one day.'

'Pigs might fly.'

Donelly's lip twisted; he focused his eyes for a moment upon the gaunt, mad face.

'What point would a cannibal see in television?' said Peterson suddenly.

'As much as I do.'

'It gives pleasure to some people.'

'Does it?'

'Some people must like it.'

Donelly smiled to catch the barmaid's attention. He watched two bottles being opened; then she returned to her magazine. The old woman had upset her drink and was trying to mop it up with a ten-shilling note.

'I was glad to hear your opinions upon TV. A writer should meet all sorts.'

'You're not a writer.'

'I might be.'

'With science anything's possible.'

'Don't you think I will be?'

'About the same time you pay taxes – '

'You're one of those people who measure success by the number of copies sold,' said Donelly. 'It would surprise you, wouldn't it, that there are some writers too good to be published?' He turned his back on Peterson and looked at the old woman. 'Too good,' he repeated, 'Stendhal was dead before he was published.'

'It didn't do him much good then, did it?'

Donelly raised the glass to hide his face. 'You would say that.'

'I don't see the point in writing a book if it isn't published until after you're dead.'

'He didn't plan it that way.'

'There may be a reason why he wasn't published; perhaps he was awful. I dare say he was.'

Donelly looked at his finger-ends. 'I don't know.'

'There you are.'

Donelly moved his glass round in empty circles. The bar was filling. The blonde wives and girl friends of men starting the weekend were drinking Drambuie. Somebody soon would suggest a bit of music, making it necessary to shout.

'She works so hard, poor thing, I'm sure she overdoes it.'

'Do you really think so? Do you really think so?'

'What I think is so nice is she's just the same as you and me. I feel she gets up in the morning feeling just like US.'

'And even *more* so.'

'When her sister was married she didn't bat an eyelid, did she?'

'She did not.'

'She never batted an eyelid – though you and I noticed a thing or two, we noticed which way the wind was blowing.'

'Yes, she takes after her granny – She was a grand old – '

'Lady, SHE was.'

'A real – '

'Lady, with a heart of gold and a – '

'To match, yes, she was. I don't think ordinary people could hazard a guess. They're a grand lot. So homely. You feel that they're just like US.'

Peterson glanced round the bar, unwilling to leave. This was his place now it was crowded: the lighters being flicked; smiles spread on faces like jam; the beer spilled in frothing continents over the bar-top. This was the fug of normality, where he should be. But Donelly condemned the idea of staying longer. He put his glass down and buckled the belt of his mac.

'Aren't you going to have anything to eat?'

'No. Come on,' said Donelly, 'let's go and desecrate St Luke's.'

3

Donelly stood back and contemplated his work:

> Our Fellowship Circle has at last succeeded in conjuring up the devil. Incubi and succubae were discussed, and 'Can devils procreate' was a question put before the meeting. Our distinguished speaker submitted his views to the audience, one of whom, a doctor, held that so-called 'incubi' were actually some form of illness such as flatulence: the devil had nothing to do with it. One speaker, in defence of devils, stated from the experience of satyrs, fauns, and telchines whom he knew, that it was possible for devils to have carnal intercourse with human beings. Another speaker denied the Devil and all his works and said that, in any case, he could not procreate for lack of semen, blaming it upon the voluptuous imaginations of human beings. Our distinguished guest advised members of the audience to protect themselves against the onslaught of demons by sleeping upon their sides, and by the regular emptying of the seminary vessels.

'Hurry up,' said Peterson, 'we're going to get wet.' He sat on his heels against the wall and watched Donelly at the glass-fronted case.

Under the street-lamps wet circles were appearing upon the stones. St Luke's was indistinguishable from the warehouses among which it stood; only a small gold cross in the tangle of stonework gave it a sense of purpose. In the paved yard stood the Wayside Pulpit. Beyond young voices were singing of martyrdoms, crosses and thorns. A piece of silver paper drifted down, touched Donelly's shoulder, and fell by the wall. He added another drawing pin and closed the case with a click.

'This afternoon,' said Peterson, 'I saw an advertisement for an assistant at Bert an' Sid's. I thought I might apply.'

'I suppose you might,' said Donelly, looking over his shoulder. He didn't feel like arguing. As the choir's voices ran on, the bile rose in his throat. The scheme of things as it presented itself to him left no room for such hope; what ghostly life could console for the wind in this street: what reunion of the spirit atone for the rain beginning to trickle down his neck?

'What future is there for us?' he said, as they took shelter in a doorway.

'There isn't one.'

Donelly looked at him; his face was blurred by the rain: once in a while, before he was sober, Peterson could face the facts and be all that he wished.

'I shouldn't have left my job,' he was saying now. Such moments of self-knowledge, when they came, did not last long. 'That's true, isn't it?'

'Why, are you any worse off?'

'It would have been . . . where's this going to lead?'

'Six feet underground – the same place as the other.'

'Not me,' said Peterson, 'I'm going to join the smoke-nuisance over Golders Green.'

A group of men coming off overtime shift plodded along the pavement, disappearing beyond St Luke's.

'They've never had it so good.'

'There's no need for them to work overtime if they don't want to.'

'How do you think they're going to pay the instalments on the new three-piece suite?' He wanted to shake Peterson by the neck, to rub his nose in the fact that the beaten track had its miseries too. 'Are they happier than you, d'you think? Once the superficial comforts are stripped away, the same discontents are discovered.'

'Oh well,' said Peterson, 'nothing's ever as bad as it seems.'

Until he spoke Donelly might have imagined a victory: but the moment passed; it had been no more than a chink in his optimism.

'I wonder how the vicar will react to this joke?'

He'll write to the papers complaining of teen-age morals.'

'And not without just cause.' Donelly turned up his collar against the rain and they walked away. 'It was a thought about that job,' he said, taking Peterson by surprise.

But Peterson wanted now to erase the words he had spoken, to prove himself wrong. 'No,' he said, 'I'll give the job a try – the one with Hart.'

He laughed as though he had escaped from a great danger. For the rest of the evening he wouldn't have a care in the world. Having been brought so near to the truth, he was determined not to think: his glimpse of a bottomless pit sent him scurrying to opposite extremes. No one was going to persuade him that life was as hopeless as it appeared. Like a child he stepped in puddles breaking the image of his own face as it swam in each.

'You should have listened to *Children's Hour*,' he said, 'you'd be surprised what the Rabbits are doing.'

'Herbert and Irene?'

Peterson put an arm across his shoulder. 'They live in a flat above a rubber-goods shop.'

'Sort of pest-control?'

'Yes – Herbert is such a prig, imagine writing to the *Rabbit Fanciers' Gazette* to complain of being solicited by a white rat.'

'And Irene dying her ears blue and having her tail lifted. What can you expect of the children: I'll bet young Wilfrid ends up a transvestite . . . '

Perhaps I'm wrong, thought Donelly, perhaps I'm wrong about everything and it's better not to face reality at all. And yet reality had a habit, sooner or later, of turning up just the same – that was what most people intended: ultimate disillusionment to coincide with death.

'Let's go to the arcade,' he said, 'they've got a rifle range now.'

Peterson lifted his hand with a doubtful gesture. 'I don't know whether I want to. We used to go there a lot but – '

'I know,' said Donelly, 'she left about a month ago. How much did you owe her? I shouldn't worry too much.'

'Two pounds ten. I did mean to pay her back.'

After the privacy of the street the main road strung

its cut-price shops and sodium lights above glittering puddles. The noise from a dance-hall puffed out like talcum powder as they crossed the road. Ten yards further on Donelly stopped outside a pub.

'There's Hart,' he said; 'I don't want to see him tonight.'

Hart caught sight of him, but made no sign of recognition, standing against a telephone box waiting for his dog to finish peeing. He had a bedraggled gingery beard that he had been trying to grow for six weeks. A woman came up to use the box and he shifted. Donelly watched him exchange a joke with her as she opened her bag to search for coppers.

Along the pavement girls were toting their breasts like revolvers; those who had not brought boy-friends with them waited to be picked up. You could tell the school-girls by the way they walked in their unfamiliar shoes. A few youths leaned against shop-fronts with hungry, vacant faces; wearing short jackets and pointed shoes after a day in overalls, they were desperate for a girl but didn't want to admit it. Among them walked Donelly in his worn jeans and beer-stained mac. To show his contempt, he put out his tongue at two girls. He could hear them giggle when he'd gone by.

Music blasted out as they neared the arcade. A girl in red trousers shrieked as a card shot out of a machine. Donelly pushed down a plunger and gazed at five chromium balls.

'Cigarette?' he heard Peterson say.

He drew back the knob and released the first ball. Surely he isn't interested in her? Three naked blondes chased by an ape lit up on the glass screen.

'I don't mind if I do.'

'My name's Steve; what's yours?'

'Mine's Josie.'

Donelly shot the second ball with a vicious kick; it span round without touching a single light.

'Steve's a nice name. I've never seen you in here before.'

'I haven't been for a long time.'

'Really?'

'Have you been here long?'

'Since seven o'clock.' She looked away sadly.

'Going to stay here all night?'

Donelly watched a fourth blonde and half the Matto Grosso appear.

'Jean and I thought of going next door.'

'For a Coke? You don't want to spend all night on your own.'

'I'm not on my own, and you're getting fresh. If I was on my own, it doesn't mean I'd let myself be picked up by the first boy that comes along.'

'Come off it,' said Peterson, turning to watch the blondes being joined by three anacondas and a party of head-hunters. 'Wouldn't you like a Coke?'

'I've already had two.'

'Have another.'

'I might. Is your friend coming?'

'I don't think so.'

'Oh, then I couldn't; I'd feel awful leaving our Jean.'

For the first time Donelly noticed, standing under the punchball, a thin girl scratching her head.

'She's shy, you see – I brought her in here to take her out of herself: I couldn't leave her.'

157

Peterson sighed. 'Does she want to come?'

'I'm sure she'd like to.'

'Couldn't she find someone else?'

'Oh no,' she said, taking a tube of sweets from her handbag, 'and if I left her alone I'd feel awful. Go on, have one.'

'Thanks,' Peterson said.

'Why won't your friend come, isn't Jean good enough for him?'

Peterson lowered his voice. 'He doesn't like girls.'

'What's the matter – he's not one of those?'

'No, but he was once jailed for indecent assault.'

Donelly shoved the plunger hard, shot a ball up, and leered at Jean.

'You wouldn't mind me taking Josie away from you, would you?' said Peterson.

Jean shuddered and for a moment he thought she was going to be sick: it was her way of being amused.

'She's shy,' said Josie. 'Just a minute.' She put her face close to her friend's and whispered.

Jean stopped scratching and shuddered again.

'That's settled then,' said Peterson.

'If your friend'll take care of Jean.'

Donelly lit up a volcano in eruption and completed the picture.

'It wouldn't be any fun without Jean.'

'Don't let's bother,' said Peterson. 'I'm going to shoot: would you like a compact, comb-case? I'm a pretty good shot.'

'You'll have to be – they don't give nothing unless you get a bull's-eye every time.'

'I learned a thing or two in the army.'

'You've been in the army? I thought you were still at school.'

'Are you?'

'No, me and Jean freeze peas.' She giggled. 'Come on, what about a packet of Weights?'

The juke-box began to play. Peterson picked a rifle, looked down the barrel, and hit a bull's eye. Josie put her arm around Jean and hugged her. Peterson swung his rifle, sighted again and fired. He didn't look up; he was too serious to speak. Josie studied his hands: they were broad with tiny hairs on the knuckles. He pushed a packet of Weights along the counter to her, began again.

'Steve,' she said, 'get that comb for Jean.'

He paused in the act of taking aim. 'What did you say?'

'Oh, it doesn't matter; come on, let's go and have a Coke.'

He shook his head. It was the only thing he could do well, shooting pellets for worthless trash. His eyes strayed back to the target. 'In a bit,' he said, 'when I've finished here.'

'Jean and me have to get up in the morning.'

'If you don't want to stay,' he said, 'you can go.' He fired: it was a bull's-eye, and then another. A small crowd gathered. He pointed to a powder-blue compact with a heart on the lid, put it in his pocket, and handed the rifle back.

'Where are you going?' said Josie.

Donelly felt a vein in his temple begin to throb; he put up a hand to touch it, expressing his hatred of the thin whine, the B.O. disguised with cheap creams, the pathetic attempts at glamour.

'Are we going to have a Coke or aren't we?'

'It's too late,' said Peterson.

'You might offer to take me home.'

'And what about Jean?'

'Your friend can take her – she only lives a few streets away.'

'You don't mind?' said Peterson.

Donelly scowled.

'What are you going to do with that compact?' said Josie.

'Why, do you want it?'

'If it was offered . . . '

'I'm giving it to a girl.'

'What's her name?'

'I forget.'

She put her arm through his and cuddled against his shoulder as they walked on. 'Never mind,' she said 'it's a very common-looking thing.'

At the end of the street Josie and Peterson said goodnight and wandered off down a side turning. Donelly gripped Jean's arm and swung her to the inside of the pavement; he almost had to push her along the flagstones: without Josie she seemed to be lost.

After the rain the sky was clear. Through departing cloudbanks the moon was bone-white, making each crack in the stonework look like a surgical operation. Donelly stared at the sky, his brain stirred by half-remembered words. With one hand he caressed a piece of chalk in his pocket; the other touched Jean's wrist.

'You don't talk much,' he said, with contempt in his voice.

'There's not much to say.'

He grinned, gripping her wrist. 'Like to see me again?' he said.

Tears of gratitude filled her eyes.

'Come to the pictures on Wednesday?'

'I'd like to.'

He let go her arm and she stumbled. A bus went by and she shivered.

'Cold?'

She nodded as though he might take off his coat.

Donelly stopped in the shadow of a wall to light a cigarette. 'What kind of films do you like?'

'Oh, all kinds.'

He peeled the cigarette from his mouth. As they passed a wall, he brought out the piece of chalk and wrote Ban American Atom Bases. Jean sniffled to herself. 'Do you go dancing?' he said.

'No, but I'd like to.'

'Haven't you got a regular boy?'

She shook her head.

They walked on for a time. He didn't speak; he was trying to imagine her disappointment when she didn't see him again. They stopped in the shadow of a block of flats and he saw her lips waiting. He drew her close, pretending desire; she was naked under her sweater and he could feel her breasts through the wool. He put his hands up and made a slight movement: she didn't appear to notice even when he found the nipple. She was so passive her helplessness made him long to kick. Feeling a prick of unwilling excitement, he drew his hand down: he wasn't going to be caught giving pleasure to any little half-wit. They walked on.

'Don't you get sick of all this?' he said.

'All what?'

'Life, living.'

She looked surprised. 'No,' she said.

'Women never seem to.'

The thought irritated him. When they reached the flats where she lived and were waiting for the lift, he chalked up on the door an indecent rhyme: 'Is it true what they say about Eton . . . ?'

In an anger which took him by surprise, she snatched the chalk and scribbled out what he'd written. There was a scuffle, and she threw the chalk into the street.

Donelly swore, kicked her hard on the ankle, and walked away across the threadbare turf whistling a Gershwin tune.

4

Hart pulled his dog to heel, touched as a policeman passed by a feeling of panic. He turned off the road and decided not to walk after all. The stalls in the market were just being set up. Retracing his steps he called a taxi. The traffic had stopped at the lights, jammed bumper to bumper. The signals changed, a car partially mounted the pavement and disappeared leaving an odour of burning oil.

Hart licked his lips: I could have been killed, he thought; the realisation came as a shock. 'There are people who'd like to kill me, but they wouldn't do it in that way. The driver brought his taxi over to where he stood. Hart felt sick; the smell of the car's exhaust still stayed in his nose.

'Where to?' said the driver. And when Hart told him: 'That's just round the corner.'

'What business is it of yours?'

The man shrugged.

Hart sat back, watching the Saturday morning crowds slide past him, the housewives shopping. If they were knocked down it would be an accident. His hands were shaking. He looked at the clock and tried hard not to think. He had better have a bodyguard, someone whose job depended on keeping him alive: he should have protection, and he couldn't go to the police, they would ask too many questions, about Evans for instance. As he paid the driver he thought of death; it worried him more than he might have imagined.

The smoke blew up from St Pancras, he looked at the towers and was reminded of railway platforms and saying goodbye. He felt a long way from home.

Murdock, waiting for him, caught his arm and said, 'Come in here – she's re-decorated it again.'

Hart nodded. The room was empty, or so it seemed at first sight. A canvas-coloured carpet stretched from wall to wall; two hard stools and a high-backed settle stood like a careful reconstruction in a museum.

'What's happened?' Hart spoke for the first time.

Murdock pulled a cigarette-box from behind the curtain. Absorbed in lighting a cigarette, he didn't speak for a time. 'Looks a treat doesn't it?' he said, inhaling and placing the match on the arm of the settle. 'It's Daisy; I can't do nothing with her, she read an article by some whore in the *Sunday Pictorial*.'

He knelt on the carpet. Hart thought he might be going to pray, until he wrenched at a drawer under the settle and brought out an ash-tray.

'It was all I could do to stop her taking the curtains down. I'm terrified she might start on the bedrooms; bed's the only place now I can go to be comfy.'

'You want to be firm with her.'

'It's alright for you, you're not married. I tell you it's like this all over – except the bathroom: she's tarted that up with wallpaper and a carpet.'

Hart examined a small cupboard.

'Thirty quid that cost me.'

'Where's the old stuff?'

'Upstairs. The attics are full of it – all those stuffed birds and china shepherdesses.' He made, as he spoke, the furtive, rather futile gestures of an elderly woman.

'I'm thinking of dividing the house into flats; she can do what she likes down here.' He puffed at his cigarette. 'Look at that other stuff – we didn't get half what we paid for it, bloody Victoriana!' He picked a shred of tobacco from the carpet, using his fingers as tweezers. 'You ought to see where we eat: it wouldn't surprise me next if she rests 'er 'ead on a block of wood.'

'What's she thinking of?' said Hart, feeling ill at ease.

Murdock took his arm and guided him across to the window. 'I don't know. We'd be down to the floorboards, but in this house they're not good enough.'

Hart was bored and waited for him to change the subject. Abruptly Murdock stopped talking as though he sensed the boredom.

'I've something in the other room that'll interest you,' he said. Taking Hart's arm, he guided him out across the hall into a room where, upon a shelf, were stacks of books in plain-coloured covers. 'Here,' he said, pressing one into his hands.

Hart opened it, there was a photograph of a woman in riding breeches. 'Looks interesting,' he said.

'Yes,' said Murdock, 'read it, read it aloud.'

Hart blinked, he needed glasses for reading: the print was blurred. He turned on – An Adventure in Beauty for Adults, packed with alluring routines. Behind him he heard his dog scratch at the door.

'Go on,' said Murdock. 'I'll see to Biscuit.'

Hart let his eye stray down the page:

He shuddered, a goose was walking over his grave. The woman in the frontispiece was almost a symbol; hugeness was the quality he most admired. His eyes began to water, again he thought of those afternoons in the dark, watching a screen that had shown life and death but had never taught him to make love to a woman successfully.

'Go on,' said Murdock, 'you've not come to anything yet.'

He emptied an ash-tray out of the window with a faraway look on his face.

Hart flipped through the book at random:

Louisa Jassel's experience is similar to that of 11,000 girls who will graduate this year as State Registered prostitutes. The minimum age for acceptance is eighteen, and they spend the first few weeks finding out how well they are fitted for the work. During the full three-year course, she is given clinical instruction and practical experience. She attends lectures by recognised pimps and panders, she takes a short course of specialised training in a particular disease, she also learns something of the work of the lesbian and androgyne. Prostitution today offers a full and absorbing career, and there is a constant demand for . . .

Hart made a movement that might have been panic. 'No,' he said, 'I can't read any more.' He closed the book; he wanted to take it away and read it in private. He caught Murdock looking at him.

'I'll wrap it up for you, if you're taking it. I'll let you have it for thirty bob.'

There was something spinsterish in the way he ran his bookshop, his hands fluttering over the volumes of learned sexology like an old maid with her china. He gave Hart a smile and hurried off through the door. Hart could hear him calling, 'Daisy, have you let Biscuit off his lead?'

Another voice answered and there was some kind of an argument.

'Lock him up, I've told you to.'

A tinkle of glass and a dog barking.

'Daisy, do something! I'm sick and tired of – '

Hart closed the door. Then Murdock came back with Daisy; she wore a plastic apron over a colourless dress, and her hair was going thin.

'D'you like my new ideas?' she said.

'Frank's been telling me. It's a bit bare.'

She pouted at Murdock. 'Well, Helen thinks it's very nice.'

'Oh, Helen.'

'You know she doesn't agree with me often.'

'I'm not going to argue, Daisy.'

Hart stared into the distance while Daisy told him about her new electric cooker. When this failed to interest him, she left the room; her voice echoed back along the passage, talking to Biscuit, singing snatches of song. The rattle of saucepans died away as a draught slammed the kitchen door. Hart caught Murdock looking at him – in a minute he would have to answer questions: how was the club doing, did he think Daisy was certifiable, were the police making trouble? And at the end, the salesman in him coming to the top: 'Are you going to buy that book?'

Hart said 'Yes,' so Murdock wasn't interested any more.

He thought of the week-ends they had had him staying with them at Holland-on-Sea; it hadn't brought him any closer, he was still a stranger. Behind his back they talked about him and laughed at his vices.

If they were both murdered in their beds, thought Hart, I wouldn't care.

Poking her head round the door Daisy said, 'There's a phone-call for you.'

He followed her out of the room, across the hall, feeling a twinge of fear: it might be Evans. He watched her close the kitchen door before picking up the receiver. 'Is that you?' he said.

The answering voice was blurred and indistinct. 'This is Evans.'

'Everything all right?'

'The stuff has arrived.'

'You didn't have any trouble?'

'A search . . . they found nothing though.'

'What's the matter?'

'They didn't suspect – I don't think so. They never found nothing.' Evans was truculent.

Hart looked sideways; he was receiving from Evans' whine a sense of superiority, he was weaker than Evans but Evans was stupid: he depended on Hart's brains to get him out of an awkward situation.

'. . . the ship's been held up for a couple of days.'

'Listen,' said Hart, 'get rid of the stuff; better lose it. We don't want too many questions asked. Is that clear?'

'It's a waste of money.'

'I'll worry. Don't take any risks.' There was almost affection in Hart's voice: he had attached himself to the biggest boy in the school. Like a leech he clung on to the memory of insults being avenged.

'I'll phone again,' said Evans, 'there's somebody here. If I can't get the stuff through . . . '

Hart listened to him saying goodbye and hung up.

'Nothing wrong?' said Murdock.

'No, that was Evans.' There was a proprietory note in his voice.

Murdock emptied the ash-tray again and then replaced it on the settle between them.

'I see your point about separate flats.'

'It was just an idea, it'd never work – after all husband and wife, one flesh, you know. She'll get tired of this; they always do.'

'Why don't you put your foot down?' said Hart.

'What do you know about women?' Murdock became faintly asthmatic.

The enmity in his voice made Hart feel uncomfortable.

'I wonder,' he went on, 'if you've ever seen a woman without her skirt except in those books.'

Hart laughed loudly. He felt his face flushing. It wasn't difficult to guess at his virginity: such things couldn't be disguised. The light in Murdock's eye was the same as Bryson at school explaining a smutty story:

the gloating over another's inadequacy. Hart knew that Murdock had been led to the altar a virgin, had been as apprehensive as any girl on his wedding night: now he sneered at him from the security of a wife.

'I give in to Daisy,' he said. 'But she knows who wears the trousers.'

'I bet she does,' said Hart.

Murdock looked at him, but could detect only a desire to please.

Hart blinked. Murdock wouldn't hit him for certain: that was one advantage of growing up. He couldn't push his head down the lavatory-pan as Greene had once done.

'It must cost you a packet, this decorating.'

'That's marriage for you,' said Murdock, 'if you want a thing you've got to be prepared to pay for it.'

'Yes.'

'You ought to get married yourself.'

'I will one day.'

'Don't leave it too late.'

Murdock smiled; he had got the last word in, like a woman. Funny how husbands grew like their wives – it didn't often happen the other way round.

'How about tomorrow afternoon, are you coming over for a game of whist?'

'I might. I've a lot to do.'

'You're busy these days.'

'Yes,' said Hart.

'I'll bet you'll be opening one of those clubs in the West End soon – you'll be deserting Daisy and me.'

'No, I'll never do that.'

' . . . we wouldn't be good enough for you then.' Murdock was determined to feel slighted.

Hart listened and wondered why he still visited them: the habit of two years ought to be broken with less reluctance. He tried to disguise his impatience.

'I expect you're wanting to push off,' said Murdock.

'There's one or two things I want to get done before lunch.'

'You're itching to stick your nose in that book – that's what it is.'

'No, I'm going up to the club,' said Hart. He was trying to think of the right phrase to get him out of the front door onto the pavement; two years had not lessened this uneasiness. He lost track of what Murdock was saying.

'Drat the thing,' said Murdock, as a ginger cat brushed by his feet and he stumbled against the banisters.

The telephone rang.

'It'll be for you, Phil; no one ever rings us.' He lifted the receiver, then passed it on to Hart.

'Hallo?'

'I'll go and see what Daisy's doing about dinner, she'd sit in there on her backside and not care if it was midnight before we eat.'

He went in, a frowsty figure in trodden-down carpet slippers and none too clean cardigan. At the kitchen door he turned back.

'We'll expect you tomorrow. Usual time.'

'It should have been locked,' Hart was saying. 'Why weren't you there?'

171

Murdock's voice interrupted him, he put his hand over the mouthpiece and nodded. The kitchen door slammed.

'Get the police,' he said. 'How much damage was done? – No, don't bother; I'll be there in half an hour.'

He put down the receiver, irritated. He didn't want to say goodbye to Murdock, but he remembered his dog was tethered in the kitchen. He closed the front door and walked back along the hall.

'Alright?' Murdock said, turning the wireless set down.

'Somebody broke in the club last night – a drunk probably. My office doors are kept locked.'

'You were lucky.' Murdock stood by the sink with one hand on the knob of the wireless.

He's disappointed, Hart thought, that the place wasn't ransacked.

Daisy, outside in the garden, was pegging a dress on the line. She waved a hand in a red rubber glove at Hart, then disappeared behind the wash-house. When she came back into sight she was shaking a wet blouse. The clothes on the line blew out in a gust of wind; Hart watched her trying to reach the line as it lifted out of her grasp.

Murdock switched off the wireless and picked up a paper: the dog had made a mess under the table, but he hadn't noticed it yet.

They had been for a walk and stolen a volume of philosophy, two ballpoint pens, and a reel of cotton: Donelly had thrown the cotton at a child. As they turned the corner of the street, they saw the club surrounded by dubious lodging houses. In a glass case outside were details of membership, also the cards of several girls – including Sandra who claimed to be a teen-age model.

'They ought to call it the Teddy-Bear Club,' said Peterson. 'And there should be a sign up over the door, a teddy-bear with a flick knife.'

'That's good,' said Donelly, 'you should tell Hart.

'It was only a joke.'

'Never mind, Hart likes jokes.'

'What happens,' said Peterson, 'if I don't get this job?'

'You'll get it alright.'

'Oh, it won't matter if I don't, I can still answer that advertisement.' He knew he could rely on Hart taking a liking to him on sight.

They went into Hart's office but Hart wasn't there.

'He's going to give you the job.' When Donelly spoke, it was in a tone of impatience. 'There's no reason to think about the advertisement.'

Peterson blinked.

'Do you want the job or don't you. Because if you don't, we'd better get out of here.'

'I've already told you – '

Peterson sniffed round the room like a dog. One wall was papered entirely with Royal tarts: Marie Walewska, Diane de Poitiers, Marguerite Bellanger, Lily Langtry and in one corner – John Brown.

'Whose are these?' he said, examining the bookshelves.

Donelly ran his eyes over the titles: *Five Desperate Hours*; *Miss Pierce, Headmistress*; *The One-Eyed Woman in Cabin 10*. He opened one and shut it again.

'Pornography!' said Peterson, as though he might have said, 'This is disgusting.'

The depth of hypocrisy defied belief. Donelly imagined him preaching morality to one of his pickups, seducing a girl for reasons of health.

'Does your boss collect this stuff?'

'You saw Murdock's bookshop over the way, there's masses of this stuff there.'

'Books like this are – ' he sought for the right word. 'Degrading.'

'You talk like a Labour M.P.'

'Give me a cigarette.'

Donelly lit it for him, leaning forward, aware of an effort to keep the match steady.

'So you approve of all this?'

'I never take sides. You'd better save your indignation for Hart; tell him, don't tell me. By banning these books you won't ban frustration.'

'No one would be safe if you made the laws.'

Donelly shrugged. 'You're a nitwit.' Peterson was in his element laying down the law to people he met in pubs: people like himself, half-educated, half-baked, half-cut. He drew down his mouth in a deep grimace. The street cries drifted in of an old man selling paraffin.

Peterson opened a drawer in Hart's desk, and found a dozen dog-whips.

'It's like a pet shop. They're almost new, except this one. Does he keep dogs?'

'He has a retriever. You saw it last night.'

'Why so many whips?'

'I suppose he's had more than one dog in his time.'

'But why buy a new one for each dog?' He stared in the drawer at a ream of paper, a few envelopes and a book of stamps. He slammed it and opened another. A bottle of whisky: he took a swig and coughed.

He passed it across to Donelly who drank and handed it back.

The other drawers were empty.

'Does he get all his books from Murdock?'

'I suppose so,' said Donelly. 'It's a lonely life, he doesn't have many friends.'

'What about women?'

'Only the ones round the club.' He sat in a chair looking up at the iron bars on the window, aloof from Peterson who was prowling around the office.

Peterson noticed his silence and was resentful. Donelly had the power to make him feel like a child. He picked up a pen and began to clean his nails, saying, 'We could get him six months if we told the police.'

'Let him alone.'

It wasn't like Donelly so openly to take sides against him. He took out the bottle, drank again, kicked the drawer shut with his foot . . . What did he

175

really know of Donelly's mind. For an atom of time he realised how little one human being ever knows another. Was there anything Donelly wouldn't do, for example? He didn't think so.

Donelly's face was blurred in its angles by a day's growth of beard. His jacket had a small tear on the sleeve.

'Can't you take a joke?'

'You weren't joking,' Donelly said, 'don't try to be clever.'

'I don't think I'm fitted for this job.'

'He's not a difficult man, I've told you. For you he's a walk-over.'

Peterson put down the pen. 'Why bother about me?' he said, 'I'm all wrong for you.'

'I'll be the judge when to throw in the sponge.'

'What must I do to deserve it?'

Donelly laughed. 'I'll stick to you like glue. It's not easy to break a habit.'

'Let's get away from here – ' Peterson held out the bait half-seriously. 'Those girls I pick up, they don't mean a thing. Wouldn't that be best? Make any excuse to Hart – '

'No,' said Donelly, 'you take the job.'

'But it wouldn't work; I might punch the bastard in the guts, anything.' He pointed. 'What's through there?'

'The kitchen.'

'I thought it might be the torture-chamber.' He speared the pen into the desk and watched it quiver. 'This is a funny set-up; I can't put my finger yet on what's wrong.'

'Don't try.'

'You said that Hart was on the level – '

'Are you such a good citizen? He at least doesn't make schoolgirls pregnant.'

Peterson went slack-lipped and stared at his feet. 'How does he make his money?'

Donelly ignored the look in his eyes. It might have saved him a lot of trouble if he'd spotted at this point in which direction Peterson's ideas were taking him. But a car rumbled past and the chance was missed.

Peterson stopped talking. Out of the clubroom came the sound of dance-music.

Donelly sighed.

'We could have another drink,' said Peterson.

'Yes, if he notices any missing he'll think it's the char.' It was time for appeasement.

Peterson opened the drawer, but the sound of a voice made him close it again. He straightened up, unsure of the next move. His fingers played uncertainly round the desk.

As Hart entered, he had his charm ready. The folds fell into place, the well-oiled machinery began to spin. What was there in Hart's appearance to cause him fear? The weasel face, the white shirt, the striped tie – more dandruff than hair. When Hart passed, Peterson caught a whiff of eau de Cologne. His fingers were stained with nicotine, a little powder was caked on his chin. What was there in this to make Peterson tremble?

He felt the smallest flicker of glee.

Hart smiled at him as he tied the dog's lead onto the window-bars.

He smiled back, ready for anything now.

Hart fiddled with the dog-leash, as though wishing to prolong the moment.

'You've shaved your beard,' said Donelly.

'Yes . . . it wasn't very successful, you know.' He unbuttoned his gloves.

In the club a girl began to sing.

Donelly gave Peterson an encouraging nod. Hart took off his coat and hung it up on a hook behind the door; his actions were slow and deliberate, those of a man filling in time. His thin face showed fear and embarrassment.

'This is Peterson,' Donelly said.

Hart swallowed, his large Adam's apple jigged up and down. 'I've got work to do at the moment,' he said. He pulled at his tie to loosen it. 'I'd like to see you tomorrow. I think I can use you.'

He noticed the pen sticking into the desk, pulled it out and examined the point with his finger.

'Tomorrow then,' Peterson said.

'In the morning.' His manner was stiff and formal.

Peterson smiled. 'About eleven.'

'Yes. Goodbye.'

Peterson stood outside the door for a moment. He heard Hart say:

'He looked a bit scruffy, your friend; I suppose he'll do. Does he know . . . '

The voice faded away through the wood. He couldn't hear Donelly's reply. Hart said something about the police, then there was silence.

As he went through the club, he saw a youth with a painted face. Two women were dancing together.

Middle-aged men stood listening to the soft farmyard
noise of canned music.

6

Sunday. A minute or two after nine o'clock. Donelly decided to shave. From the window he saw the advertisement hoardings peeled and warm in the sunlight. He didn't want to die on a day like this: the sun created a world that seemed better. He wiped the mirror free from steam, and drew the cold blade across his cheek; he needed a new one. On the window-sill a daffodil in a green bowl was beginning to grow, it had not been expected to live; but it defied him, pushing thin shoots above the soil. Plants and animals couldn't reject life. He rinsed his razor, deciding to take a bath.

Lying in the warm water, he hummed a tune, flicked soap over himself and stared at his navel. The house creaked, there was a patter of plaster, the gurgling of a pipe. Outside a car backfired. One day he would shoot himself, he was living already in the future: the hole in his temple blackened by burning. He'd never handled a gun in his life, but that was no problem: as long as the trigger were pressed, the instrument did the rest. That was how he'd kill himself when he got round to it. No violence, no effort required.

He lay for a second hardly breathing, the glimpse of his own corpse had been so bright.

Bells began to ring; there was never silence for long in this street. An idea started to form in his brain. When he went, he'd take others with him: five or six at least. Something for the Sunday papers to talk about. You could shoot five people down before they'd recovered their wandering senses. Perspiration ran on his shoulders in drops. The idea staggered. Why not cure the population problem by even so small an amount? It seemed as though he had cut himself free from everyone at that moment.

A kind of embittered happiness made tears come into his eyes. He pulled out the plug and stood up.

As he dried himself, he could see the crowds watching the bodies covered with sheets, see the police opening their notebooks – asking one another how to spell 'holocaust'. He started to dress, pulling his shirt on over his head, not noticing that he'd forgotten to dry himself properly. He closed the door of the bathroom behind him. Peterson was still in bed.

He thought for a moment that Peterson might detect the fantasy in which he had been indulging. His limbs felt as though they were under the influence of a drug. But in Peterson's eyes he saw not the faintest glimmer.

The instinct to tell him became unbearable.

'I'm going to shoot five people.'

'When?'

'I don't know, I've not got a gun – and then of course I must be in the right mood.'

Peterson smiled.

'I'll kill myself afterwards.'

There was something in Donelly's face – 'Are you feeling alright?' he said.

'Don't be so ridiculous.'

'But *why*?'

181

'The world,' said Donelly, feeling the absurdity of discussing the matter while tying his shoelaces.

Peterson shoved back the sheets and got out of bed. 'Civilisations rise and fall, men remain the same – stupid.'

He wasn't going to take Donelly seriously. Society changed, but men were alright at bottom.

'Oh well,' said Donelly, his mouth stiffening in an effort to ignore the familiar optimism.

'I'm going to shave,' said Peterson, 'I'll meet you in the gardens in half an hour.'

'Don't be late.' Donelly put on his jacket and went downstairs.

His mind reached back, checking his thoughts. He wondered why the world was permitted to carry on. Why didn't God scrap it and begin again? He might love thieves and adulterers, but how could even God love the wives of stockbrokers and the pigs who run and are run by materialism?

The sun was hot in the gardens. A few good remarks and a lot plagiarised from the Hellenes don't make a religion. If people had leisure and were taught what to do with it – taught to use their eyes for more than staring into a goldfish-bowl.

He moved away, deafened by the sound of a wireless set from a basement flat.

God knows, the sooner the Bomb fell the better. And one day, with a finality beyond the axe, docks and fool's-parsley, brambles and thick primeval green will cover the cathode tubes and traffic signs. Only the mice and beetles in the semi-detached villas will know the perfection of those Mod Cons.

Donelly beat his fist against his head to stop thinking.

To his surprise it worked. He noticed once more the warmth of the sun, encouraging stunted flowers. He moved to another seat and watched children playing a game with chalk-marks on the paving. The smoke from a chimney rose straight in the air, an omen of good weather.

On the point of lighting a cigarette, his attention was caught by several men running towards the canal. A woman screamed. A priest pushed his way through the crowd. (Did he perhaps anticipate extreme unction?) Six choir-boys in surplices came down the steps of St John the Evangelist. Nothing happened. The men walked back along the path. The crowd dispersed, disappointed. They had been ready to be in on the death, but it was a false alarm. The priest in his soutane shooed the choir-boys back inside. Donelly slid down in his seat.

'Covered in slime,' a woman was saying, 'got it all over her shoes – the little madam.

'It gave her a fright,' said a man, 'she won't go along there in a hurry.'

He patted the girl on the back; it was like a bad film.

The woman smiled and began to talk to somebody else.

Donelly spotted Tusker Makarios outside the gardens and waved him in. He wore black jeans and smoked cheap cigarettes. He had with him a boy about twelve, who wore the same jeans and smoked the same cigarettes: one knew that both before long would end in a police court.

'Where are you going?' said Donelly.

'Nowhere.'

'What's *he* doing?'

Tusker watched with contempt as the boy closed the gate.

'He's joined the scouts. He thinks he ought to behave himself.'

'What's his name?'

'Derek, he lives in our block.' He pulled the stump of a cigarette off his lip. 'Got a fag on you – that was my last?'

Donelly gave him one.

'He'd better have one too, he'll moan if he don't.'

'Take the packet.'

'No, these two'll be enough.' He wandered among the flower beds. 'What are these called?'

'Crocuses.'

'Will they get bigger?'

'No.'

'Then they're no bloody good.' He prodded about him. 'What's going to come up here?'

'Tulips.'

'How long'll they be?'

'Oh, the end of April.'

'That's too bloody late.' His face fell. 'We can't wait that long, and people don't seem to fancy these crocuses; we tried last year.'

'Yes,' said Derek.

'What happened?'

'We got a tenner for a whole morning's work.'

'No bloody good,' said Derek.

'There used to be two lovely ducks on this lake.'

'Did there?'

'We had them with sage and onion.' A look of discontent passed over his face. 'It'll be better when the roses are out; we made a packet last year. Nobody wants these little things.'

'There are some narcissus in Regents Park – get a 30 bus to Warren Street.'

'How much is the fare?'

'Threepence or fourpence.'

Tusker did a rapid calculation. 'Lend us two bob? I'll pay you ten per cent.'

'It's no good in the daytime.'

'Well, lend us two bob anyway. He can put on his uniform, pretend we're doing a job on the flower beds.'

Donelly stretched himself. 'Don't you get any pocket money?'

'Not much.'

'If you want any money,' said Donelly, 'you can always touch Mr Hart.'

'He gave me a quid last time,' said Derek, sucking his thumb.

'Thanks for the florin,' said Tusker, walking away, followed by Derek, his tight black jeans making him look ridiculous. 'I'll let you know if I want any more.'

A cloud had covered the sun; Donelly shivered. It was beginning to rain.

Peterson stood looking out. A squall of rain hit the pavement. An old man playing a gramophone picked it up and walked away. A gust of wind blew a piece of paper behind him, circling, performing a dance.

It was twilight in the street; the rain drummed on the bonnets of cars. A light was switched on in a basement flat and a bald-headed man in his underwear appeared. The wind blew a box along the canal, raised it and sailed it into the water where it sank. A cyclist passed, his cape yellow and dripping, his tyres sizzling on the wet road. Peterson stared with unseeing eyes at a tide of match-sticks.

A woman pushed by him into the street. 'It's stopping,' she said, 'it was only a shower.'

Peterson wanted someone to talk to, to banish the thoughts from his brain. A little dint sharpened between his eyebrows. With his mac buttoned he felt warm and uncomfortable. The woman came back, shaking an umbrella; somewhere a dog barked, a door slammed. There'd be a rainbow soon. He caught sight of a thin figure hurrying up the street.

'Crane,' he called, 'Crane.'

Crane came over. 'What are you doing?'

'I live here.'

'Then why are you standing outside?'

'I was going to meet Donelly.'

Crane shook the water out of his hat. 'It's a strange neighbourhood to live in,' he said. 'I don't come here often – only by way of business.'

He put down his collar.

'That man over there now, what do you make of him?'

'The one with the gramophone?'

'Yes.'

'He seems harmless enough.'

Crane raised his eyebrows. 'He looks like a pimp to me. A clever idea the gramophone, it diverts attention.'

Peterson gave him a quick look. 'What do you think he has in the horn, heroin?'

'Not at all,' said Crane: 'there are more brothels round here than you would suppose.'

'It seemed a reasonable guess.'

Crane looked at Peterson's scar. 'It must have been quite a fight,' he said.

'A fight?'

'The scar – '

'Oh yes.' Peterson touched his chin.

'The man's in Pentonville, isn't he? Did you lose much blood?'

'About a pint, I believe.'

'It looks a small scar.'

'They had to give me a transfusion – the razor went very deep. His gang had switched all the lights out, I'd fallen in front of the bar and lay there fainting from loss of blood.'

Crane took out a handkerchief and blew his nose. 'I see; it's as well to be able to look after yourself.'

Peterson took a deep breath. He sensed a trap. 'It's stopped raining,' he said, 'I must go.'

'What do you know of this club where Donelly works?' Crane patted his pockets, forgetting which one he had put his handkerchief in.

Peterson looked at the neck ringed with lines and grooves.

'I don't know anything,' he said.

Crane eyed him. 'You must know.'

'Nothing that would interest you.'

'You never can tell,' said Crane, edging out of the doorway.

Peterson walked beside him along the street.

He strode with his legs apart, as though anxious not to catch his heels in the turn-ups of his trousers. 'I'm on a little assignment,' he said, 'private, you understand?'

'Yes.'

'It's just a hunch I had but it might pay cash.

'What's all this about?'

'So you're interested?'

'I might be.'

Several thoughts had struck Peterson suddenly; dim ideas gathered momentum.

'As a matter of fact, I might be interested.'

'A nod is as good as a wink,' said Crane. 'I could be mistaken of course, and no harm done then, but with your help I might get my teeth into something big.'

Peterson nodded.

'You've been in the club. What's it like in there?'

'Not much to write home about.'

'Anything suspicious?'

'He's got a few blue books, a collection of dog-whips – '

'A pervert!' said Crane, his eyes widening.

'These club-owners are all the same. What else to report?'

'There were women dancing together.' Peterson racked his brains.

Crane stared at him with a wondering air.

'I'll give you thirty per cent of what we make. Here's my telephone number.'

He thumbed through a wallet and put it away.

'I don't seem to have a card on me at the moment.'

'Here's a pencil – ' Peterson handed over a broken stub.

Crane tore a piece off an envelope. A paper-clip fell to the ground; he picked it up and replaced it in his wallet.

'There. If I'm not in you can leave a message. Always ring from a public call-box, it's safer.'

'For whom?'

'For everyone. Where are you off to now?'

'To the club.'

'At this time on a Sunday morning?'

'Donelly thinks he can get me a job.'

Crane gripped his arm. 'You'll be even more valuable on the inside – I'll give you forty per cent. I must see you again this morning.'

'Why?'

'For your report. What time will you be through with Hart?'

'What kind of thing would I have to report?'

Crane lowered his eyes; his nose had become inflamed. 'Report anything out of the ordinary.'

'How many per cent did you say?'

'Forty.'

'How much?'

'There's no need to be mercenary.'

'You can't expect me to take risks without compensation.'

'Forty-five. I can't say fairer than that.'

'It's a deal then.'

'Alright.'

Peterson almost had to run to keep up with his enormous strides. At the gates he stopped. 'I'm meeting Donelly in here,' he said.

'Well, goodbye, I'll be in the milk-bar outside the tube station at half past one.'

Peterson walked down the path. Looking back, he could see Crane outside the gates, moving his nose from side to side like a compass needle. He followed the path through the gardens, forgetting Crane as Donelly appeared, He didn't want this job with Hart, but there was no avoiding it now: he was in a situation from which he couldn't escape.

The sun came out, and ahead of him a bird splashed in a puddle. Donelly, waiting for him by the shelter, said 'Where have you been?'

'It came on to rain.'

'I thought I saw you talking to someone by the park gates.

'No.'

Donelly sighed as they went out of the gardens into the street. A placard announced the memoirs of some accepted whore; 1,070 Frenchwomen tell their love secrets, said another. They picked their way through dried vomit, past men with polythene buckets washing second-hand cars.

'I thought we were going to the club?' said Peterson.

'No, to his house; that's what he told me last night. He doesn't often go to the club on a Sunday.'

The entrance to the block of flats, when they reached it, was in need of painting. The hallway smelled of cooking and cats. Peterson glanced at the row of bells: Macdonald, O'Dwyer, Macbride.

'Blacks mostly,' said Donelly.

'He's probably forgotten we're coming,' said Peterson.

'He hasn't forgotten.'

Peterson felt he was being swept along by a tide. He need only to say No and he was free. 'Perhaps he's out.'

'Don't be balmy,' said Donelly.

Peterson leaned on the banisters touching wood. He could imagine Hart reaching for a dressing gown, walking down the passage. The door opened. His opportunity had been missed.

'Come along in,' said Hart.

I can't refuse now unless he wants me to do a murder; but hired assassins are chosen with more care. He dismissed the idea as unlikely.

'Sorry we're late,' he said, 'I got caught in the rain.' He looked at the chandelier with red-fringed shades, looked down at the carpet, turned upon Hart a smile of disarming frankness.

'I'll wait in the other room,' said Donelly, 'you don't want me around.'

Peterson watched Hart sit comfortably in a chair.

'I hear you were in the army in Cyprus.'

'That's right.' He was in control of the situation.

'There's no job for you at the moment in the club, but when I open my new one . . .

You're thinking of it?'

'It won't be for a while, a year, eighteen months.' Hart leaned back against a cushion. 'Donelly tells me you're reliable. I need someone that I can . . . rely on.'

He appeared reluctant to carry on: then the lines of his face slackened, his muscles relaxed.

'Donelly thinks you'd be useful. Were you in Cyprus long?'

'Just over a year.'

'National Service?'

'Yes.'

'I was in Egypt,' said Hart. 'Do you smoke?'

'Thanks.'

Hart passed a box over, saying in a firm voice, 'I'm not too good at explaining things. It's awkward, you see.' He was apologising before he began.

'Are you being blackmailed?' said Peterson.

'God, no!' Hart laughed and looked at his shoes. 'Whatever made you think that? It's only that I've been wondering lately if anyone wanted to get at me in some way . . . ' His voice trailed away; he was unconvinced himself. 'I need a bodyguard – one reads about such things in the papers every day. I want a young fellow like you to stand by me. You know what I mean?'

Peterson nodded.

'It was like this,' said Hart, 'I was on the pavement waiting for a taxi . . . '

'I see what you mean.' There was a second or two while Peterson collected his thoughts. 'Nobody nowadays,' he said, 'can afford to be without protection.'

'At the club,' said Hart, 'I'm so accessible, so . . . '

Peterson stabbed his cigarette in an ash-tray and gave him a ruthless look. 'I think you're wise. You need a bodyguard, just for your peace of mind.' Now he stepped before the audience, confident. 'If you have enemies who can be tough, you must show them that you can be tougher. I was a crack-shot in the army. Can I have a gun?'

'A gun,' said Hart, 'I wouldn't have thought of a gun. Have you got a licence?'

'Yes.'

'Oh dear. Well, we'll see about that. I'd like you to call for me here in the evenings at half past seven, when I take my dog for a walk.'

He hurried on to the details of the arrangement.

'I shan't need you much in the daytime – mostly at night.'

'I'm satisfied,' Peterson said. 'Have you got a car?'

Hart nodded.

'Bullet-proof?'

'No, I think it would be too expensive.'

'In *Gunsmoke*,' Peterson said, 'they had somebody locked up in a Turkish bath.'

'No,' said Hart, 'it wasn't *Gunsmoke*; I'm not sure of the title, but it was with Lauren Bacall. There were spies and the other side locked her up in a steam-house, where she was baked. He wrinkled his forehead. 'No, I think she was rescued. I can't remember.'

'Like Fausta,' said Peterson.

'Who?'

'Her husband - he was a Christian, he locked *her* up in a steam-room and had her grilled like a fish.'

'That doesn't sound very Christian.'

'It was a long time ago.'

Hart looked out of the window into the branches of a sycamore dripping with moisture.

'And someone,' said Peterson, 'had been slipping her a length, I think.'

'Was there a film?' Hart stared at a church spire pointing against the clouds.

'No, it was a book. And there was only that bit that was interesting; the rest was about an old girl who was looking for something.'

'Did she find it?'

'I think so. There was a lot of witchcraft.'

'Witchcraft?' said Hart. 'Now I'm interested in that. There's a film on at the Roxy, I think I shall go. You'll be coming with me of course?'

'Yes,' said Peterson. 'Do you go to the pictures often?'

'Fairly often, but not as much as I did at one time.'

'I used to go every afternoon when I was at school,' said Peterson.

'Did you?' said Hart. 'So did I.' He looked at Peterson. 'I wasn't any good at games,' he said, 'were you?'

'Not bad,' said Peterson. 'This film we're going to see, what's it about?'

'It's in colour,' said Hart, 'I think it's about the Crusaders.'

'Plenty of blood?' said Peterson.

He drew a bow, released an arrow, died clutching his throat. The sun lined the twigs of the sycamore with globules of light; the spire rose into a patch of sky. His future was suddenly bright.

'Plenty,' said Hart, 'from the look of the stills outside.'

'I'll see you at half past seven,' said Peterson, getting up.

He made for the door.

'Will you let me drive your car?'

'Sometimes.'

Donelly came in. 'Everything settled?' he said. 'That's good. Here, take this home with you – ' He fished for a book in his pocket. ' – it's that Nietzsche we pinched on Saturday.'

7

'Nietzsche,' said Crane, 'why, what a coincidence.' He leaned across the counter and ordered another orangeade. 'I wouldn't have thought Nietzsche was your cup of tea.'

He watched Peterson put the book on the counter, his eyebrow raised in surprise.

The accent of patronage in his voice stirred Peterson. 'Oh yes, I've read them all. Kierkegaard, Swedenborg. The lot.' A vision of stolen books came into his mind. 'I get a lot of help from the great minds of the past.'

Crane stuffed his handkerchief into his pocket and looked at his fingers: the knuckles stood out like stones.

'Would you like a sandwich?' He took a sip at his orangeade. 'All fat,' he said, 'this ham. Anything to report?'

'No.'

Crane poked at his sandwich and took careful sips. 'Do you like his books'?'

'Whose?'

'Nietzsche's. Do you think the Outsider theory has a religious solution? There seems no other way out of the impasse, does there? Perhaps you believe there is?'

He pronounced the words with deep satisfaction.

'No, not really. So that's what you are – an Outsider.'

Crane nodded. 'I'm an essential Rebel.' He paused while he searched his mind for jargon. 'I'm out of harmony with the Universe. Oh, excuse me,' he said. His nose had begun running. 'I'm always catching colds. What a coincidence that you've read Søren.'

'Who?'

'Kierkegaard. Do you think the Regina Olsen episode had much effect on him?'

Peterson hesitated.

'And what about the attacks in the Corsair?'

Peterson glanced through the window. 'About this collection of blue books,' he said.

'This what?'

'The collection of blue books that Hart has.'

Crane pressed his lip between his teeth. 'It's not important,' he said, 'if we pay too much attention to the blue book business, we may scare the big game away.'

'What is the big game?'

Crane put down his glass with a thump. 'I'm not certain yet.'

'I can tell you where he gets his books – '

'Can you?' Some of the orangeade dribbled onto his tie.

Peterson blew out a cloud of smoke; it shaded his eyes and gave him a mysterious look.

'Murdock's bookshop,' he said.

'Where's that?'

'Just along the road from the club.'

'Good,' said Crane. 'Where does Hart live?'

'I don't know the name of the road – north end of Bloomsbury.'

'Ah, you were probably being led round in circles. Take note the next time you go there: try and familiarise certain landmarks; anything that catches your attention, fix in the memory. But what ever you do, don't let them suspect, I know I'm being a bore but – I wonder if you're familiar with the section on boredom in *Either/Or*?'

'No.'

Crane shook his head. 'These are dangerous people with whom we are dealing. But danger, as Fauconberg said, is the stepping-stone to truth. Do you know his work at all?'

'I'm afraid not.'

'Fauconberg. 1781 to 1840. There's a translation in Everyman by a woman called Stewart; it's odd you've never read it.'

'I must have missed it,' said Peterson.

'You're not one of these people who only read anthologies, are you?'

'No. I'll have to be going, it looks like rain again. Anyway I've an appointment.'

'I'll be expecting to hear from you,' said Crane, 'you have my number.'

He drew on his gloves.

'I'll go first. We mustn't be seen together.'

He threaded his way through the customers to the door. Peterson saw him move aside as two women entered, and then he was gone. He followed him out; he had to run to keep up with him.

'Ah there you are,' said Crane. 'Do you think that's wise? Never mind, we must be more careful in future.'

His legs splayed out as he walked; his feet thrust from side to side.

'I must tell you about a play I'm writing,' he said: 'a dialogue between Queen Elizabeth the First and

Second, putting my own opinions into the mouth of the one, and those of the *Daily Express* editorial into the other. I must get a bus here, I live in Canonbury you know.' He looked sourly about him. 'I'm trying to organise an Outsiders' club; nothing's finally settled yet, but I hope to have readings and lectures. Do you think Wilson would join?'

Peterson took a deep breath. 'I must go,' he said, 'it's started to rain.'

Crane waved a glove as he turned the corner.

Grey light fell on the canal, giving its surface a silvery sheen. How many things become bearable on a Sunday afternoon. Cigarette cartons and broken bottles assume forms more potent than glories and grandeurs gone. Peterson rattled his keys in his pocket. A girl's heels on the pavement behind him made a startling noise. Thunder sounded like a gong. The sky almost reached the darkness of night.

Peterson screwed his eyes up, ran his thumb round the edge of his key-ring, inserted the key in the lock. As he closed the door he heard the sound of a tap running; he must have left it on. He took off his mac.

This life's alright when you're young, he thought, I'll hang on with Hart for a bit – try and save from what he pays me; perhaps I'll get something from Crane. I'll make clean break with Donelly one day, but not till I've a couple of hundred in the bank.

He opened the wardrobe, hung his scarf on a hook. Donelly's dressing-gown had fallen on the floor, he picked it up. He remembered with longing Francesca's breasts beneath her white blouse when she danced, her pale-coloured lipstick, the way she let her skirt ride up to the knee. I'll tell her I bought her the compact. He felt in his pocket for Donelly's book, took careful aim, threw it on top of the wardrobe. He switched on the fire and began to take off his clothes.

If only I could get hold of the money, I could have the best of both worlds. The blurred snapshot of Francesca came into his mind. He lay flat and started to do his exercises, toes touching the back of his head, head brought forward until it lay on his knees. For a few moments he breathed heavily; he was alone: there was no one for whom he might put on an act. He thought of Crane. He tried to imagine the house in Canonbury where he lived, reading his books, while his mother cooked meals and his father sprayed the hydrangeas.

Unaware of the draught from beneath the door, he closed his eyes and unaccountably fell asleep.

8

What sauce! Crane thought, as he pushed his way through the workers streaming into the station.

He repeated the phrase, the book clutched beneath his arm pressing into his ribs. He looked at the clock by the Gents lavatory, it was half past nine. I wasn't born yesterday, I know a fake outsider when I see one. The German philosophers had been soiled, dragged in the dust of ridicule. If he'd had less self-control, he'd have given the lie to Peterson: the thing to do was play cat and mouse, throw the man off his guard, lead him on.

The trap needed to be dug by an expert.

When the time came to administer the *coup de grâce* – he would not be controlled. It was not the first time that he had detected a crypto-beat, a fraudulent rebel, a man whose anger was not strictly on the level. There are so many whom no one calls but themselves. He would seem the innocent flower, but be the serpent beneath. He opened his book and began to read to calm his annoyance.

The sentences refused to convey any meaning. He hoped Murdock's bookshop would be open. If it were not, he must wait: there was a pleasant garden nearby where he could sit and settle his nerves. And would he find Murdock alone; an assistant might prove an unguessed-of complication.

He turned through a small square. The soil smelled clean after yesterday's rain; mounds of broom pressed against the iron railings.

Murdock's bookshop had an entrance at the side through a glass door: it was dirty and Crane couldn't see anybody inside. Ranks of paper-backed semi-pornography blocked his view. He closed the door quietly and walked to the counter. On a high stool was a young woman knitting; if her hair had been longer, she could have been an effeminate boy.

'May!' he said, 'what are you doing here?'

She looked up. On the counter in front of her lay a French nudist magazine, open at an illustration of two women hosing a car.

'What do you mean. This is where I work.'

On the wall behind her there was a door marked Private.

'I thought you worked at Smiths',' said Crane.

'Not since last October.'

'I certainly never expected to find you here. Why did you leave Smiths'?'

She shrugged. 'I was tired of the books: nothing but war memoirs and C. P. Snow.' She took off her glasses and snapped the case shut. 'It was good clean fun while it lasted.'

Crane's eyes rambled over the muscle-boy magazines. He took in the out-of-date books by Havelock Ellis and Marie Stopes. 'By the way, you were at Mavis' party, weren't you?'

She flushed. 'I left early.'

'Ah, you were fortunate. It wasn't Mavis' fault, and I don't think much damage was done.'

She was silent.

Crane came round the counter and looked at her magazine. 'Is that part of the stock?'

'I must have something to look at while I'm knitting.'

'How are you getting on with the drama group?'

'We're doing a German play.' She smoothed a wisp of hair over her ear. 'It's very experimental.' She twisted round on her stool. 'I say, leave those books alone, what are you doing? – this play is rather your line of country I should have thought, all about incest in the early days of aviation.'

'Do you sell much of this stuff?' said Crane, pointing to the highly coloured shelves. 'Have you an "*enfer*"?'

'A what?'

'A section of special volumes . . .'

'We're strictly above board,' said May, 'there's nothing like that here. We work for our living. Crime, interesting art studies, anthropology – all legitimate. There are more expensive works in the back room at thirty bob, translations of nineteenth-century novels about hermaphrodites – '

'Thirty bob seems pretty steep.' He examined a book cover showing a black-haired ruffian with a whip.'

'*Pride and Prejudice*,' May said. 'People pay just for the cover.'

'They'll be disappointed by Parson Austen's daughter.'

'It might teach them something. When are you starting that club of yours? I suppose you'll be having poetry readings? Rimbe and Verlomphe and so on. Mind you, this play we're doing takes all my spare time.'

'Don't you find amateur drama a bit soul-destroying?'

'Sometimes perhaps, but you'll like this play. Come and see a rehearsal.' She rummaged under the counter. 'Better still – it's on next week; come and see it. What about Wednesday? Two at five bob, I'm sure you can find someone to bring.'

Unwillingly he handed over a ten-shilling note.

'Come round to my dressing-room afterwards.'

'Shall I?'

'We'll have a drink. But if you have Mavis with you of course . . . '

'Now, May, I really came to see Murdock.' He slipped the tickets into his pocket. 'If I see Mavis, I'll tell her I met you.'

'You needn't bother.' She indicated the door. 'He's in there.'

Crane stepped behind the counter, opened the door, and found himself in Murdock's office.

Murdock, looking up from a Science Fiction magazine, narrowed his eyes as they focused on Crane. He had a plate of biscuits by his side. 'What can I do for you?'

Crane leaned against the door, watching Murdock's teeth crunch into another biscuit. He touched the wood with the tips of his fingers.

'Who are you?' Murdock said, 'and what do you want here?'

He held a biscuit half way to his mouth.

'I wonder if you could help me. I hope I've come to the right place.'

'My assistant had no right letting you in.'

'I was told you might help me.'

Murdock brushed biscuit crumbs off his lap with a magazine.

'I'm interested in unusual books.'

'All my stock's on display.'

'Not those kind of books – "curiosa", if you understand me.'

'I understand you only too well. I keep nothing of that sort.'

'I don't mind how much I pay.'

'My assistant will help you to choose a book. She knows far more than I do about the stock.'

'Are you sure I can't find something in here?'

'What is it you're after?'

Crane fluttered about in the doorway and came to the point: 'I'm interested in rare editions.'

'What do you mean?'

'I'm a student of physiology.'

'Try Charing Cross Road.'

'I've been told to contact you.'

'By whom?'

'You're very suspicious. Do I have to bring a letter of credit? I can be trusted.'

'I don't know what you're talking about.'

'Ah, I think you do. This isn't the first time you've been approached in this way.' Crane leaned back against the door. 'I'm willing to pay.'

'I haven't the foggiest idea what you want.'

'I want art studies.'

'Phaidon?'

'You choose to misunderstand me. I'm interested in the nude, without veils – they must be books published for the connoisseur.'

'Male or female?'

'I'm not particular.'

Murdock's eyes became slightly dilated.

'I might be able to find you one or two, but you don't expect me to display such things in the window, it's not an artistic neighbourhood.'

'Will these books be – stimulating?'

'Oh very, I should imagine.'

Murdock licked a crumb of biscuit from his upper lip. The telephone rang. They heard May lift the extension.

'And will there be life-size enlargements?'

Murdock beat a tattoo on the desk. 'Who did you say sent you?'

'I'd prefer not to discuss it.'

'How do I know you're not from the police?'

'Do I look like a policeman?'

'It depends,' said Murdock. 'We seem to be talking at cross purposes.'

'What an extraordinary thing to say! It's just that I heard – at a club I belong to – my friend is the soul of discretion. I'm sure if I gave you his name, you'd be prepared to do business.'

'Why don't you?'

'You must find it very cramping, this censorship.'

'You say that I know him?'

'I'm sure you do.'

Murdock spread out his hands. 'I know so few people.'

'His taste is for illustrated classics.' Crane sniggered. 'And *what* classics. Can't you help me, I know you'd like to?'

Murdock shifted his magazine, the pages rasping beneath his fingers. 'What exactly – '

'Come now,' Crane said, 'don't keep me waiting all day.'

'What you require is difficult to come by,' said Murdock. 'I might be able to oblige you, but not today. I can't put my hands on a book of that type at the moment.'

He opened a drawer and slid forward an envelope.

'How about these? Unusual angle shots: guinea, a set of five.'

'Very interesting. I'm sure I'll be most enlightened.' Surprised at his sudden victory, Crane paid him, picked up the envelope, and opened the door.

He had expected to have to invent more details to put Murdock at his ease; he felt his ingenuity wasted.

'It's been a pleasure meeting you,' he said. 'I hope I shall see you again.'

Outside in the shop he paused before racks of primary-coloured book-jackets. May was busy on the telephone. He put the postcards in his pocket and smiled; it had been an expensive morning. He went to the door and let himself out.

The sun was shining, the light had an air of Spring tenderness, dwelling on the terraced houses, on gulls coming up from the Thames. How remarkably perfect life seemed. The smell of hot coffee suddenly made him yawn with hunger. He searched through the coins in his pocket, and in the call-box on the corner dialled a number.

'Is Peterson home?'

'He's in bed,' said Donelly, 'is it urgent?'

'I'd like to speak to him.'

'Who is it please?'

'Crane is the name.' Small clicking noises came over the wire. 'Hallo, is that Peterson?'

'What do you want?'

'I'm sorry if I disturbed you.'

'Is that all you wanted?'

'Anything to report?'

'Give me a chance.'

'All square and above board?'

'Look, I've just got up – I had a late night. Of course I haven't anything to report, I'd ring you if I had.'

'I wonder, Peterson, whether you like the theatre?'

'Why?'

'I've a couple of tickets for an amusing play; I can't go myself.'

'I'm at the club every night.'

'Would you like them?'

'Except Wednesday.'

'These are for Wednesday: I'll post them to you. – I've been doing a little research on my own account – you were right about Murdock.'

'I know I was.'

Crane blinked at himself in the mirror. 'He's sold me a packet of pornographic postcards.'

'What are they pictures of?' said Peterson. 'Or can't you tell me over the phone?'

'I haven't examined them yet.' He began to doodle on a directory. 'They're the first piece of evidence: we shall build it up link by link.'

From the corner of his eye he caught sight of a woman waiting outside. He drew a girl with long hair, a pair of scales, a domed roof, a sword.

'You're not short of cash? When we pull off our scoop, I'll give you fifty-fifty – we don't want to spoil the ship for a ha'porth of tar.' He drew a rowing boat and added shading. 'As long as you accept that I'm in charge.'

'Yes,' said Peterson, 'I'll ring you again. O.K?'

'Very well,' said Crane.

A wave of irritation swept over him. The sword of mockery is sharp, but its blade is double-edged.

'So long.'

He put down the receiver. The woman glared at him as he stepped into the street. He lifted his hat politely; she looked surprised.

All the seats were taken in the gardens. An old woman heaved herself up and tottered off; Crane walked with relief to the vacant place.

Now to open the envelope.

Disgust welling up, he bowed his head in the attitude people use for prayer. As at the centre of a cyclone there was complete calm. Like a problem in mathematics, you could work it out many ways – the answer remained the same. Admiralty Arch, Piccadilly Circus, Trafalgar Square and the Changing of the Guard did not constitute a breach of the postal regulations.

He tossed the envelope away. It touched the railings and was lifted through them to roll on the roadway beyond.

9

The carpet swallowed Peterson's footsteps as he stared at the long-faded photographs: Garbo, Coleman, Gable. Here the archimandrites of the 'thirties collected dust, heads posed as though they guessed their curious immortality, among the unmistakable smell of decay. The empty corridors augured the waning of a cult; so Venus, Jove and Diana watched their temples crumble, the paint curl in strips from the sanctuary.

He noticed several boys from his old school, their haircuts elaborate. Behind him were empty rows. It would have been depressing to calculate the cinema's takings.

'Has this always been a picture-house?' he said.

'I think so,' said Hart; 'they had an organ once.'

'Those were the days.'

The music played, bringing to mind gas-mask cases and rouge on high cheek-bones: nostalgic music for yellowing idols, for fox furs and nude shoulders, for black moustaches and glossy hair.

Peterson lit a cigarette and watched the smoke curl upwards. 'Are we going to see the whole programme?'

'What do you mean?'

'It'll be very long, I've a telephone call to make at half past four.'

'We'll go,' said Hart, 'when we've seen the news and trailers.'

An old man rustled sweets in a cellophane bag. A boy in a sailcloth jacket turned and tried to attract Hart's attention.

'Do you know them?' said Peterson.

The younger boy was eating an ice.

'He's Greek,' said Hart, 'a friend of Donelly's.'

'Don't encourage him,' Peterson said, 'they'll come and sit with us in a minute.'

The boy's eyes were turned in their direction again; Hart smiled at him distantly. The only people in the building were under sixteen or over sixty: it was as if it were a ritual reserved for childhood and old age.

The lights faded, the music shut off; the Gents and Exits glowed. A tin of liver salts darted across the screen; point and counterpoint sang a threnody of purgation. A bubbling glass appeared, the dirge changed to joy, the heavenly voices soared.

I must ring Francesca, thought Peterson, make a date for tomorrow.

An appeal was made, collection boxes brought round. The main feature came on. 'What was her telephone number? Peterson found his thoughts wandering: he felt in his pocket but only Crane's number came to light.

'What's the matter,' said Hart.

'Another cigarette?'

'Thanks.'

The twelfth century. Saladin behaved like a cad. Richard Cœur de Lion, one day in Sicily, heard Phillip Augustus speaking of him in a way that opened his eyes. Up to now women had played no part in his life, but that evening Berengaria came to the Island. Pretty

211

and unapproachable, she seemed to offer everything that he had missed. The Crusade set sail next day. Unwilling to cause her pain, he delayed telling her of his love. In the combat of rival tyrannies Hollywood had underlined startling parallels with the world today.

With a sigh of relief Peterson recalled Francesca's telephone number. The Crusaders took Acre. He glanced at the clock, it was four fifteen. 'I can't stop after this,' he whispered.

Hart nodded. 'It's nearly done now.'

In her tent Berengaria waited; Richard rode up in a glitter of armour. Capped teeth flashed against hectic suntan, twilight over the desert, procrastination of rape reached its climax. The violins became ecstatic and it was over.

'If you want to stay . . . ' said Peterson.

'No, no,' said Hart; 'that boy will come over if he sees I'm alone.'

'I'd tell him where to get off if I were you.'

'He tries to borrow money.' Hart glanced back at the screen. 'This film took three years to make, the actor playing the king died.'

'What a waste of time,' said Peterson.

A few people emerged with them, blinking, into the sunlight.

'I'll use the phone over the road, by the under-takers.'

'I'll wait,' said Hart.

'Where are we going afterwards?'

Hart looked thoughtful. 'We'll go to a place I know; Donelly may be there.'

'I'll only be a minute,' said Peterson. The pennies dropped, he could hear his number being rung. He watched Hart walk up and down. Why wasn't she answering? He remembered her cheap scent, her plump little buttocks. He wanted the feel of her lips, her neck, her feet. He swallowed hard and his mouth went dry. A voice at the other end said 'Hallo?'

'Is that you?'

'I should think so.' Her voice was hard.

'Look, Fran,' he said, 'I didn't forget; it's this new job I've got at a night-club.'

'A night-club?' She sounded awed.

He pulled at the tip of his nose, thinking of lies. His eyes in the mirror stared back at him. 'What are you doing?' he said.

'Sitting on the stairs.'

'No, I mean – is it any good for today?'

'Not now.'

He swore under his breath.

'Everyone wanted to know who I was waiting for.'

'I know – I'm sorry. Have you got a powder compact?'

'Why?'

'I've bought one for you.'

'Describe it to me.'

'It's pale blue with a heart on the lid.'

'All the girls have them. They're from the shooting gallery, aren't they?'

'I'll give it to somebody else,' he said, 'I'm sorry.' Her lack of guile made him ashamed.

'Don't worry,' she said, 'the thought was there. If you like, I'll give it to Marjorie for her birthday.'

'O.K. I'll bring it along.'

'I was wondering what to get.'

'When am I going to see you?'

'I don't know.' She paused for a moment. 'You're sure you don't mind?'

'That's not what I want to talk about – ' His hunger for her became unbearable.

'Don't forget to bring it along.'

'When am I going to see you?'

She laughed. 'How about tomorrow?'

He tapped his fingers against the glass. 'Can't you take the morning off school?'

'No.'

'How about in the afternoon? Can't you come round to my place at night?'

'Better make it a quarter past four.'

'I'll see you then – '

'Outside the gates as usual.'

'So long – '

They were reluctant to hang up.

Her voice dropped to a whisper. 'Be on time.'

''Bye,' said Peterson. He replaced the receiver. He had a vision of girls walking in twos and threes out of the concrete playground, their lipstick hastily applied.

Hart hurried forward.

'Where are we going?' said Peterson.

'This way,' said Hart. 'That boy's following us. He tries to sell me things: I don't know where they come from. What's the mark on your chin?'

'My scar,' said Peterson. 'It was the time they threw a bomb at my C.O.; he was killed outright. They thought I was dead too or I would have had it. I was unconscious for days.'

Hart smiled.

Peterson glanced at him, unsure of the next move. They stopped at a zebra crossing waiting for the traffic to slow down. 'Is anything wrong?'

'No,' said Hart.

'You didn't believe me?'

'Did you expect me to?'

'What was the mistake?'

'None at all,' said Hart, walking across the road in front of the cars. 'I have an instinct for these things; that's all. Quick, before he can follow us!'

'Who?'

'Those boys.' Hart darted into a crowd of workers. 'They've been walking twenty yards behind; now they've lost us.'

Peterson frowned. A feeling of panic stirred in his brain. Hart was smarter than he had supposed; perhaps he was smarter than any of them had supposed.

'I've never used that line before,' he said; 'it's always a razor-fight.'

'Stick to that in future.'

'It was a piece of tin in the canal. I was bathing.'

'Look out.'

Following with a jungle tread came two figures in narrow jeans.

'Let them catch up with us,' Hart said.

A poster caught Peterson's eye: DUCHESS STRANGLED.

Tusker sidled up, picking a shred of tobacco from his lip. 'Don't you walk fast?' he said.

Hart said, 'Why aren't you at school?'

'His mum wrote a note. He had to go to the infirmary.'

'Does that excuse you?'

'Somebody had to go with him.'

'I see.'

'Didn't you take an afternoon off when you was at school?'

'Not often,' said Hart. He opened the door of an espresso bar. 'We're going in here.'

'So are we,' said Tusker. He ran his fingers over his hair.

An LP throbbed a number from a musical; they were surrounded by long-leaved plants.

'I'll go to the counter,' Hart said. 'The waitress is busy.'

They could hear her talking.

'Oh, Herbert doesn't work –

– you didn't actually *think*?

They live off the National Assistance –

– it's quite adequate. And Doreen has her job at the –

Yes, yes.'

Derek ate a lump of sugar; Tusker pulled the leaves from a fern.

Hart came back with May.

'This is May, and this is – '

'Marian.' The blonde woman smiled; a few beads of sweat lay on her upper lip.

' – Lottie has gone to see Erica, but I couldn't face the idea. After all one gets quite enough lesbians in books without actually meeting a *real* one.'

'Have I sold you a ticket yet?'

Hart shook his head.

'You know Daisy?'

'Yes.'

'And she hasn't sold you one?'

'No. I'm busy every evening. Except Wednesday.'

'You must come and see us. Have you a ticket on you Marian?'

'I may have.'

'You should have seen Marian's Lady Macbeth,' May said. 'Though as it was played at the Camden Road Polytechnic, I don't suppose many people did.'

'May – '

'And you've never seen a single thing we've done?'

Hart shook his head. May glanced at Tusker, murmuring to herself 'extraordinary'.

' – not a single play. You're in for a treat. Daisy used to be a member.'

'Daisy did?'

'Ages ago, didn't she Marian?'

'Ages ago,' said Marian.

'But you wouldn't think that nowadays; if it's not her Old People's Homes, it's her Women's Club, or her Handicapped Girls.'

Tusker looked across at the waitress.

May said, 'What are you trying to do with those leaves – weave them into a mat?'

He stared, open-mouthed. A fragment of icing trembled on his lip; rubbing his finger across the bristles of his cheek, he frowned.

'You must come to a performance,' May said.

'I'm busy,' Hart said.

'Not Wednesdays.'

'No, not Wednesdays.'

'Have you a ticket on you Marian?'

Marian rummaged in her bag.

'It's rather special; a German play: banned when Hitler came to power. The man who wrote it was suspected, not without just cause, of being loopy.'

'It's a lovely play,' said Marian.

'Lovely,' said May.

She lifted her coffee to her chin.

'In one scene I have to express wonder that I should be sitting inside a gigantic goose's egg.'

'A what?'

'A goose's egg.'

'They've had it on the telly,' Tusker said.

'I don't think so.'

'They had a preview before Christmas.'

'Did they?'

' – about an egg; from the Palladium. He didn't think much of it.'

He nodded at Derek, drank the rest of his coffee, and stared through the foliage into the street.

Hart said, 'It sounds interesting.'

'I have a theory – you see it isn't a real egg, but a symbol of frustration. In a sense we all live in eggs.'

'Why a goose's egg?'

'A goose expresses stupidity.'

'Yes.'

'For so many people life is spent in an egg. When we break from the egg we're free; it's as simple as that. Most people spend their lives trying to be born, and die unhatched.'

'Is there a plot?'

'If you come to the play you'll see. There is a haggle over maidenheads – which I suppose you might describe as a plot.'

'When are you doing it?' said Peterson.

'Next week.'

'I'll take a ticket for Wednesday,' said Hart.

May didn't speak; her eyes widened.

'That's good of you.'

'Here's one for Wednesday,' said Marian. She handed him a square of blue card with a tragic mask printed on it.

'Come to my dressing-room afterwards,' said May.

She buttoned her shirt and clipped on the bow tie: her winding up gestures. She pushed back her chair.

'Do come.'

Marian said, 'So many people buy tickets and don't turn up.'

'You will, won't you?'

'Yes.'

The door swung open; they waved as they passed the window.

'Excuse me.'

Her hair streaked with silver, the manageress craned her neck over Hart's shoulder.

Tusker rose to his feet, the table rocked; he looked down at Hart.

'It was an accident.'

'It's ruined,' the manageress said. 'Look at it. You ought to be ashamed of yourself.'

'I'm terribly sorry,' said Hart. 'We were talking – I had no idea what he was doing.'

'What about our plant? He's almost cut it in half.'

'I'll pay for it.'

Hart put his hand in his pocket to feel for his wallet.

'Wait for me outside, Peterson, I'll be with you in a minute.'

10

In the bathroom, lying in tepid water, he might have been dead and in a tomb: secure from the prostitutions and second-rateness of life. He heard the thump of a newspaper in the hall; noises from the street were reduced to half-heard sounds, remote, meaningless.

His last crime needed to be exact. Nothing must be left to chance, no accidental detail unallowed for. He didn't want to clutch at straws, make more excuses for staying alive. He was filled with nausea, with self-disgust.

Paradise to lie in a steaming bath for ever: the right temperature eternally provided. Centuries might pass, civilisations rise and fall; what would he know of it. Gaugamela, Lepanto, Actium, Roncesvalles, Ypres: war after war, stupidity after stupidity; it wouldn't matter to him.

The door slammed; a window had been left open.

And now that life was almost past with its many futilities and small corruptions, feeble joys and pleasures and astonishments, love and hate were levelled to a single point of no importance. He stared upwards until his neck ached and his eyes swam. The meaningless and absurd life situation into which he had had the misfortune to be born was over. His books were no use. Who cares what a philosopher who has done nothing but live in his slippers says about this world or the next?

He thought, planned, waited, and waiting plunged back into dreams. Old memories and dim associations, the crowding words of poets, tapers burning in the twilight, glittering images, self-luminous, suggestive. This world is void of purpose, of volition, it is a dead immeasurable engine, pounding out indifference into space.

He reached for a towel, pulled the plug and went into the bedroom.

The battered wardrobe, the stolen books lay around him; his dressing-gown hung on the door; the daffodil had withered, given up the ghost. To live appeared infinitely more desirable than to die. He gave the low whimper of an animal caught in a trap.

He put on the light and went to the window to close it; a wind was blowing, stirring the leaves of the daffodil, wrinkling the canal's surface: one might mistake the movement for life.

The woman upstairs had her wireless on. It sounded like Brahms. Donelly shook his head. It was odd because she was a lousy common pig-faced rattle-brained whore who couldn't tell a violin from a douche-bowl.

I've just cut the throat of a dear friend of mine,
She talked of Castelnuovo-Tedesco all the time.

He knelt and rooted among his books.

He felt dizzy; he had been drinking too much. He looked in the mirror: his skin was pinkish and flushed, and he was pale round the eyes. He couldn't find what he wanted.

An expurgated school edition of *Hamlet* and half a sausage stood on the shelf. He took the sausage and ate it, lifted the *Hamlet* and threw it out of the window. A worker on his way home looked up. Donelly made a face. There is no fate worse than that of being excluded by pressure of circumstances, by necessity to work long hours, from all possibility of leisure.

He climbed on the bed; it seemed unnecessary to get off again.

Working for what? For a better world? For a merry-go-round of more production. It was wrong. All of it. Everything.

I want – And his thoughts ended. He lacked courage to die and courage to live. He wanted a sign. Any excuse, O Lord, any excuse.

He scrambled to his feet, opened Evelyn Waugh's *Ronald Knox*, tore out several pages and went into the lavatory shutting the door with a bang.

11

Peterson was late. It was deliberate; he didn't want to wait, stared at by girls, whistled. The sunlight touched his bare arms and made them appear gold.

She stood on the steps, and he was defenceless before her. Francesca. She had the air of a child expecting a present, not a woman anticipating a lover.

She ran over to him; the yard was deserted. She lifted her face and they kissed: he could smell her hair as it brushed his cheek. He fumbled in his pocket and brought out the compact: the mirror was broken.

'It doesn't matter,' she said.

The sun disappeared from the sky; the deceptive warmth of Spring vanished.

'Aren't you cold?' she said.

He shook his head, swelled his chest to make the muscles stand out, looked at the sky. He glanced at her sideways and kicked at a stone.

'I don't feel the cold,' he said. 'I'm a swimmer. I've a layer of fat under the skin.'

Outside the tobacconist's was a slot-machine; he tried it: a coin tinkled and he pulled out a roll of peppermints. There was a constraint between them, the uneasiness of people whose first excitement is over.

'Where are we going?'

They turned into the gardens, the branches hazed with early green, a motor-bike backfired, pigeons wheeled from the path.

Her hand was sticky. 'Can we go to your place?'

Peterson pressed her knuckles. 'Is it any good where you live?'

She shook her head.

They stopped by an iron seat. Peterson kissed the side of her neck. She said, 'Mum would have a fit if she knew.'

'About me?'

'Yes.'

They sat on the seat, she leaned her head on the slats; the strap of her brassiere was visible through her blouse.

'What's your new job like?'

Peterson ran his finger down the side of her breasts, feeling the flesh give beneath his touch. 'I'm a bodyguard.'

She moved her position; there was an inkstain on her finger, her lipstick was smudged like badly applied crayon. 'It sounds funny to me.'

He put his hands over her breasts and said, 'I get well paid.'

'Isn't it dangerous?'

'No,' he said, kissing her.

'It must be, or why would anyone pay a bodyguard?'

The sun dropped behind the houses, beams of light shone from basement windows. Shadows unwound about rooftops and balconies; chimneys melted against the sky. He shivered.

'Are you cold?'

'A bit.'

'They close the park at five.'

Peterson kissed her again. She put her fingers round his wrist; he nuzzled the side of her neck with his nose. It was astonishing to think he could be jailed. She took the initiative with assurance. He felt relief when she let go. She flicked open her compact; Peterson rubbed the red stain from his mouth.

'Where are we going?' she said, running her tongue across her lips.

'I'll think of some place.'

She snapped the compact shut and smoothed her hair.

Peterson was silent, staring at the canal between the houses. It was dark. It would have been possible to see the stars, if the lights of the city were switched off.

Far above the glow, world upon world, nebulae, comets and moons and trabants and blackness and nothing. All that dark and down here not a piece of waste ground or a corner. Peterson dug his hands in his pockets; Francesca put her arm through his. He flinched from the thought of exposing her to Donelly. He would stick on a label like a butterfly, he had a cruelty of insight which knew no scruple.

They walked out of the gardens; a policeman was knocking on the door of a house: the last light had gone from the sky.

'Let's have a coffee.'

'What time have you got to be back?'

'Don't worry.'

A group of scouts came down the road. They walked in a squad behind their leader, who explained a point of law to a new recruit:

'You f – ing well have to do a f – ing good deed every f – ing day. If you don't you can f – off out of our f – ing troupe.'

'I must be back by eight,' Francesca said.

She moved a plate shaped like a shell to one side; it left a smear of ice-cream on the table.

Peterson stared through the window at a bus waiting for the traffic-lights to turn green.

'We'll go back to my place. Donelly may have gone to the club.'

'If you don't want to be bothered – '

'Don't take any notice of the things he says.' He tried to give her a warning. 'He's not a bad sort.'

'He can't eat me, can he?'

'No.'

He stared past her. He felt an affection for Donelly; the idea of taking this girl to bed seemed to dwindle in importance. Never to be tied to an alarm clock, the sun enjoyed in summer, the frost in winter, untrammelled by false wants.

'Can't you get another job? More secure. Less – dangerous?'

'Don't bother about me,' he said. 'You may never see me after tonight.'

'I'm safe, you can trust me.'

'Where will you end?' he said, feeling morals stir within him.

'I'll get married.'

'Who to?'

'You.'

He laughed. 'You're not old enough.'

'We could wait.'

It was an illusion. A feeling of despair crept across his body; he sensed the wheels working, preparing an end that did not include their being together. This was all they were allowed, before levers were pulled, threads gathered and cut. She leaned her head on his shoulder; her hair stirred as he breathed.

'Come on.'

They climbed the stairs and stopped on a landing. Peterson opened the door and paused, reluctant to go further. Donelly appeared in the opening. His breath smelt of beer, his cheeks were wet and red from having been rubbed by a towel.

'I've brought Francesca,' said Peterson.

'Yes. Excuse me while I put my clothes on.'

They stood in the hall while he tucked his shirt into his jeans.

'Have a peppermint?' said Francesca.

'Has Steve been robbing slot-machines again?' His smile remained fixed like a limp line across his face. 'No one would think he was dishonest – he looks so unsuccessful.'

Peterson said, 'Is there a drink?'

Donelly went into the bathroom and came back with two bottles and a glass.

He wrenched the tops off with an opener.

'You can have the glass. Steve and I are used to sharing things.' He gave a meaning look. 'Was your mother reading Dante?'

'No – the *Seventh Veil*. Don't you remember?'

'It was before my time.'

He replaced the opener on the table, handed her a glass, hardly bothering to conceal a grin when she sipped and shivered.

'Been to the pictures lately?' He wouldn't use her name.

'I went last night.'

'What was it about?'

'King Richard – you know who – '

'On his way to the Crusades did penance for sodomy.'

'They missed that part.'

'It might not film well.' He watched her. 'Do they teach that at school now? They spend so much on education, I hope you get your money's worth.'

He stared at his bottle with unsteady concentration, pretending a drunkenness he hadn't reached, avoiding Peterson's eye.

'I thought you'd be at the club,' said Peterson.

'I'm late.'

He put the bottle to his lips, drank, and dribbled.

' – Crane was on the phone for you.' He wiped his chin.

'What did he want?'

'He'll be outside the club tonight. He'll have the tickets with him. What tickets?'

'Some tickets he's giving me.'

'Are you taking her?'

'No.'

'So Crane's giving you tickets? Nobody ever gives me anything. I haven't your charm.'

'Hart has tickets too; he'd like to go with us. He paid for his.'

'Hart going to the theatre?' Donelly finished the bottle and put it down. 'How friendly you two are, as thick as thieves.'

'It's an expressionist drama.'

'It'll be a change from *The Archers* – though, Jesus Christ, they're expressionist enough.'

He put his jacket on, changed his mind and took out an old mac. Picking up a book, he read aloud: ' "Sheds new light on Mary Tudor".'

He flung it from him.

'I do wish you wouldn't steal such rubbish.'

'Do you steal these books?' said Fran.

'Steve does,' said Donelly. 'I wonder sometimes if he isn't – you know. Such a worry he was to his mother.'

'She's dead?'

'Dead? She's in Holloway. He was a worry to her before she became a worry to him.'

Peterson said, 'For God's sake talk sense. My mother lives in Romford.'

'He's embarrassed,' said Donelly, 'so we won't talk about it. Romford – that was a good touch.'

'What do you do with these books?'

'Do with them?'

'Yes.'

'Well, some of them – ' he picked up the copy of *Ronald Knox*. ' – I wouldn't like to tell you quite frankly.'

'Supposing anyone found out?'

'They don't,' said Donelly, grimacing into the mirror.

Peterson winked at Francesca and shook his head.

'I think it's terrible,' she said.

'We're public benefactors in a way. We steal – the shops order more – the publishers are pleased – everyone is happy. We finance literature. We are a sort of Maecenas.'

He kept his malice under control.

'You wouldn't even begin to understand the real reasons why we do these things.'

'Do you understand yourself?'

She wandered round the room, touching things, wrinkling her nose in disapproval.

'Do you know what subreption is?' said Donelly.

'No.'

'To obtain something by misrepresentation. That is what our civilisation does – it holds carrots in the air to make donkeys work. Do you know what it wants in exchange for a house, a car, a larger house, two cars, a television set in every room?'

'No.'

'It wants their lives.'

She sat on the bed; Donelly stared down at the top of her head.

'And by kidding the donkey as to how many carrots it needs for a happy life, it gets what it wants.'

'People are happier today than they were.'

Donelly's eyes watered in emotion. 'They are so busy working they haven't the time to be unhappy; so busy watching television and driving round in cars, they haven't the time to think. That isn't the same thing at all.'

'I won't argue,' she said.

'You can't.'

Donelly watched her; he ruffled his hair for a last time.

'I have to go.'

He made no attempt to say goodbye.

'So have I.'

'Stay here. I'm sure you can find some way of entertaining yourselves.'

Peterson said, 'I'll see you later?'

Donelly nodded, leaning against the door. 'You know I think you want to get rid of me. Perhaps I shall stay and watch.'

He was not laughing; his face looked hopelessly past them at the window. And this is Hell, nor am I out of it. His wretchedness was contagious; he ought to carry a bell like a leper.

He hummed a tune to himself between clenched teeth. 'I'm off,' he said, his eyes moving over Francesca as though she were invisible.

He was gone. They heard his footsteps in the hall; the door slammed. They were alone.

'I knew it was dangerous,' she said.

'What?'

'Your job. Mixing with people like him.'

'Donelly's alright.'

'Is he?'

She wandered about the room: she could be inquisitive now, free of Donelly's eyes.

She wiped a smear of dust from a photograph. 'Is this you?' she said.

'No.'

'Who is it?'

'I don't know. We pinched it – from a secondhand shop.'

'What use is it?'

'It's funny; don't you think so? Look at the uniform, those teeth. How could you think I ever was like that?'

'People change.'

'We've a painting of the Garter Ceremony in the lavatory; would you like to see it?'

She shook her head. 'I don't think I shall come here again.'

Peterson swept a chair clear; she refused to sit down.

Kneeling on the rug she said, 'Kiss me.'

He bent forward and put his arm round her neck; it was an awkward position.

'Put the light out,' she said, 'we can see by the fire.'

12

Peterson found the letter by accident; Hart had pushed it under the blotter. He read it. He knew nothing of Evans. He wasn't interested, it didn't concern him.

An idea gnawed at his brain, refused to be thrown aside; half-formed notions stirred; he was irritated by the nebulous.

A light came on in the passage.

He thought of his doubts and his reluctance, and knew he had been right.

'Hallo,' said Donelly.

Peterson looked up. He might feel sorrow for innocent victims, but Donelly had none. They were so many fools to him; why should he cry over people who hadn't the will-power to resist temptation? It was the fools themselves that felt sorrow for their fellows. The wise man protected by wisdom had no need of pity.

Donelly said, 'I missed Hart. Is he here?'

'No,' said Peterson; his face cast a sulky shadow.

'Can't she afford a better lipstick? It's all over your collar.'

'She wants me to leave this job.'

'What a small amount of conscience makes a coward.'

'She doesn't think it's safe. I'm not sure myself.'

He watched Donelly's reflection in the glass over the books. He had no resolution in him now: the wheel that had spun so rapidly a few minutes ago had slowed to a standstill.

He tugged at a zip on his pocket. I'm fighting a losing battle against unaccountable odds. I shall give up. I shall die. Not like Donelly, but from wavering inertia, from an awareness of a future stretching into infinity of life going on, entangling him in a deathless battle, a lifeless progression of detail.

Donelly's skin had a sheen, as though it had been dipped in milk.

'I've always been doubtful – '

'She talked you out of it.'

I'm not happy about this place; Crane says it's a cover up.'

'Did you imagine it wasn't?'

'I thought it was a joke.'

'You've read a little,' said Donelly, 'but not enough. You know nothing. Less than nothing. We live in an age of miraculous discoveries. Darwin is dead. God created man suddenly; in a crash of thunder he was. It is even possible that you are right and I am wrong.'

'It's so – insecure.'

'Still worried about the day after tomorrow?'

'Not this year, or next. But the future. There are things – '

'I don't understand you.'

'Can't you care at all?'

'No.'

Peterson said, 'The life you choose is likely to bring you no more happiness than mine.'

'There are different kinds of misery.'

'You don't want the same things as me.'

'What do you know of my wants?' said Donelly.

'You don't want a home life and children.'

'I do if I can have them in decency. Not three flights up, and a sink full of nappies. Getting married is fine if you go to the club to escape the bitch. Where we are it's different. I don't need to tell you.'

'It's not so bad,' Peterson said.

His eyes wandered to the faces on the wall: lips perpetually smiling, breasts round and full, waiting for Titus, Louis, Bonaparte and Charles.

'Have you always known Hart was crooked?'

'Yes.'

'I found out a few minutes ago.'

'What have you been up to?'

Peterson took the letter from his pocket and passed it across.

'He can't get away with this.'

'Don't pretend you have a conscience. It doesn't worry me what his business is. Why can't he get away with it?'

Peterson shook his head. 'A man ought to have a conscience. None of your books will justify this. It isn't a matter of convention. Conventions occasionally have right on their side. We can't let him get away with this.'

'Don't stick your nose out too far.'

'Fran was right. You are dangerous.'

'Give me that letter.'

'We know everything from this letter. Not enough to put him inside, but plenty to set the police on the right track.'

There was sweat on Donelly's forehead.

'He might make it worth our while to keep quiet,' Peterson said suddenly.

Donelly laughed. This was Peterson's morality: a desire to be in on the racket.

'What are you laughing at?'

There was no fathoming the shallow mind. Donelly shrugged. Was the Peterson he had known a mirage? Had he imagined a decency?

He said, 'Don't blackmail Hart.'

'Would you stand by him?'

'If you try blackmail.'

'It's the obvious thing to do.'

'You won't play fair by your own standards,' said Donelly. 'Be honest or dishonest. Choose.'

Peterson was muddled; his ideas, once so clear, were now no use; he murmured something and looked sheepish. The pose of straightness was difficult, and the role of blackmailer dangerous.

'You're not coming in with me?' he said.

'You're on your own.'

'Should we go to the police?'

'If you wish. He'll guess who told them. I won't be involved.'

'Think of the opportunity,' Peterson said.

He smacked his fist into the palm of his hand. 'What's a few hundred to him?'

'A lot.'

'I can't throw this chance away. I can clear out. Hart will never see me again. How much do you think I could ask?'

Donelly listened; it wasn't real. He wanted to brush Peterson from his mind like a gnat; he wasn't worth the bother of thinking.

'It's fool-proof,' said Peterson.

'It will need to be.'

'He can't risk going to the police. I'd ask for more than I expect to get. That's sense.'

'Is it?'

'Crane will help me.' He had remembered Crane; he became excited.

'You really think he will help?'

Peterson stood, biting his lip, concentrating.

'Hart won't be able to refuse.'

'Don't be a fool,' said Donelly.

He had lost interest; he was not curious any more: the worlds they lived in didn't touch. He had not been able to rub even a particle of truth onto Peterson.

'Do you think you'll get away with it?'

Peterson put the letter under the blotter.

'I'll wait a bit.' There was a deceptive calm in his words.

'Don't tell Crane.'

'No,' said Peterson, 'no.'

Donelly noticed the look in his eyes; he didn't care now.

Peterson said, 'All the same – it isn't right.'

'No.'

Donelly stood up, stretched himself, and left the room.

13

Approaching the theatre in darkness the car slowed down, hesitated, seemed to be feeling its way along the road, and then shot forward.

'Christ!' Donelly said. 'Watch out.'

'Sorry,' said Hart.

'What's the matter with you?'

'It's Biscuit. I'm worried about Biscuit.'

'Let me take over.'

'No. It's alright. I'll be careful.'

The raindrops spat on the windows in which Donelly could see himself reflected.

'I didn't know whether I ought to come,' said Hart.

'Why not?' said Peterson.

'It's Biscuit – '

'Biscuit? What's wrong with Biscuit?'

'She's ill. I've been sitting up with her all night.'

Donelly wound down the window a slit and threw out his cigarette.

'What's wrong?'

'Last night she was off colour – so I took her temperature.'

'You took a dog's temperature?'

'Why not?'

'I didn't know you could,' said Peterson.

' – it registered a 105. The vet says it's Hard-pad.'

'Hard-pad?'

'What's that?' said Peterson.

Hart braked suddenly. They were flung forward.

'Let me take over,' said Donelly.

'No. It's quite alright.'

'What's Hard-pad?'

'It's a disease,' Hart said. 'She should have been immunised at four months.'

Outside the theatre Hart locked and parked the car. The rain settled into a drizzle. Almost the first thing they saw – as though it were a reminder of what they had come for, or a portent of the evening – was a poster showing a woman asleep in an egg.

'There's half an hour yet,' Hart said. 'Let's go and have a drink.'

The pub had a false, shabby atmosphere: stools upholstered in red leather, one or two Japanese lanterns hanging over the bar: it was an odd mixture.

As he passed, Donelly looked through the glass window into the lounge and saw a sweatered girl with loose hair looking up at an old man and listening, and smiling.

'Well, what do we all want?' said Hart.

'Light ale for me,' said Donelly.

'Same here,' said Peterson.

Hart made tentative gestures towards the barman who was in conversation with an elderly woman in tight, dark trousers.

'But my point is *this* – '

'Quite, quite.'

'Quite.'

'Two light ales, please,' said Hart, 'and a double whisky.'

'Just one moment, sir.'

'You do see my point?'
'Oh,' said the elderly woman, 'I do. That's just the trouble. I do see your point.'
'I can't – '
'Run away and serve the gentleman, Harry.'

The barman came across to Hart. 'Two light ales and a double whisky, sir?'
'Yes.'
'Nasty weather.'
'Yes.'
Donelly watched two labourers playing darts. A tall man wearing a green-spotted bow tie was talking to two women; a man, wanting to get to the bar, said 'Excuse me,' and pushed past.

'Well can you imagine it – ' the man in the bow tie said. ' – two days to go and NO Juliet?'
'God! how absolutely – '
'No JULIET. I gave up – very nearly. I nearly gave up.'
'Whatever did you do?'
'Whatever did I do? I can't remember.'
'But you must be able to remember.'
'Yes, Fred, don't be silly – of course you remember.'
'Well I naturally only meant – '
'Never mind *what* you meant – tell us what happened.'
'We asked Moira. We had to ask Moira.'
'MOIRA – how awful for you. How absolutely.'

241

'Fred! don't tell us she took over from – '

'Wendy. She did. Even though it was – most unsuitable.'

'So that's why – '

'I certainly do sympathise with you, Fred. Now when we did *Pericles* we had to ask Moira to play – '

'Yes. I saw it. Wasn't she AWFUL. Wasn't she? I just sat back and died.'

'As a matter of fact I thought she was bloody good.'

'We all have our opinions.'

'Fred – '

'It's quite uncalled for. Moira's a nice little actress – '

'Yes. Little – '

' – when she's not – '

' – that's her trouble. Little. Small. Quite wee.'

' – flustered. And naturally when she has had time to rehearse. And when she has a decent producer. Naming no names.'

'I think we'd better be going. There's only five minutes.'

'Are you coming Wendy?'

'Oh, do come on. Do come on.'

Hart gulped down his whisky and asked for another. One of the dart-players scored a bull's eye.

Somebody was saying seven inches from Donelly's ear: 'His aspirations were a good deal less complicated than you like to think.'

'What's the time?'

Hart looked around for the clock; then glanced at his watch. 'A quarter to.'

'The curtain's up.'

'Yes.'

'We may as well stay here and go in at the beginning of the second act.'

'I suppose so,' said Hart. 'Another?'

'Same again.'

'Same again for me.'

There was a pause in which Donelly looked round. He had a feeling of tiredness – a feeling that the evening might go on for ever. He had had too much to drink already: he had a headache coming. A girl in a blue dress leaned out and lifted her bag.

The bar was full of smoke and fumes and talk. The light shone full on the elderly woman in trousers, she was by herself, holding a glass and staring in a gloomy way into space.

Hart bought a sandwich and began to eat it.

At a quarter past eight the man in the bow tie came back with the two women.

'May, of course, was – '

'BLOODY.'

'She's not as bad as that.'

'I have seldom *seen* – '

' – such a bad performance. 'Why did they give it her? Now why? She's quite unsuitable, and – '

' – she's got flat feet.'

'What are we having? Wendy? Pam?'

'A gin and orange.'

'Same for me.'

'Speaking personally, Pam, I think Fred is the most – '

'Yes, Fred, yes. Well gin and It then. I really don't mind.'

' – bitchiest man I've ever met.'

'And he's not queer.'

'Definitely not.'

'I should say not.'

'I should most certainly say NOT.'

Hart went over to the liar and watched for a few minutes, trying to catch the barman's eye. He came back with three more drinks.

'I think we ought to go now.'

'Why?'

'The second act begins at half past.'

'It's twenty-five to.'

'Oh, dear,' Hart said. 'What shall I tell May?'

After the second interval he said, 'We must see some of it.'

They crossed the road to the theatre's foyer; it was very quiet: the quiet of a foyer upon which the curtain has risen. They waved their tickets under the nose of the usher.

The attendant in low tones told them the play was nearly over.

'You're a bit late.'

'Are we late?'

'Curtain comes down in fifteen minutes.'

'We'll see the end, won't we?'

'It hardly seems worthwhile to me.'

'Just in time for the end.'

Another attendant opened the door for them; a torrent of light poured towards them. They were shown to the gangway. Three people were sitting in their seats and had to move.

Donelly turned to watch the scene on the stage: May was sitting upon a bidet and sawing at a violin. It was difficult to follow the dialogue: they had arrived at some kind of climax.

Do you concur that the world is run by the talent-less, by the speculators, the soulless, the spiritually sick?

Do you agree that the world is chock full of incompetents, the stupid, thoughtless, the blunder-ing bunglers, and those who cannot see beyond the end of their noses; those who boggle, muff, and botch all opportunities.

It is run for the benefit of those who founder, loppet, stumble, trip and put their feet into all situa-tions; who betray ideals, make fools of themselves and the people they would fool; for the benefit of those who strain at gnats and swallow camels, who aim at crows and kill nightingales.

Do you now agree that it is better to leave the world to the maladroit, the slatternly, the unteach-able, the apathetic, the mob, the political gerry-manders, to temporization?

Isn't it better to hang oneself than to suffer the spectacle of the world careering on through space and time, carrying with it such a load of –

stop.
STOP.
(*A man comes from the audience*)
I am from the Lord Chamberlain. I forbid you to use the next word.

Why not?

The next word is obscene.

You don't think it adequately expresses the mass of humanity?

I am not qualified to give an opinion. I merely wish you to use an alternative expression.

Very well.

Thank you.

Carry on.

Isn't it better to hang oneself than to suffer the spectacle of the world careering on through apace and time carrying with it such a load of –

Yes.

You've convinced me.

Let us hang ourselves.

The difference between men and animals is that men can end their lives, animals cannot.

Goodbye, Stanley.

Goodbye, Arthur.

Good – oh, dear!

What is the matter?

Nothing – nothing – only –

Not regretting your decision, are you Jenny?

No.

Well?

I shall never now taste the veal we were having for lunch.

Ah, well.

Goodbye, Jenny.

Goodbye, Arthur.

(*Three nooses descend*)

Fasten your nooses please.
GOODBYE.
GOODBYE.
GOODBYE.
Goo –

The curtain fell; the audience gave a gasp of surprise. Hart turned to go and picked up a programme someone had dropped.

'We must see May,' he said.

They went round to the pass door and through behind the scenes; a gust of size and greasepaint hit them. Hart asked a man in a dressing-gown where May's room was.

'May's – oh – it's number two.'

Hart knocked and May answered it.

'HALLO! Isn't it nice to see you. Come in.'

There were several people in the room. 'You know Marian and Bill, don't you?'

'I do indeed.'

'And how did you like the show?'

'It was a – very pleasant evening. Very pleasant.'

'What are you going to do now?'

'Well – ' said Hart, 'bed, I suppose.'

May raised her eyebrows; everyone in the room laughed.

'We're all going on somewhere.'

'Where?'

'We haven't – '

'We haven't decided yet,' said a thin woman.

'Why not come to the club?'

'The club?'

'My club.'

'Oh, but that would be WONDERFUL.' She turned and shouted, 'Mr Hart says – '

'Wonderful.'

'Don't bother taking your things off. No one will notice.'

'Alright,' said May.

Everyone bundled into Hart's car and drove to the club through the rain.

14

May sat back in the chair: under the shades her face was pink.

'You saw the second act, didn't you?'

'Yes,' said Hart.

'Tell me exactly where you came in. I can give you the gist of what happened till then.'

'I think I understood.'

May blinked at him over her glasses.

'Marian hasn't got a drink – '

Hart put his hand across his mouth to control a burp; he was out of his depth.

'Is that Marian?' said Donelly.

'Yes.'

He carried a drink across the room; Marian was arguing with an old man.

'This is Dennis.'

'Hallo.'

'Hallo.'

Dennis laughed; it was an extraordinary sound; his lips opened showing a set of old-fashioned false teeth. Marian's mouth set in a line.

A glass somewhere was dropped; there came a squeal and a burst of laughter.

May lifted a hand and waved, pointing to the seat beside her.

Marian edged away from Dennis, who followed her across the room – remembered his drink and went back for it.

Marian said, 'God save me from him.'

'You were a bit off colour tonight Dennis,' said May.

'I was off colour.'

' – take my advice, inhale before you say your lines – if you don't want to be accused of flatness. You do tend to have a monotonous voice.'

Dennis tottered forward waving a glass of gin.

'I like that, May. You were perfectly bloody tonight. I had to go into the kitchen till you'd finished. It was humiliating.'

Donelly closed his eyes; his head ached. Peterson lit a cigarette.

'We're all under-rehearsed.'

'Are we ever going to get a prompter? I don't believe there's been one since the dress rehearsal.'

'Yes there has. She wasn't there tonight – You must have seen her – a hump-backed woman, somewhat Indian in appearance.'

'But that's Petronia Moore. I understood she was playing a part.'

'Playing a part! I suppose she might be able to walk on; if anyone gave her a chance, which isn't likely.'

A man called Findley came over. The party drifted into twos and threes.

'Did you see *Uncle Whuppity*?' said the man called Findley. 'The whole atmosphere reminded me of a harebell.'

'I was too busy,' said May.

'For Christmas we did *The Rainbow Cat.* Miss Clutton-Brock did want to revive *The Fairy Flute* but I said You can't do that old thing again, Miss Clutton-Brock, my grandmother was in that fifty years ago. Do you know what she said? she said, What's good enough for your grandmother ought to be good enough for you. And I said, You may not know it, Miss Clutton-Brock, but fifty years is half a century. What do you think she said to that?'

'I don't know.'

'Nothing. There was a complete and splenetic silence.'

'Miss Clutton-Brock paints, did you know? She once showed me a very fine still life of some mackerel in a bucket.'

'Did you see her Cleopatra out at Potter's Bar?'

'I was busy.'

'She came forward in pink satin trimmed with flounces of lace, and died with her legs sticking in the air.'

'In Shakespeare?'

'God! No. Nothing so trite. Dryden.'

' – everyone liked it – from what the papers said.'

'What the papers said; you can never tell anything from what the papers say.'

'It was amazing – a really lovely performance by Marian here as Octavia. It seemed to have a most aphrodisiac effect: my cat had three kittens immediately afterwards.'

'Was your cat a member of the audience, May?'

'No.'

'Then I don't see how the play had any effect on your cat.'

The record came to an end. People called for an encore. Someone switched the lights out; someone else put them on again.

Peterson was drunk.

A woman in a brown beret was taking a census of the room. She had begun twice, each time the crowd moved.

The loudspeaker's volume increased: there were cries of Turn it down.

Peterson said to a blonde, 'Come on,' he said, 'I'll show you over the place.'

'It's quite small,' she said, 'I've seen all I want. '

She leaned over and listened long enough to gather what the conversation was about, then picked up Dennis' glass and drank from it.

'My head aches,' she said.

Peterson heard Findley say, 'I do wish I could like Miss Clutton-Brock's acting, because I do like her.'

'I can't possibly see how the play could have any effect on your cat's performance.'
'Oh, be quiet, Dennis.'
'Miss Clutton-Brock is famous in her way.'
' – she's mentioned twice in Irene Vanbrugh's auto-biography – '
' – if *that's* any credit to her.'
'If I were to write my theatrical memoirs they would be the best-seller of a decade. *Lolita* in reverse.'
'Yes, May, we all know you work in a bookshop.'
Dennis put out a hand knotted with veins and picked up his glass.

'Have you pinched my gin, Phyllis? – well, I do think it's a bit thick.'

May said to Hart, 'You never told me where you came in.'

'Oh,' Hart said, 'it was where – '

'Dennis saw the original production in Berlin, didn't you – you old whore?'

'Yes.'

'What was it like?' said Findley, 'better or different?'

'I suspect it was better.'

'Actually,' said May, 'I'm sure our production was far superior. Dennis can't remember from one year's end to another what anything is like.'

She lapsed into silence.

'There, Dennis, you've made May ratty.'

'She certainly seems to have fallen into a stupor all of a sudden.'

'Either that or she's squiffeh.'

'I think she's drunk. May's not listening, are you, May? May's cross; she hasn't spoken for ten seconds.'

'Oh, shut up, Dennis.'

'Good, May's found her tongue.'

'I love that hat you're wearing, May,' said Phyllis, after a pause.

'I copied it from a little thing at the Victoria and Albert.'

For some moments they examined the object of black felt surmounted by one or two artificial greengages.

May narrowed her long, painted eyes.

Hart went to the lavatory; when he came back May was sitting on his chair. She moved, and he bumped against the table making a tinkle of glass.

'What point did you say it was, when you came in?'

'Dennis was making a speech about – '

'Did you miss the bit where all the characters sit in a circle listening to a quasi-military tune called, The Yokohama Fowl Has a Strange Incongruous Head?'

'I think we must have.'

'I love this play. It is the ultimate prophecy of our time, in which hysteria and madness are of the market-place.'

'God! How erudite, how unexpected May has become.'

'She's so intellectual,' said Dennis, 'it's a pleasure to work with May. She found this play for us. We hadn't a clue what to do for our next production; then May found this play. We can't thank her enough.' He leaned back.

'Do you remember, Phyl, how May saved our bacon with *Santa Claus, I Presume*? She took over at a moment's notice from Moira.'

He gave Hart a nod.

'She learns her lines at – lightning – speed.'

'I saw poor Moira this morning,' said Phyllis. ' – crossing the road.'

'Half a life-time of acting isn't able to disguise what's wrong with her.'

'She was very good as Juliet – though she went to pot in the potion scene. You see she was pregnant and it showed in that scene.'

Peterson said to Phyllis, 'Let me show you over the place.'

'What a worry you are. Ask May.'

'No.'

'Be a good boy and go away.'

Donelly opened his eyes. People were talking in loud voices; a woman bumped against him. He closed his eyes.

'I could show you something,' said Peterson.

'What?' Phyllis said.

'I could show you – books.'

'Books. Whatever for?'

'Be careful,' said Donelly, opening one eye.

'Oh, that kind of book.'

'Come on, I'll show you.'

'Just for a few minutes.'

Peterson took her arm and walked across the room. Hart's office was dark, he switched on the light. The telephone was lying on the table; he replaced it.

'I wonder who left it like that?'

'Marian came to phone for a taxi.'

'I shouldn't show you these.'

He drew close to her: she was a natural blonde but too thin.

'I'm not really interested.'

'Why did you come here then?'

'I was getting fed-up with in there,' she said.

'Is Donelly your brother?'

'No.'

'Are you his boy-friend?'

'Yes. '

'I'm broadminded.' She giggled.

She kissed him; her mouth tasted of soap.

'You've nice eyes, darling.'

She brushed his cheek with a fingernail.

He smoothed the material of her skirt and listened: there was a knock on the door.

'Who's that?' he said.

The girl spun round and opened her mouth. Peterson went to the door and looked outside in the passage.

It was Crane.

'What are you doing here?' he said.

'I've come to see Hart.' Crane spoke in a whisper. 'That information you gave me – '

'Who's there?' said Phyllis.

'A man I know.'

'Why doesn't he come in?'

The door opened. Crane shoved his face round the corner. He wore a riding mac, very dirty, and carried his hat in his hands; he moved uneasily, shifting from one foot to the other.

'I came to see Hart.'

'He's in there. Why don't you come in?'

'Wait here,' said Peterson. 'I'll go and fetch him.'

He pushed by Crane, slammed the door, a blare of music came in for a moment and was cut off. He picked his way over the carpet through bits of broken glass; a woman was telling him to be careful.

The group around Hart were drinking neat whisky.

'A tragedy of insanity in verse. The culmination is a great castigation scene, in which the floggee is killed. Naturally it has never been performed.'

May said, 'I'd love to put it on. What a sensation it would cause.'

' . . . a conversation between an oboe and a harp – that was a sensation of another order.'

'It takes it out of you though, I was exhausted by the second act.'

May showed the whites of her eyes.

Hart sat stiffly between them looking bedraggled; someone had run their fingers through his hair. He glanced from side to side, keeping up with both speakers.

May lowered her voice. 'The man who produced it was rather odd, but his wife was a wonderful woman: she was a professional. We only got him in because of her.'

'I saw her recently on television,' said Dennis, 'playing a juvenile delinquent.'

'Is she *young* enough?'

'There's a man wants to see you,' said Peterson. 'It's important.'

Hart said, 'Who left the door open? This is a private party, the club isn't open.'

'He wants to see you urgently.'

'Who is it?' said Donelly. His skin was stretched tight across the cheek-bones.

'Crane.'

'The man who went to Murdock,' said Hart. 'He may cause trouble. 'What does he want?'

'I don't know.'

'I won't see him; tell him to go away.'

'I don't think he'll go.'

'Kick him out, what the hell do you think you're paid for? Kick him out.'

'You'd better see him,' said Peterson.

'What do you mean? Tell him to go away.'

'You'd better see him.'

'What the hell do you mean?'

Donelly said, 'I'll go.'

Hart looked after him, and then at Peterson in surprise. Phyllis came back and sat down. The loud-speaker played a number from a new musical:

> Heigh ho, let's go to bed,
> Grandmother's turning
Politically red.
> The last rat we caught
Was the size of a setter.
> Paul's piles are worse,
But Geoffrey's are better.
> Nancy has sold that big bust by Canova
> For eighteen and six to a man in a Rover.
> Grandfather's death duties
This year are owing.
> Let's go to bed
O Christ, look it's snowing!
> Let's take our chloral and go off to sleep,
> It's the ghost's night for haunting
The old ruined keep.

As Donelly walked into the office he put his hand on the door-lintel to steady himself. He felt anger and hatred for Crane; his hatred of Peterson, of himself, was concentrated, reduced and focused upon Crane.

He turned the handle and flung open the door.

Crane was standing by the barred window. Down the passage came the noise of the music:

        The view has been utterly
    Spoiled since the Folly
    Collapsed in the night
    Upon poor Lady Molly.
                Lord Bertie has taken to driving a hearse;
                Paul's piles are better,
    While Geoffrey's are worse.
                The waste-pipe is blocked,
    And the peacock's dropped dead,
                Switch off the lights, dear, and let's go to bed.

'What do you want?' said Donelly. He came forward, swinging the door shut behind him.

'I want to see Hart.'

'You're going to see me.'

Donelly put his hand on Crane's arm and tried to steer him to the door.

Crane shook him off. 'I want to see Hart.' He was firm.

                By selling young Desmond
    We could fill our coffers,
                But Saudi Arabia's turned down
    Our offers.
                So thank God the V and A's buying that po,
                Edward the Peacemaker gave to Aunt Flo;
                Three cheers for old Florence,
    We're back in the red:
                Drink up your Horlicks and let's go to bed.

'I want to see Hart,' said Crane, twisting his hat in his fingers.

Donelly put out a hand and clutched at the empty bottle on the desk. He held it like a club; he swung it and brought it down on Crane's head. The glass cracked, it split into pieces, the pieces fell on the floor. Crane sagged. Donelly caught him and brought his knee up into his stomach.

Crane fell under the shelf of books.

Donelly's forehead was damp as he reached for a handkerchief, opened its folds with a flip. His heart thudded against his chest. He watched the blood trickle from a cut on Crane's head, over his hair and onto the floor.

He leaned on the desk, breathing heavily; he felt no sympathy for Crane, no regret: he wanted to do something more. His whole body shook; he raised his toe and kicked Crane in the ribs, again and again.

After a while he went into the club-room and told Hart what had happened.

15

Her cheeks were pressed against the railings; there were ten minutes in which to talk. Peterson watched the girls in the playground. Without her make-up Francesca was pale, her lips dry and cracking.

'You shouldn't have come,' she said.

'Do you want a bar of chocolate?'

'Did you buy it?'

'Yes.' It was too late to tell the truth.

'Unwrap it for me.'

Peterson took off the silver paper and put a square of chocolate into her mouth.

Love is a thing that comes quickly; it is sudden: like the ice, which trapped the mammoths eating grass.

A window-cleaner stopped climbing his ladder and looked down on them. The teacher on duty moved towards the gate.

Francesca said, 'Is she coming over?'

'No.'

He rolled the silver paper into a ball and tossed it through the bars.

'Don't do that. We're supposed to keep the place clean.'

She put out a hand and held his. There was nothing to say. The future did not exist. Before she reached the age to marry, he would be tired, have seen too many of her faults. He wanted to hold her, to kiss her lips, to lose himself in the warmth of her body.

'Do you love me, Steve?'

'Yes.'

'Really?'

This was the face that launched ships for him; he needed those lovers of whom he had never heard to speak through his mouth: he was dream-ridden, and this dream would not last longer than the others.

'I wish I knew what to do.'

'What about?'

'My job, my life – you.'

She didn't understand; he wasn't able to express himself in terms she could grasp.

'She'll be ringing the bell in a minute.'

'When are you going to see me?'

'I don't know. Phone me.'

A wind had sprung up, driving the clouds across the sky, a few spots of rain fell.

'You haven't got a coat.'

Peterson held out the rest of the chocolate. 'Want any more?'

She shook her head.

'I don't either.'

He threw it away. A dog came by, sniffed it, and licked.

'Your job *is* dangerous, isn't it?'

He thought of Crane, of violence. Did he care if Crane died? He had nothing to do with it. He saw Crane, dumped on a bomb-site, with half a bottle of gin poured down his throat. What loyalty did he owe to Crane?

'No. It's not – dangerous,' he said.

Francesca looked over her shoulder towards the quadrangle.

'Are you giving it up?'

'I may.'

In dreams complications didn't exist; he had glamour without risk. A gunman without a gun. Now he had a gun. The gun Hart had given him.

How complex is the machine, directing insignificant actions towards an end. The coming times develop from the past: the future is born into the present. Events move in one direction and are cumulative.

A bell rang.

The girls wandered back to the school door.

'I'll have to go,' said Francesca.

He watched her. She ran up the steps. He was alone.

He dropped a half-smoked cigarette to the ground and stepped on it. He made his way back to the flat. The dusty stairs greeted him, the empty milk bottles, the door. He pushed his key into the lock.

Donelly's face was a blank, he showed no concern, just weariness.

Peterson stared at the books; they had nothing to do with him. I'll go away and it will all come right.

'I'm leaving,' he said.

'Leaving?'

Donelly shrugged: they had nothing in common, they had grown apart.

'The club. I'm going away.' He took a deep breath. 'This has nothing to offer.'

He gestured towards the biscuit crumbs on the frayed carpet, a glass stained with dried beer, a copy of *To the Lighthouse*.

'If Crane doesn't recover,' he said, 'you're in trouble.'

Donelly ignored him. 'I suppose she persuaded you?'

'No. I've been thinking for myself.'

'When are you going?'

'Tomorrow.'

'Why not today?'

'I want to see Hart – for money.'

'Crane ought to have been a warning.'

Peterson shook his head. 'He'll be keener than ever to keep out of trouble.'

'He doesn't use kid gloves. There's Evans.'

Reluctantly Peterson faced the thought.

'What did you think he was paying you for? You should have kicked him out.'

'I don't like that kind of thing.'

Donelly said, 'I hadn't realised you had scruples. You're a fool. Your class can't afford them – they don't come on hire-purchase; you buy them outright. And for that you need plenty, not hundreds but thousands.'

'Lend me a pound or two,' said Peterson.

'No.'

Peterson sat on the bed; he was tired. His mouth set in an obstinate line.

'Then I shall go to Hart.'

Donelly stretched his legs, touching the edge of the fireplace with his toe; rain spat on the windows. It was almost dark.

'Then go to Hart,' he said.

16

The number of wreaths was large. One would expect the deceased to have been well-known in social circles.

From the Officers and Men of the Royal Horse Guards, Remembering Thee.

H.R.H. Prince Friedrich Hilda of Ballenstein, To Stephen, Inamorata Felix.

From the Duchess of Norwich, loved and remembered every day.

Prince Yovanovitch Wessolowsky, treasured always.

From the Old Etonians, à la Recherche du Temps Perdu.

Madame de Chateaubriand-Necrophile, sadly missed.

From Brigadier General Sir Harold Frensham, nothing but memories now.

Charles Lloyd Turner, M.D., D.P.H., Consultant Pathologist, never fading sorrow.

From Count Vielcastel de Said, and still thy presence goes before me.

Mrs Wackenroder Wainwright-Forbes, to commemorate the passing.

From Dom Rodriguez de Babrillo Pedrodagasca –

> – clusters of loving memories,
> sprayed with many a tear,
> to me who loved and lost you,
> bring your image near.

And on its own – a heart: scarlet and miraculous perfection of roses, and a white card:

Eternally yours, Margaret.

Donelly stood looking at the flowers. His bank balance had gone; the roses were out of season and expensive: the last laugh had to be correctly played.

He noted the housewives, attracted by a funeral. He noted that Hart was missing. The vicar mumbled the service. Donelly wanted to laugh. A great feeling of peace swept over him; he had been given his excuse.

A woman in the front pew sniffed, patting a handkerchief to her eyes.

The coffin was lifted and carried out of the door. The woman moved after it. Donelly had an insane desire to kick her backside.

He stared at the floor, tears pricking behind his lids. Soon peace. God had answered his prayer – provided a gun and an excuse. Thank you, God.

He giggled.

Peterson's beauty smashed for ever. The car made a nasty mess, inextricably mixing his charm with the paint on the mudguard.

Sic transit gloria Stepheni.

I wonder who's kissing him now?

All those hopes were gone; Francesca widowed before marriage; those children massacred: the great abortionist had done his work.

It was over. The housewives left the church. He was alone.

A voice said, 'He was young, I believe?'

Donelly turned. The curate, a small man with a bald head, came towards him as though he wished to lock up the church. He had expected the place to be empty.

'The toll of the roads,' said the curate. 'A tragic accident. Was he your brother?'

'He had no relatives – only his mother.'

'I noticed there were few mourners; I was surprised.'

'Surprised?'

'The wreaths.' He looked at Donelly with inquisitive eyes.

'They were from – friends.'

'In this neighbourhood . . . '

'It's de rigueur to live round here: didn't you know?'

'I have no contact with the world.'

'Surely it's your job?'

'I don't understand.'

'To have contact with the world.'

The little eyes peered at him. 'Not with the world of fashion.'

'I see.'

'Aren't you following him to his last resting place?'

'No.'

'I wondered – why more of his – friends – weren't here.'

'What are friends? They desert us in the hour of need. I think Augustine had one or two things to say on the subject. You would be better acquainted with him than I.'

The curate nodded and shuffled on the stone floor.

'So sad,' he said, 'such a tragedy.'

'If he had lived,' said Donelly, 'I think you would have liked to know him. He was very interested in your Christian Fellowship Circle.'

'I should have been delighted to meet him.'

The curate put the key he was holding into his pocket.

'Was he a soldier?'

'Why do you ask?'

'One or two of the wreaths struck me as having – a military flavour.'

The scrawny neck wobbled above his dog-collar.

Donelly said, 'His dealings with the army were not precisely – Do you understand? A love passing that of woman. You know the book of Kings?'

The curate coughed, throwing a little phlegm into his throat.

'Of course.'

'It's my vade-mecum. We used to read it together.'

He paused; the curate could not mistake his meaning.

'I feel life has nothing more to offer.'

'I am here to help those in need.'

'You?' Donelly let surprise dawn.

'Perhaps I could call on you. There may be things you need to tell a clergyman.'

'Are you – married?'

'No.' The curate put an arm across his shoulder. 'Come and see me tomorrow at the Clergy House. You know our denomination.'

'You'll be hearing from me.'

'Good.' The fingers tightened for an instant upon his shoulder, and relaxed.

'I'd like to give you something now for the church. Have you an organ-fund?'

'We have no organ.'

'I see.' Donelly's face twitched. 'Goodbye.'

On the canal the children threw bricks at floating bottles. The sun was shining. In window boxes daffodils gleamed, pale and ethereal; stucco and iron drowned in a haze.

The women gathered their shopping bags, their baskets; the funeral was over.

'If they have pork-chops, I'll get spinach. And if they have lamb-chops, I'll get green peas.'

Donelly kicked at a stone. How I'd love to throw a bomb and blow the knickers off those fat women.

Peterson's death was a joke. Life was a joke, beauty, culture, civilisation – death. Spring, the universe, God – all jokes. – Christ! – who laughs?

His head ached again. Thoughts rotated inside. Pain, disease, unendurable knowledge, fear, filth. I want to die. Cowardice, Christ's blood, hell. That is all I want.

He threw the card of the Rev. Thomas Mason into the gutter: he wouldn't expose his soul to an inquisitive rat of a man who thought he carried God around in his pocket.

He bit his lip, a sweetish taste came into his mouth.

A pigeon flapped by and let squirt a fall of dung.

O Spirito Sancto!

He took a deep breath and glanced at his watch. It was then he saw Francesca.

'I rang the club,' she said, 'they told me.'

'Aren't you at school?'

'I'm supposed to be.'

She looked more than ever like a doll left out in the rain; without her make-up her complexion was bad, her skin pale and blotchy. Her expression sullen rather than tragic.

'I must be going,' he said.

'What happened?' she said. 'He was run over?'

'A car mounted the pavement – he was waiting for someone.'

'Who was he waiting for?'

'The man driving the car. A man called Evans.'

She looked startled.

'Did you imagine it was an accident?'

She understood: she was not as surprised as he had hoped.

'He was making a fool of himself,' he said.

'I liked him.'

'One can like a fool – love even.'

There was a redness about her nose, she might be going to cry.

'I must go.'

He took a revolver from his pocket, released the safety catch, put it back. All naturally, with calm. It was a few minutes after two thirty.

A drunk, walking in the gutter, swore; he was trying to find his way somewhere but had forgotten the address.

Donelly caught the stink of his breath as he passed. Which is worse, fruitless running or aimless drifting? Evil to look back on, nothing to look forward to, and pain in the present. The faces passing seemed to him pale, with a hunger not physical, mixture of brute and human, devouring and defiling: long claws and bird mouths, fat hips and loins.

This universe is held in tension
        by inhibition of desire,
But when, like flies in summertime,
        the void trembles with fornication
Its elemental body is shirted with
        aboriginal fire.

For a moment the sky was gone. The street, the clouds, they were all gone, and where the blueness had been was darkness. He was tired. His eyes closed – opened. And what rose above him was a wave. A stone wave, tumbling and plunging; a wall so high that it touched the sky. The earth spun.

– Have you heard the news?
What about the news.
– Have you heard the news?
The Foreign Office states –
– it's all a mistake.

He wanted to die. To get back to a dim memory of a better place. In his heart each man carries some lost Paradise, a ruined world of submerged continents. He wished to return. A deep roaring drummed in his ears.

And then suddenly the spinning had stopped. The roaring gone. He stood still.

He stared through the window. Wonderful things, books; letters, white, black, yellow. Manes of horses curling in spirals like a whelk-shell. He would never steal or read them now.

Sweat beaded his forehead; his face ran with oil and light. Thrashing streamers hung from spires. Long minutes passed. His muscles ached. During a lull in the wind he heard distant muffled sounds of music.

He weren't no saint
       (those engineers are pretty much alike),
And his smile was pensive and childlike
       (as I frequently remarked to Bill),
– the hot black breath of the burning boat
And God isn't going to be too hard
On a man that died for men.
– till cherubs swing their snowy hats
       and saints to windows run.

The wind hummed. At intervals the music from the city. The noise struggled upwards. The stillness had exploded into roaring life. His lips trembled. His mouth compressed into a bloodless line and his hands opened and closed at his sides. He walked in an area of trees and fountains. What marvellous vistas, squares exact and precise, idols higher than Achilles staring into water. His reflection moved across glass.

He stumbled on the pavement. Suicide is an insult to the body; it is self-hatred, which dries up energy and makes life infertile. He would be fixed for ever in a dead and withered sterility. And when time ceases, will there be nothing to know but the follies and discontentments of the past?

His fingers touched the handle of the pistol in his pocket.

White bannered, armoured like insects, the towers of the city lay among a cascade of broken walls.

Over bulges, crags, buttresses. The stone caulked with gold. Golden needles, chasms, inches of gold, ricks, golden chains, gold-covered slabs of concrete. And now my captain.

The gun was in his hand.

Two women came towards him, laughing and talking. He steeled himself. He turned the revolver on them. They began to scream.

His fingers curled around the trigger.

In the split second before the bullet moved along the barrel, he noticed the street – his vision was now clear; people ran, hiding in doorways, away from him, out of control.

He closed his eyes and fired.

And then he was conscious no longer, he plunged into blackness.

17

Geometric patterns moved across his field of vision; colours diamond-clear, intense: he was conscious of a jug as it came towards him, of fingers curled around the handle, of flowers springing from its lip.

A drop of water splashed onto his face as the nurse put the jug on his locker.

'I always think a room looks undressed without flowers,' she said.

Donelly felt a tug of pain.

'How many fingers have I left?'

'Don't worry.'

She came to the side of his bed.

'I want to know.'

'You're going to be alright.'

'I want to know.'

'Doctor will tell you tomorrow.'

'Just answer me.'

'Keep calm.' She jingled the keys in her pocket.

Donelly closed his eyes. Christ! I'm locked in here with a madwoman.

'How many?'

'Well – we had to amputate two. We saved part of the other.

'Thank you.'

'Everything is going to be alright. You're to have visitors this afternoon.'

'A visitor?'

'Yes.'

'Who?'

She smiled. 'You'll see.'

Donelly pressed his lower lip between his teeth. She couldn't answer a straight question. He lifted his arm and stared at his bandaged hand.

The nurse teased the flowers into shape.

He said, 'Who is coming?'

'You'll see.'

'Is it my mother?'

'Have you a mother?'

'Yes. It's my father I'm not sure about.'

'Tell me,' she said.

She sat down; the starch rustled; she waited.

Donelly sighed. 'You wouldn't understand.'

'I would.'

He looked at her. 'They said I was crackers in the reformatory.'

'You've been in a reformatory?'

'I never had a chance.'

'Why not?'

'I can't tell you.'

'I think you'd better get the whole thing off your chest.'

He nodded. 'I've done wrong, nurse. Did I hurt anybody?'

'You did no harm – except to yourself.'

'I'm glad.'

'It must have been a very old gun.'

'It belonged to my grandfather. He used it on the Somme.'

'You had a lucky escape.'

Donelly sighed again and closed his eyes.

'I'm going to reform,' he said.

'I know you are.'

'How can you know how I feel?'

She didn't answer; her apron rustled as she moved.

'I've been so mixed up inside – so confused. But I don't feel bitter any more.'

She leaned down and touched his hair.

'If you're truly sorry,' she said, 'they'll let you off lightly.'

'Do you think so?'

'I'm sure of it.'

'Mother will be so glad. I've caused her a lot of pain in the past. Has she been here? I don't want her to find out.'

'I don't think she's been. Sister would have mentioned it.'

He stared at the walls; cool and green.

'Why do they keep the door locked?'

'What makes you think the door is locked?'

'It is.'

'No.'

'Yes.'

'I wouldn't let it worry you.'

He wriggled his toes in the bed. 'Why – I'm not dangerous.'

'I have to lock it.'

'You've been told to?'

She nodded.

'Who told you?'

'I must go. I've such a lot of work.'

'Won't you answer my question? I get so worried lying here, not knowing. It's a desperate feeling.'

'I've done all I can.'

She looked at the jug of flowers.

'Yes.'

' – the police told us to lock the doors. That is why you aren't in a main ward.'

'Thank you.'

'You've a – little – trouble to face with them.'

'Is it the police who are coming this afternoon?'

'Yes,' she said, surprising him with a straight answer. 'Doctor says you're well enough. You won't be in here much longer.'

'I'll be in Wormwood Scrubs.'

'Don't worry.'

'Where else?'

Attempted murder is a serious charge. He remembered Crane. Manslaughter too.

'I've ruined my life, nurse.'

'You're young. You'll get over it.'

'I was doomed from the beginning. I want to tell you. I never had a chance.'

He could feel her backside pressed against his knee.

'What is it you want to tell me?' she said.

He sighed and made a weary gesture. 'I don't know where to begin.'

He wished for a way to shake her to the soul; admitted there was none; bit his lip.

'I've been misunderstood.'

'In what way?'

'No one ever took the trouble to teach me right from wrong. I never had any love.'

'What about your mother?'

'My mother was an ape, and of course, she couldn't give me the attention I needed. I never knew who my father was.'

In the dim recesses of her brain she heard what he said, but the meaning was transmuted by alchemy into a harmless phrase.

She smiled and shook her head.

'I'm sure if you tell this to the people in charge of your case, you'll be surprised how sympathetic they'll be.'

She bent down to tuck in the blankets.

Donelly's heart was an atom about to explode. He felt an impulse, and there was no reason now to deny them. He lifted the jug of flowers, and, with a suddenness which surprised him, emptied it over her head.

She sprang to her feet, drops of water spraying from her starched white hat onto her shoulders. She stood for a moment mopping herself with a handkerchief.

'I'm surprised at you,' she said. 'I was trying to help. I'm not going to tell Doctor this time. I shall leave you now – and I hope you feel ashamed of yourself. When I bring your lunch in I shall expect an apology.'

Donelly closed his eyes and heard her turn the key in the lock.

It was like this for the Incas, the Aztecs, and the pure-blooded Polynesians, for the golden-bearded kings of Atlas and the legionary upon the Wall. For Genghis Khan and Savonarola too – though he may have thought he was different; for Alexander, bringing fire by night to Persepolis.

They had ignorance and accepted custom in Alba Longa, Megiddo, and Ilion: they had chicken-hearts and sleek ideals upon those topless towers. Youth has been betrayed and tears shed for its loss too often and too long ago for anyone, any more, to feel anything.

The endless spinning of the wheel; the perpetual closing of a circle.

God laughs and snaps his fingers . . . The only thing for a man to do is to imitate God and snap his fingers too.

Works of Joe Orton available from Methuen

ISBN	TITLE	PRICE
☐ 0 413 74900 2	Between Us Girls	£6.99
☐ 0 413 41460 4	Head to Toe	£6.99
☐ 0 413 45180 1	Loot	£6.99
☐ 0 413 36680 4	What the Butler Saw	£6.99
☐ 0 413 34610 2	Orton: Complete Plays	£9.99
☐ 0 413 73650 4	The Orton Diaries (edited by John Lahr)	£8.99

*   All Methuen books can be ordered online at www.methuen.co.uk. They are also available through mail order or from your local bookshop.

Please send cheque / eurocheque / postal order (sterling only) Access, Visa, Mastercard, Diners Card, Switch or Amex.

Expiry Date .... Signature ....

UK customers please allow £1 for the first book and 50p thereafter up to a maximum of £3 for post and packing.

Overseas customers please allow £1.50 for the first book and 75p thereafter up to a maximum of £5 for post and packing.

ALL ORDERS TO:

Methuen Books, Books by Post, TBS Limited, The Book Service, Colchester Road, Frating Green, Colchester, Essex CO7 7DW.

NAME ....

ADDRESS ....

....

....

Please allow 28 days for delivery. Please tick box if you do not wish to receive any additional information   ☐

Prices and availability subject to change without notice.